Praise for Susannah B. Lewis

Della and Darby

"Lewis's heartwarming latest (*Bless Your Heart, Rae Sutton*) follows twin sisters as they attempt to find themselves and overcome the past in their stiflingly small Mississippi hometown . . . Lewis captures the vulnerability and humor of their relationship. This light jaunt has surprising emotional depth."

—PUBLISHERS WEEKLY

Bless Your Heart, Rae Sutton

"Settle in for an enchanting tale featuring a delightful cast of characters. At turns humorous and heart-wrenching, Lewis's novel delivers on themes of forgiveness and restoration. Wise, witty, and full of Southern charm, *Bless Your Heart, Rae Sutton* is as refreshing as a tall glass of sweet tea on a hot summer day!"

—DENISE HUNTER, BESTSELLING AUTHOR OF
THE RIVERBEND ROMANCE SERIES

a Weekend on Allyson Island

Other Books by Susannah B. Lewis

Fiction

Della and Darby

Bless Your Heart, Rae Sutton

Nonfiction

How May I Offend You Today?

Can't Make This Stuff Up!

A Weekend on Allyson Island

Susannah B. Lewis

THOMAS NELSON
Since 1798

Published in Nashville, Tennessee, by Thomas Nelson. Thomas Nelson is a registered trademark of HarperCollins Christian Publishing, Inc.

Thomas Nelson titles may be purchased in bulk for educational, business, fundraising, or sales promotional use. For information, please email SpecialMarkets@ThomasNelson.com.

Scripture quotations are taken from the Holy Bible, New International Version®, NIV®. Copyright © 1973, 1978, 1984, 2011 by Biblica, Inc.® Used by permission of Zondervan. All rights reserved worldwide. www.zondervan.com. The "NIV" and "New International Version" are trademarks registered in the United States Patent and Trademark Office by Biblica, Inc.®

Publisher's Note: This novel is a work of fiction. Names, characters, places, and incidents are either products of the author's imagination or used fictitiously. All characters are fictional, and any similarity to people living or dead is purely coincidental.

Library of Congress Cataloging-in-Publication Data

Names: Lewis, Susannah B., 1981- author
Title: A weekend on Allyson Island / Susannah B. Lewis.
Description: Nashville, Tennessee : Thomas Nelson, 2025. | Summary: "They've come for a birthday celebration . . . but they'll leave celebrating themselves"—Provided by publisher.
Identifiers: LCCN 2025033424 (print) | LCCN 2025033425 (ebook) | ISBN 9781400347384 paperback | ISBN 9781400347391 epub | ISBN 9781400347407
Subjects: LCGFT: Christian fiction | Novels | Fiction
Classification: LCC PS3612.E9867 W44 2025 (print) | LCC PS3612.E9867 (ebook)
LC record available at https://lccn.loc.gov/2025033424
LC ebook record available at https://lccn.loc.gov/2025033425

Printed in the United States of America

25 26 27 28 29 LBC 6 5 4 3 2

As iron sharpens iron, so one person sharpens another.

Chapter 1

CELIA KATE STOKES flipped through the pile of mail that her youngest child, Tucker, had brought inside and dumped on the kitchen counter, which was already cluttered with books, papers, pencils, and artwork. One envelope stood out among the bills and junk mail. Even before checking the return address, she recognized who the sender was by the elegant black envelope adorned with gold trim. Something as sophisticated as this must have come from Mrs. Moira Allyson.

She ran her thumb beneath the shiny seal and pulled out the matte-black invitation. A slip of vellum paper fell to her hardwood floor, sticky with syrup from the morning pancakes and glitter from Sophie's latest art project. She settled onto the leather barstool at the counter and reached for her cell phone. As CK ran her fingers through her light brown hair, Gemma Gardner's loud Southern drawl belted out a "Hey!" after the third ring.

"Have you been to your mailbox this morning?" CK asked while reaching for her Golden Girls mug of tepid coffee and pressing it to her thin lips.

"Are you talking about Mo's invitation? I grabbed it out of the mailbox on the way to work this morning and just opened it. Are you able to go?" Gemma asked.

Celia Kate shrugged while organizing stacks of construction paper on the counter. A weekend at Moira's beautiful waterfront home on the Georgia coast sounded relaxing, but the thought of leaving her family to fend for themselves for three long days left her feeling a bit skittish. "I don't know. Are you?"

"I would love to get away for a few days. School has only been in session for a month, and Carolina's senior year is already stressing me out. There's so much to do, not to mention how expensive it all is. I'll have to sell a kidney to afford the yearbook photos. My high-maintenance daughter is asking for a photo shoot at Swan House. Who does my kid think she is? Princess Di?" There was nervous tension in Gemma's voice. "What about you? Can you cut the cord and pull yourself away from your children for an entire weekend?"

CK rolled her eyes at her best friend's remark. "I didn't know it was a crime to care for your children's needs."

"Yeah, yeah." Gemma sighed. "So when is the last time you even talked to Mo? It's been over a month for me."

CK took another sip of coffee and then replied, "She texted me a few weeks ago about her garden. She wanted to know if it was too late in the season to transplant a hydrangea. There was no mention of her birthday or a party, though. We only chatted for a few minutes. She must be keeping busy."

"Well, that's good to hear," Gemma said. "I've been meaning to check in with her, but between work and Carolina's demands, I just haven't found the time. I'm a terrible friend, I guess. I'm surprised I even received an invitation."

"That isn't true." CK looked out her kitchen window at the grove of magnolia trees in her side yard, their waxy green leaves swaying in the wind. "You know we can go months at a time without speaking to Moira and pick right back up where we left off."

Gemma, in her rich-woman impersonation, said, "It's sure to be an extravagant affair, darling. I imagine we'll have European facials and mud baths, and we'll be sent home with Louis Vuitton goody bags filled with caviar." Then she shifted back to her normal voice. "I could definitely use a spa weekend. Mo always serves the best food too. Do you remember those fancy hors d'oeuvres at her Christmas party a few years ago?" Gemma sighed. "I haven't looked at a snail the same way since."

Celia Kate grimaced. "I can do without the snails, but I could use some pampering. I'll have to check with Sean and see if he can handle the kids all weekend."

"You don't have three toddlers, Celia Kate. Sean can handle the kids."

CK couldn't stand the sight of the glitter and crumbs scattered on the hardwood floor any longer, so she stood from the barstool and headed to the utility closet to fetch the dust mop. "I wonder who else she's invited."

"I don't know, probably her sorority sisters. Maybe her sisters-in-law," Gemma continued. "Hopefully not MerryLee, though. That windbag never shuts up. I'm still traumatized by that girls' trip we took a few years ago. Remember? She started talking the minute we left Savannah and didn't stop until we pulled into the rental on Hilton Head. I literally fell to my knees and kissed the ground when I got out of the car. I'll need more than snails to get through a weekend with Chatty Cathy. I'll need vodka. And lots of it."

CK laughed while she swept the glitter and debris on the kitchen floor into a little pile. "I'll talk to Sean and get back to you. If we do go, I'll drive. I want to get there in one piece. On our last road trip together, you got a speeding ticket on the way to Biloxi and on the way back."

"If you ain't fast, you're last," Gemma said, then hung up.

CK placed her phone on the farmhouse kitchen table, emptied the glitter and crumbs into the trash can, and sighed in relief at the sight of clean floors.

"Hey, Mama, think I could get a snack? Reading about the Spanish Inquisition and torture and executions really works up an appetite," her oldest child, Silas, asked while walking into the room.

She placed the broom and dustpan back into the closet, turned with a warm smile to her towering sixteen-year-old son, who stood at six three, and offered him a choice between peanut butter and jelly or homemade chicken salad. He asked for chicken salad and a couple of chocolate chip cookies. She got busy fulfilling her boy's order.

~

THE CEILING FAN turned slowly above the sleigh bed, its gentle whirring the only sound breaking the thick silence of the night. Outside, the crickets had fallen quiet. Tunnel Hill, Georgia, had shut down hours earlier, tucked in behind porch lights and locked doors. But CK lay wide-eyed in the dark, one hand on her chest and the other gripping the corner of the quilt her grandmother Sue had made decades ago.

Sean's breathing was soft and even—annoyingly steady, if she was honest. He could fall asleep in the middle of a thunderstorm or with the TV still blaring. CK had never understood how he managed it. *He doesn't worry because I do it for both of us*, she thought, not unkindly, just truthfully. That was how their marriage had always worked.

But tonight the silence clawed at her, and she hated it. It brought with it too many bad memories. It was the kind of quiet that hung in the air before the phone rang, before everything changed. Tragedy didn't shout; it whispered. It crept in like fog.

Her thoughts were quick and chaotic, always landing back where they usually did these days: Silas. *He's sixteen going on what? Six?*

He was smart and sweet and funny in a dry, clever way. But he was also so irresponsible. He had failed driver's ed. He'd lost two phones and the birthday money his uncle had given him. And Lord help Celia Kate, she had let him get away with too much. She'd babied, softened, coddled him much too often.

She pressed her fingers to her temples and tried to ease the tension. What if he never matured? Would he end up living in their basement, waiting for her to bring him leftovers, until he was thirty? And worse—would it be her fault?

Sean shifted, mumbling and turning his face toward her. He was still asleep and still at peace. The man could sleep through a tornado. And, mercy, she sure did love him. But sometimes she wanted to shake him awake and yell, "Help me worry! Help me fix this!" But she knew he'd just pull her close and say, "He's a kid, CK. He'll figure it out. Just give him time." Or maybe he'd say, "It's your fault he is like he is."

Time will work it out. That's what everyone always said. Time didn't hold her boy accountable. And time didn't fix everything.

She had learned that the hard way—from people who never came back, from losses she still carried like stones in her chest.

The blue numbers on the digital clock blinked. It was 1:54 a.m. now. She stared at the ceiling, arms crossed, heartbeat loud in her ears. Stillness and quiet would never mean peace for her.

It would always be the moment before everything changed.

Chapter 2

Erin Pepperell turned the key on her assigned unit in the cluster box and pulled out a weighty stack of envelopes. She scrambled up the stairway, unlocked the hunter-green apartment door, and once inside, hastily secured it with double bolts and chains. The apartment was small, the kind people rent only when there's no other option. The carpet was rough, the plumbing shoddy, the neighbors unpredictable. But it was hers. And while she lived there, no one screamed at her for not folding the towels right. No one grabbed her wrist too hard, or slammed doors, or broke plates because dinner wasn't hot enough.

She tossed her purse and keys onto the small kitchen table and felt a wave of discouragement as she thumbed through the bills. Grabbing a pencil from a cup on the counter, she jotted down her and her son PJ's take-home pay on a scrap of paper, carefully considering their expenses. After she made some calculations, she couldn't help but feel concerned about having to live on the number she'd written down.

Erin's financial worries were replaced with curiosity when she looked at the luxurious embossed envelope, recognizing the elegant handwriting as belonging to Moira Allyson, her boss. With her head cocked in confusion, she carefully opened it to reveal an invitation to Mo's fiftieth birthday celebration. The itinerary on the back of the sophisticated cardstock promised a weekend of delicious cuisine and pampering at Moira's coastal home.

For a little over a year now, Erin had worked for Mo three days a week, and her responsibilities included cleaning and running errands. She often found herself with nothing to do and then was tasked with polishing silver that would never be used or rearranging already immaculate closets. But as Erin scanned the invitation, she thought surely Mo could use help with preparations for an entire weekend of entertainment, and yet she hadn't mentioned a thing to her about it.

Erin sank into the shabby love seat in her cluttered living room and kicked off her worn tennis shoes. Her feet, exhausted from a ten-hour shift at the convenience store, welcomed the relief. As she leaned back, she picked up the phone and dialed Moira's number.

Two rings, three, and finally, an answer. Because Mo sounded tired when she breathed, "Hey, Erin," into the phone, Erin assumed she must have just finished a cycle workout in her state-of-the-art gym overlooking the Intracoastal Waterway . . . or she was at the bottom of that evening's bottle.

"Hey! I didn't want to wait until I came in to work tomorrow to ask you about the invitation I received in the mail today." Erin nervously tucked her short black hair behind her ear, which was lined with studs from the lobe to the cartilage.

"Oh, I'm glad you got it. I had to search for your address on the internet, so I wasn't sure I sent it to the right place." Moira hiccupped, which ruled out the fatigue in her voice being the result of an intense cycling session. "I hope you'll be able to make it."

"I'll be there if I'm not scheduled to work at Family Pantry.

Even if I do have to work at the convenience store, I could clean the house and prepare the food before I—"

Moira interrupted with a laugh. "No, Erin. You've misunderstood. I'm not asking you to work at the party that weekend. I'm asking you to attend as my guest!"

Erin's eyes widened in puzzlement. Although she and Moira came from vastly different socioeconomic backgrounds, Moira had always been kind to Erin and never acted like a superior, snobby, or holier-than-thou boss. They often carried on friendly conversations about their sons and the television shows they both enjoyed. However, Erin didn't believe their relationship was close enough for her to be considered a guest at Moira's birthday party.

"Hello, Erin? Are you still there?" A clinking noise echoed in the background—a familiar sound of glass tapping against Moira's wedding ring.

"Y-yes, Moira," Erin stammered and sat upright on the lumpy love seat. "Thank you for the invitation. I just assumed—"

"I know you're my employee, Erin, but I think of you as a friend as well. I'm inviting you as that friend. I hope you will come."

"It sounds like a wonderful time, Moira. I'll be there if I can. Thank you again."

She tossed her phone aside and shook her head at the strange turn of events. The thought of mingling with Savannah's elite made her heart race. These were the kinds of people she was used to serving, not socializing with.

—

A SHOUT ECHOED from the alley below—it was sharp, angry, and too close. Then came the crash of a bottle, followed by laughter that was high and unsteady. Someone was revving an engine, and tires were squealing. Erin flinched under her thin blanket, her heart pounding before her mind caught up. She lay stiff in bed, staring at the ceiling, which was cracked in three places. One arm clutched the blanket up to her collarbone, as if it could shield her from the outside world. She waited and listened. The sounds outside faded into the usual hum of distant traffic, the occasional dog bark, a siren farther off. Still, her thin body wouldn't settle.

She glanced at the bedroom door, which was barely open. Down the hall, PJ's door was shut. The nineteen-year-old had fallen asleep in the living room earlier while watching football highlights with his headphones on, his large feet hanging off the end of the thrift store couch before he finally mustered the energy to drag himself to bed. He was a good kid—too good for the life they had to endure. He was far too aware of things that no boy should ever have to bear. Enrolled in trade school, he was learning the ins and outs of auto mechanics. He contributed to their income by working at a fast-food restaurant within walking distance of their apartment. They brought home enough to cover the bills, but nothing was left over.

Erin exhaled, slow and tight. Her body ached, not from anything new, but from everything old. She had scar tissue in her mind, in her muscles, and in her heart. Peace hadn't come just because she and PJ left Phillip and their old life behind. The echoes of that life still whispered to her in the quiet—in the way she flinched at raised voices or the way her hand sometimes hovered before turning a doorknob, like she still needed permission to move.

Her stomach growled. She had skipped dinner again without realizing it. More than anything else tonight—more than silence, more than food, more than money, more than safety—she wanted sleep. Not just rest, but the kind of sleep that didn't feel like surrender. She wanted the kind of sleep where she didn't dream about the past.

She turned onto her side and raised her knees to her chest. The air was cool, and the moonlight cast soft shadows across the chipped walls. She closed her dark eyes, and her breathing slowed just enough to drift, not into a full, deep sleep, but into that in-between place where nothing hurt for a little while.

She'd take that for now.

Chapter 3

NELL REHMAN WAS completing the last steps of her two-mile morning walk, and she thanked the good Lord for the cooler temperature today that didn't leave her drenched in sweat or out of breath. She slowed her steps and intently watched the tracker app on her phone as she approached her long, winding driveway, which forked off the gravel road in rural Chatham County, Georgia. The app's icon of her daughter's face showed her slowing down to zero miles per hour, safely arriving in the dorm parking lot after the drive back from an off-campus class. Taylor merging onto the freeway to get to the veterinary science building on Tuesday mornings always made Nell anxious.

Relieved that Taylor was back on school property, Nell slipped her phone into the pocket of her light gray windbreaker. Suddenly, a nagging concern overtook her mind, prompting her to grab the phone once again. Quickly opening the app, she followed Taylor's footsteps across the large parking lot to make sure she safely reached the dormitory. Distracted by the phone screen, Nell failed to notice a twisted branch left on the driveway from last night's storm and stumbled over it. Although she managed to steady herself and avoid a fall, the unexpected jolt left her heart racing. Before tucking her phone back into her pocket, she watched a few more of her little girl's steps on the screen.

Nell stopped to get a stack of mail from the redbrick mailbox. On the very top was another army recruitment letter—straight to the trash it would go. If Tate saw it, he'd take it as another sign to run off to serve his country and leave his parents and the safety of his hometown behind. Next in the pile was an embossed envelope with Moira Allyson's return address neatly stamped on the back flap. Still standing at the mailbox, Nell opened it to find an invitation to Moira's home for her fiftieth birthday celebration. Surprised that she'd even received it, Nell put the invitation in her left hand, alongside the army's prompting for her only son, her baby boy, to "be all he could be." She continued her walk toward the house—toward the trash—where both were destined, as both were invitations to a bad time.

THE CLOCK ON the nightstand glowed red in the dark: 2:12, then 2:13, then 2:14 a.m. Nell lay on her back, her green eyes wide open, staring at the ceiling as the minutes ticked by. Beside her, Chip snored softly, one arm draped over the blanket, his breathing slow and steady. The sound made her jealous—a reminder that at least one of them was sleeping.

She turned her head toward the window, where the pale glow of the moon brightened the blinds. The house was quiet, and the world outside felt even quieter. But her mind wouldn't settle.

She thought of her strawberry-blonde girl being over two hundred miles away at the University of Georgia, too grown up for a curfew and rules and too far away for Nell to pop in with a hug. The news that appeared on her social media pages daily hadn't helped ease her worries—all that talk of danger, campus crime, and girls going missing, topics she refused to google after dark.

And now Tate—her sweet boy—included the army in nearly every conversation. She pressed her hand to her chest and felt her heart thudding with worry.

"Lord," she whispered into the silence, barely moving her lips, "I need you tonight."

All she could hear was the steady hum of the fan and Chip's soft snoring.

"I gave you my addiction, Lord," she said on a breath. "I laid it at your feet, and you broke the chains. You got me through the cravings and the shame. You s-still do," she added, her voice cracking. "Please, Lord, I need that same strength again."

She reached for the Bible on her nightstand, its edges worn from use. She also grabbed her phone and brightened the pages with its light. The Bible naturally opened to Psalm 121—the one she'd clung to during the hardest days of her recovery.

"He who watches over you will not slumber," she read silently as a tear slipped from the corner of her eye and onto her pillow. "You're awake when I can't be. You're watching over Taylor. You're walking beside Tate." She claimed these truths out loud.

She placed the tattered book back onto the nightstand and folded her hands over her chest, letting the verse settle over her like a blanket. She didn't feel better—not exactly—but she felt held. And maybe that was enough for tonight.

She closed her eyes, knowing sleep might not come easy. But also knowing she wasn't alone in the waiting.

Chapter 4

MOIRA ALLYSON SAT in a wooden chair beneath the live oak and watched her two white long-haired cats at the water's edge. Their green eyes tracked a dragonfly hovering over the surface of the lake, and their fluffy necks jerked in response to the bug's movements. Dove entered hunting mode, crouching down on her front legs like a tiger stalking a gazelle in the brush. Pearl sat beside her, focused on the insect's every move but not yet ready to pounce. In an instant, Dove leapt from her back paws, reaching for the dragonfly with her long front leg. She missed, however, and the dragonfly quickly fluttered away. Pearl cut her eyes toward her sister almost mockingly, then walked toward Moira.

"It was just too fast for you, old girl," Moira said to her friend as the cat jumped from the soft grass into Moira's lap. Pearl remained at the water, watching intently for the flopping tail of a sunfish or the flicker of wings; whether a dragonfly or an egret, it didn't matter.

Moira stroked Dove's fur and took a sip from her glass before placing it back on the wide arm of the chair. She gazed at the dark, glassy water and reflected on her childhood on Lake Conasauga. Her grandfather, Ernest, owned a nineteen-foot aluminum fishing boat in a hunter-green color. She remembered how hot the green-and-white-striped vinyl seats became in the sun. She would dig into the built-in ice chest, which was stocked with beer for her granddaddy and cans of orange soda for herself and her brothers. She often tossed ice cubes onto the seats before sitting down in her shorts, only to burn her legs anyway. Granddaddy Ernest had a battery-operated radio with a cassette deck sitting on the Astroturf carpet in the boat, blaring country classics by Waylon Jennings, Hank Williams, or Charley Pride. Her grandaddy sang along at the top of his lungs, not caring that his raspy voice carried across the water and scared most of the fish away. Being out on that aluminum boat with his grandkids wasn't about fishing anyway, not really.

Granddaddy Ernest passed away when Moira was in junior high, but her father kept his father's old boat. Occasionally he would take it out of the shed, hook it to his pickup truck, and drive out to Lake Conasauga. Moira's older brothers were often too busy to spend an afternoon at the lake, but Moira never declined the opportunity. She cherished every chance to be back on that old boat with the only other man she loved as much as her granddaddy—and that was her dad, Albert.

Moira was the youngest of the Wallace siblings and the only girl, which meant she held a special place in her father's heart. He affectionately called her "Apple," as she was truly the apple of his eye. If she was with her dad, she never left a store without a piece of candy or a new toy. When she was sixteen and went on her first date with Barrett Marcum, her intimidating father stood on the porch with his Winchester rifle. While he partly did this as a joke, there was an underlying seriousness to his gesture. His protective nature toward his blonde-haired, blue-eyed little Apple was unmistakable. When Albert lost his long battle with lung cancer when Moira was a freshman at UGA, she didn't think she'd make it through.

Pearl joined Moira and her littermate, Dove, on the Adirondack chair and purred with contentment. Mo welcomed the cat before she took the last swallow from the glass and placed it back on the arm of the chair. She picked up the small yellow notepad and pen on the other wide arm and used Pearl's back as a desk. She started making notes for her birthday party coming up in three weeks.

"What in the world will I wear on the sunset cruise?" she asked her best friends resting silently in her lap. "It might be chilly. Or it might not. I can never tell this time of year. Maybe the navy jumpsuit? Or that floral maxi I haven't worn in forever? The black long-sleeved mini I ordered online?"

Dove responded to Moira by pawing at the frayed threads at the hole in the knee of her jeans.

"I haven't worn the black mini yet. No place to wear it," she said while tapping the end of the pen on the sheet of paper.

Moira was confident that she would look stunning no matter what she wore. She had been aware of her beauty from an early age, partly due to the doting she received from Ernest and Albert. Although she knew she was beautiful, she remained coy and humble. This modesty was a virtue taught to her by her mother, Louise. Not only was Louise Wallace strikingly beautiful, even into her old age, but she possessed inner beauty and wisdom. Louise often reminded Moira with a gentle smile, "Vanity blossoms but bears no fruit."

When Louise passed away ten years ago, Moira stood beside her mother's pearl-white casket, tears leaving black mascara streaks on her face. She reached into the coffin and brushed her mother's cold cheek, framed by her long silver hair, and she couldn't help but think how lovely her mother still looked at seventy-five, even beneath layers of mortuary makeup.

An egret taking flight across the brackish water startled her from memories of her mama. The cats, however, were sleeping and purring so deeply that they didn't notice.

Moira reviewed her notes and thought about the guests she had invited. Among them were her sisters-in-law: Tabitha, Penny, and even her oldest brother's wife—always a source of her frustration—the overly talkative and negative MerryLee. Moira believed that sending MerryLee an invitation was a waste of a stamp since MerryLee had always resented Mo's wealth, beauty, and talent for hosting fabulous parties, and therefore she was sure not to come. Moira decided to invite her anyway, hoping to please her brother, whom she loved dearly.

Among Moira's other guests were her childhood best friends, Celia Kate and Gemma. She had also invited a couple of her sorority sisters: Carla, who had a talent for telling hilarious stories, and Jenna, who laughed heartily at them. Two friends from church, Nell and Jess, were included as well, along with Erin, Moira's housekeeper. Erin was more than just an employee; she was like a friend who brought life and conversation to Moira's big, quiet house several days a week. She had a knack for making Moira smile with sweet compliments about her clothes and various things around the house, and those little gestures meant a lot to Moira. Over the year they'd spent together, Erin had become the person Moira talked to most regularly.

She looked over at the matching Adirondack chair beside her, a layer of dust covering the dark wood. She thought about the countless hours she'd spent right here with Jeffrey, with coffee mugs in hand. Beneath that two-hundred-year-old tree canopied in Spanish moss, much like the white long-haired cats, they, too, had watched herons and egrets take flight over the Ogeechee River and its salt marshes. It was in this spot on the banks of the water that Jeffrey had talked of retiring at sixty, by which time their oldest son would be thirty and ready to run the family business.

Moira and Jeffrey discussed one day sailing around the world on a forty-two-foot Delta Diamond yacht, complete with crew. Talk about a contrast from that aluminum boat with vinyl seating! Conversations of their future, beneath that tree, made Jeffrey and Moira Allyson giddy, like a young high-school couple. They often interlocked hands and rested them on the arms of those slatted wood chairs, where her glass was now sitting. It was unique, still being so in love after over twenty-five years of marriage.

Pearl and Dove both stretched and rolled onto their backs, exposing their fluffy white stomachs. Moira placed the notepad and pen beside her and nuzzled the limp rag dolls, saying to them, "You all miss him too, don't you?"

She thought back to that chilly spring day when she found her best furry friends, when the sun looked warm but the air was sharp and cut through your sleeves. Moira remembered clearly how the wind tugged at her lavender scarf as she and Jeffrey stepped out of the car onto gravel. They were somewhere out past Richmond Hill at a little rescue tucked behind a horse farm. It was run by a retired schoolteacher named Fran who had long white hair and wore denim skirts and spoke to every animal like it was her grandchild.

They'd only come to "look," which was what Jeffrey always

said, even though he knew good and well they were leaving with something furry. Both their golden retriever and Maine coon cat had passed the year before, and the house had been too quiet ever since.

Fran led them into a sunlit room filled with old wooden crates and dusty shelves. There in the corner were two long-haired sisters curled up together, looking like a patch of snow. Both were white from whisker to tail, and each had striking emerald eyes.

"They're a bonded pair," Fran had said. "Someone found them in a box off Highway 204."

Moira crouched in front of them, and Dove—elegant, cautious—blinked slowly, then extended one paw to touch her knee. Pearl yawned and stretched her full length. With a quick jump, she plopped into Jeffrey's lap.

"She's picked you." Fran chuckled.

"I'm a dog person," Jeffrey argued before he looked up at Moira and asked, "What do you think, Mo?"

"I think we're not leaving one without the other," she said.

He smiled, and that was that.

They rode home with the cats in a borrowed carrier on the back seat, meowing like tiny singers. Pearl became carsick halfway through the ride, and Jeffrey, unfazed, pulled over and cleaned it up without complaint.

When they returned to Allyson Island, they surprised the boys with the little snowballs. Brent cuddled Pearl on the couch while Bradford held Dove in the air like Simba from *The Lion King*. Moira recalled Jeffrey standing in the doorway, watching the scene unfold, with his arms crossed and a familiar glint in his eyes.

Moira was sitting quietly now with the eight-year-old cats and watching as the late August sun sank lower on the horizon over the marsh, transforming the sky into beautiful colors of orange and pink. She thought about the sunset cruise she had planned along the Atlantic, where she and her birthday guests would witness the same sky changing into a canvas of colors while gentle waves rocked the boat. She was determined to make every moment of the weekend special. Moira mulled over the ideas of having a bonfire, hosting a game night under the stars, or maybe painting canvases in the courtyard with Rober, her artist friend.

Drowsy, thirsty, and tired of brainstorming plans for the party, she gently nudged the cats off her lap, grabbed her empty glass, pen, and notepad, and headed back toward the house. Her steps were unsteady at first, but she quickly regained her balance as her bare feet sank into the soft, plush Bermuda grass, with Dove and Pearl frolicking behind her. The outdoor lights surrounding the pool, courtyard, and back patios suddenly turned on, triggered by a timer, casting long shadows of the oaks, palms, and palmettos across the lawn. It marked the end of another long, lonely day.

"Time to go in, girls," Moira said to her feline friends as she stepped onto the cool cobblestone patio and entered the dark house.

~

THE PALM'S FRONDS swayed in the wind, moving in and out like a steady, relentless breath outside the open window. A salty breeze stirred the white linen curtains, sending them brushing against the darkened room like a ghost. Moira lay on top of the covers in the white robe she had put on after dinner, her body stretched across the wide bed that had once held two people.

Her fingers clutched the glass of wine resting on her stomach. It was her third one since her dinner of leftover lasagna, maybe fourth, and the stem was smudged with fingerprints, the red liquid nearly gone. Her eyes, wide and sleepless, stared up at the coffered ceiling where the moonlight traced patterns in the shadows. She could hear the curtains brushing against the hardwood floor.

Jeffrey's side of the bed was untouched. Still. Always still.

She exhaled sharply through her nose and said to the white cats purring on their backs at her feet, "You'd think I'd be better at this by now."

The clock ticked somewhere behind her, loudly, in the dark. She reached over and turned it to face the wall. She tried closing her eyes, but that only made it worse. Some nights she swore she felt the warm weight of him there beside her—and then she'd open her eyes and the room would be just as empty as her arms.

She sipped the last of the wine, then let the glass roll gently off her stomach onto the mattress. It didn't break. It just lay there, hollow and fragile. She turned to her side, wrapping the sheet around her like armor, trying to block out the chill that had nothing to do with the wind flowing through the room.

Chapter 5

Gemma Gardner never appreciated the phrase "You carry your weight well," but it was one she had heard more than once. She knew what the saying implied—that she had a pretty face, round and charming with flawless milky skin and framed with bouncy brown hair, and she also dressed trendily, cute. All that was fine and well, but the expression also meant she was too big.

Gemma had been heavyset for as long as she could remember. She could vividly recall being in elementary school and her tall, skinny father sitting at the kitchen table, his brows furrowed with concern as he sternly told her mother, "You can't feed her so much, Linda. She'll be as big as a barn." Those words still lingered in her mind decades after they were spoken.

Linda, Gemma's mother, expressed her affection through cooking. Every meal was a labor of love, filled with hearty portions of meat—fried chicken or smothered pork chops—accompanied by two vegetables and bread. However, the vegetables were never served in their natural state. There was no steaming and light seasoning in Linda's kitchen. Vegetables were coated in breadcrumbs or baked into comforting cheesy casseroles. Gravy formed a pond in the center of the mashed potatoes. The homemade cornbread muffins or biscuits accompanying the meals were delicious and warm proof of Linda's culinary skills. While her mama's meals brought Gemma temporary comfort, they also contributed to the weight she carried both physically and emotionally.

Gemma pondered all of this as she sat on the couch in her office at Emory Hills Realty, gazing out at the rain soaking downtown Atlanta. The sweltering summer humidity caused steam to rise from the rooftops and roads, creating a thick fog in the air. She turned away from the view and focused on her computer, scrolling through a website in search of a bathing suit for Moira's birthday weekend coming up in a couple of weeks. The thought of trying on swimsuits in a store made her cringe, so she opted to order several online instead, hoping at least one would fit. If not, she could always return the ones that didn't work or use them as furniture covers.

"That was rude," she said, acknowledging the self-deprecating thought out loud.

The bathing suits that ended up in her cart resembled cheerleading outfits more than anything else, featuring sleeveless full-coverage tops paired with skirts. This style reminded Gemma of the customized uniform that had fit her snugly in high school. Although she didn't have the cute and petite figure of some other girls, Gemma was popular thanks to her big personality and infectious laughter. She dedicated her time and talents to various clubs, and during her senior year, she had a leading role as Rizzo in the Tunnel Hill High School production of *Grease*.

During the Friday evening performance, Gemma caught the eye of Tyler Gardner, the ruggedly handsome cousin of one of her schoolmates. His charm made other boys dislike him while girls adored him. Gemma was both shocked and flattered when he chose to pay attention to her.

"Why did you choose me?" she asked him one night only a few weeks into their relationship, while they sat on the tailgate of his truck under the Georgia stars. "You are so handsome, Tyler. You could have someone much thinner, much more beautiful."

"But you have such a pretty face," he said before he kissed her forehead and finished singing the chorus to an Alan Jackson song playing on the radio.

She entered her credit card information and slammed her laptop shut after successfully placing her order for the bathing suits. She dreaded seeing the charge from the plus-sized women's clothing company on her bank statement, as it would only lead to ridicule from Tyler. The thought of the insults he would throw her way made her roll her eyes, though she was used to it by now.

Over the years, Tyler's scrutiny of Gemma had intensified. He'd recently started counting her calories, his critical gaze fixed on her whenever she reached for sugary, high-calorie snacks. One evening at dinner a few years ago, he chastised her for choosing a glass of sweet tea instead of unsweetened.

"We're born and raised in Georgia, Tyler. Unsweet tea is blasphemy!" Gemma's Southern drawl declared.

"Zero-calorie aspartame, Gemma. Ever heard of it?"

"Cancer, Tyler. Ever heard of it?"

He smirked nonchalantly, as if he believed the love of his life consuming a carcinogenic sweetener was preferable to her being overweight. What began as playful banter over tea transformed into a strained silence, and Gemma felt the weight of his judgment pressing down on her. She recalled their disagreement each time she fixed herself a glass of sweet tea, which was every day.

Thunder rumbled over the city as Gemma made calculations in her mind. There were two weeks and three days until the birthday weekend on Allyson Island. By cutting out all sugars, starches, and carbohydrates, she hoped to lose a pound each day. However, that still wouldn't be enough to fit into the stylish, boutique corduroy pants she loved but hadn't been able to button for nearly six months. What would be the point of dieting anyway? Mo was a fabulous hostess who would inevitably indulge her guests over the weekend. The thought of eating whatever she wanted without feeling Tyler's disapproving stare brought a smile to her face.

Gemma walked over to her messy desk and picked up her phone. While standing there, she grabbed a handful of salty potato chips from a bag amid the clutter. Then she texted Mo, I'll see you on the 20th. Can't wait! XOXO

Moira immediately responded, Antonio is making his famous chocolate panna cotta. XOXO

Gemma smiled before deleting the text so Tyler would never see it.

—

GEMMA HOWELL HAD become friends with Celia Kate Hopkins in elementary school through alphabetized seating charts. As they grew older, they chose to sit together in class. In fifth grade, Moira joined their friendship after Celia Kate's twin brother passed her a note in English class asking if she would be his girlfriend. Although their middle school romance lasted only until lunch the next day, Celia Kate and Gemma continued their friendship with Moira.

Moira Wallace came from a wealthy lumber-business background and lived in a big white house on acres of rolling hills, while CK and Gemma were middle-class kids raised in middle-class neighborhoods. Despite their different upbringings, Moira was a good friend who never boasted or bragged like some of the other rich kids in their hometown. Her humility was evident in her warm smile and the genuine way she treated others, making her just like Mrs. Louise Wallace—beautiful on the inside as well as the outside.

Their friendship endured the dramatics of adolescence, and at Tunnel Hill High School, it was rare to see one of them without the others. Moira was the knockout—homecoming queen and a cheerleader too—while Celia Kate stood out as an athlete, excelling in basketball and track. Gemma embraced her role as the funny "big girl" of the trio, both then and now.

Even though the three friends remained close after graduating high school and while pursuing college, careers, and families, the bond between CK and Gemma was different. In their decades-long friendship, they never went more than a few days without speaking. They also shared secrets they wouldn't tell anyone else, not even Moira, and spoke to each other frankly, like sisters.

Gemma brushed the greasy chip crumbs from her hands and settled at her desk. She felt a sense of joy thinking about the four-hour drive from Atlanta to Savannah. With CK as her companion, a mix of good conversation, '90s music, and a car full of snacks was exactly what she needed and deserved. After all, she sold two multimillion-dollar homes in August. On top of that, she was juggling numerous stressful commitments for Carolina's senior class, including building the homecoming float, selling raffle tickets, and organizing a car wash to fund the senior dance. Tyler, of course, offered no help. When he wasn't busy selling insurance, he was off hunting or fishing . . . among other things.

~

GEMMA LAY ON her side in the king-size bed, the duvet bunched around her waist, one arm tucked beneath her cheek. The other side of the bed was cold and empty. It had been for a while now. Tyler said he had plans, but she didn't ask with whom. She didn't need to.

Her eyes burned from crying, though the tears had stopped hours ago. Now she just stared at the shadows on the wall and chewed on the inside of her cheek. She looked at her reflection in the mirror across the room. The outline of her body, covered in moonlight, made her stomach twist. She pulled the blanket up higher.

Tyler's words echoed in her head: *"Maybe if you took better care of yourself."*

She clenched her jaw and blinked hard, whispering obscenities about him in the dark. What she needed was a snack. She had discovered a box of Girl Scout cookies in the freezer earlier that day, and that was exactly what she wanted: Thin Mints and a big glass of milk. However, she didn't want to risk being in the kitchen, rummaging through the refrigerator, when Tyler finally came home. That would just be more fuel for the fire.

She turned onto her back, staring up at the ceiling. The silence pressed down on her chest, heavy and familiar. Tomorrow she would put on her blazer, paint on a smile, and sell someone their dream home. She was good at that. She was good at making things look perfect—at making strangers believe in happiness.

But tonight she let herself feel the weight of betrayal, the ache of years spent shrinking herself to make room for a man who never tried to understand her. She pulled the blanket tighter around her and whispered into the empty room, "I deserve better."

It was the truest thing she'd said in a long time.

Chapter 6

C ELIA KATE TOOK the last clean plate from the dishwasher and placed it in the cabinet before making her midmorning school rounds. Sophie preferred to do her work at the kitchen table. By this time each day, she was speed-reading through a literary classic before writing a few paragraphs on what she had retained. This morning it was Frances Hodgson Burnett's *The Secret Garden*.

"Mama, would you say Mrs. Medlock is fastidious?" Sophie asked while tapping her pencil on the table.

"I'm not sure what *fastidious* means, Sophie," CK answered as she peered over her eleven-year-old's shoulder at the beautiful penmanship on the notebook paper.

"What about capricious?" she asked, looking up at her mother with wide, cocoa-colored eyes.

"Sure, baby." CK tapped her daughter's shoulder and walked toward the adjoining dining room where she found her nine-year-old, Tucker, with his head down on the cherry table cluttered with books and worksheets.

"Up and at it, boy," she said loudly to the fourth grader.

His dark, shaggy head bolted upright, and he sleepily groaned. "Mama, I hate this. I can't do it."

Celia Kate sat in the plaid captain's chair beside him and reviewed the work he'd done so far.

"All of this is correct, Tucker. You've done a great job here." She placed the paper back on the table and gave his shoulder an encouraging squeeze. "Being unable to do something and not wanting to do something aren't the same thing. Get this done and you can go outside for a while, work on your fort in the woods. The rain isn't going to move in for a couple of hours."

He argued, "But why do I need to know how to figure sales tax? You and Dad buy everything for me."

She smiled at him and stood before saying, "The lesson is percentages and decimal places, and your dad and I aren't going to buy you another fishing pole unless you finish all your work."

"Yes, ma'am," he mumbled before the sounds of scribbling filled the room.

She knew that would motivate him because Tucker had a curious and adventurous spirit. She was thankful he would rather be outside climbing trees or catching fish than spending his free time staring at a screen—unless it was the thrill of an Atlanta Braves game on the television.

Unlike most little girls, Celia Kate never wrote "teacher" on her "What I Want to Be When I Grow Up" worksheet in elementary school. In fact, she cried most mornings before her mother dropped her off at kindergarten and struggled academically for the next twelve years. Her true passion was found on the track or the basketball court, where she thrived as a member of the 1992 Lady Wildcats, the first basketball team in school history to earn the title of 2A Georgia State Champions. CK's athletic achievements far outweighed her academic ones.

After barely graduating from Kennesaw State, CK began her career in sports medicine, a job that both paid the bills and brought her happiness. She felt at home being around athletes and never imagined she would leave a career she loved to homeschool her children.

But six years ago she couldn't ignore the signs to pull her kids from public school. At the time, CK's oldest child, Silas, was ten years old and struggling to do the same things Tucker could easily do at the dining table. Silas had severe "testing anxiety" where he would shut down and his mind would go blank at the very moment a test was placed before him. School nights in the Stokes' house consisted of cramming, reading, flash cards, and bouts of crying and frustration—from both mother and son. And because it was impossible for Silas to excel in the public school system without passing tests, he had to repeat the fifth grade. It broke CK's heart that her son was teased by his classmates and called a failure. She mourned watching her once-happy little boy become self-conscious and depressed.

That same year Sophie was in kindergarten. Her teacher frequently sent home notes complaining that the energetic five-year-old talked too much during the day, disrupting the entire class. After a loud telephone argument between Celia Kate and Sophie's teacher, CK formed the opinion that public school was a rigid environment where children were told to sit down, stop talking, and conform. She believed her kids were valued solely for their test scores and their ability to be quiet. Without consulting anyone, not even her husband, Sean, she decided to pull Silas and Sophie out of the same elementary school she had attended as a child, and that was that.

In the early days of homeschooling, CK felt overwhelmed and uncertain, often questioning whether she could successfully teach her children everything they needed to know. Sean was supportive, but she sensed that he secretly shared her concerns. Thankfully, CK gained confidence after dedicating countless hours to watching instructional videos and participating in homeschooling forums. She was grateful to discover a welcoming community of fellow homeschoolers, a group of cheerleaders who provided the support she needed.

Before long, CK's preconceived notions about homeschooled children were proven wrong. They were not socially awkward; in fact, they were remarkably articulate and often engaged in richer and more meaningful conversations than many adults. These children weren't captivated by screens or hesitant to make eye contact. Instead, they exuded confidence and curiosity. They were leaders in their own right, bursting with ambition and creativity. CK was inspired by these remarkable kids and knew she wanted her own children to become self-assured, engaged individuals ready to take on the world.

Seeing Silas happily and diligently working at his desk in the office was the sweetest fruit of CK's labor. Now sixteen, he was on the fast track to college to major in graphic design. His struggles in fifth grade now felt like a distant memory, a forgotten blip on the radar of his academic success. But feeding himself, taking responsibility around the house, getting a job—those were skills she had neglected to teach him, and his lack of self-sufficiency weighed heavily on her. By constantly catering to him—making his snacks, cleaning his cluttered room, and purchasing everything he asked for such as new shoes, gaming headsets, and music or movie subscriptions without suggesting that he should work for it—she had created a protective bubble around her older son that now felt difficult to burst.

"How's it going?" she asked her handsome boy with dark hair and eyes like his siblings.

He swiveled around in his seat and looked at his mother while she sat on the oversized corduroy chair next to the row of windows.

"It's going pretty well. I need to finish the worksheet on the stuff we went over yesterday," he replied while stifling a yawn.

"Do we need to review it again, or do you think you understand it?"

"No, ma'am." He stretched his long arms above his head, causing the Nirvana logo on his dad's old T-shirt to become more visible. "I've got a handle on it. Once I finish that, I want to work on some typography stuff for Sophie's website. I'm not happy with the layout."

Sophie had blossomed into a young entrepreneur. With each stroke of her calligraphy pen, she created beautiful handmade greeting cards and sold them on the website that Silas had built for her. She had already saved up quite a nest egg.

"I'm proud of you, kid."

"Thanks, Mom." He nodded and grinned. "Do you think you could show me how proud you are of me by washing the hamper of dirty clothes in my bathroom? I'm down to one pair of underwear, and I'm definitely not wearing Tucker's Ninja Turtle Underoos."

"I wouldn't let you anyway!" Tucker yelled from the dining room.

"Yes, son."

While she sorted her grown son's laundry that was soaked in week-old sweat from the last time he begrudgingly mowed the yard, she thought back to him being that defenseless, premature baby facing a variety of health issues. During Silas's time in the NICU, the family endured sleepless nights, anxious doctors, and uncertain diagnoses. Being in that valley nearly shattered Sean and Celia Kate's new marriage. CK leaned heavily on her faith and her mother's support to get through it. But it was no surprise that CK was so protective of her miracle child. While she also worried about Sophie and Tucker, her concerns for Silas had always been far greater.

That same afternoon, while Tucker hammered away on his tree fort, Sophie sat at the kitchen table working on greeting cards, and Silas took a nap on freshly washed sheets, Celia Kate checked the calendar hanging on the office wall to see if anything conflicted with Moira's birthday weekend. On that Saturday, Cumberland State would begin accepting scholarship essays and online applications. She was hesitant to let Silas handle this on his own. Would he answer the questions in a way that would guarantee he received more scholarship money? What about the essay? He wasn't strong grammatically, and he might need her help. She sat in the office chair, her anxious mind racing.

The reality was that if CK didn't do things, things simply wouldn't get done. Several years ago, she had dared to leave for the weekend to attend her cousin's wedding in Fort Worth with her mother. When she returned home, her house looked like the hotel room in *Fear and Loathing in Las Vegas* and her cat, Chipper Jones, had nearly starved to death. She'd also stayed at Moira's place two other times—right after Jeffrey died and for a weekend two summers ago—and each time she returned to a house where penicillin had begun to grow on the damp clothes piled at the bottom of the hamper. Removing the green spots that had stained Sean's favorite work polo was nearly impossible.

Her thought process went something like this: *If I'm not here, will Silas complete his application correctly? If he doesn't, he'll be stuck living at home forever, which wouldn't be so terrible for me to have my baby boy at home for all of eternity, but I would have to listen to Sean gripe about cutting cords for the rest of my life. Will my husband, in his usual distracted manner, remember to lock all the doors before bedtime? Or will the family be vulnerable to bad guys and thieves roaming the neighborhood? What if Chipper Jones slips out the back door, escapes into the night, and becomes prey for coyotes lurking nearby? Who will oversee the payment and shipping process if Sophie receives an order on her website while I'm away? Will Sean and the kids get to church on time on Sunday morning? Who will iron the khaki pants and button-downs? What will they eat that isn't coated in red dye 40? Does Sean know not to put plastic in the microwave?*

What about other catastrophic possibilities? What if her healthy, active dad, who now lived in Pensacola, became ill? What if her twin brother, a lineman, fell from a towering electric pole? What if her in-laws— *Stop, CK!* The flood of worst-case scenarios was too much to bear. The anxiety coursing through her made it painfully clear: She could not leave.

She continued to ponder these thoughts that evening as thunder rumbled and sheets of rain beat against the farmhouse's tin roof. Lightning flashed through the window above the kitchen sink, causing her to flinch as she turned the chicken breasts sizzling in a cast iron skillet.

"You're going to go," Sean said, breaking the stream of panic in her mind.

She looked at him standing beside her, slathering peanut butter on a piece of wheat bread.

"To Moira's party. I saw the invitation sitting in the junk mail pile, ready to be thrown away, so I know you're standing there mulling over worst-case scenarios and trying to talk yourself out of going, but you're going."

"Sean, why in the world are you fixing a peanut butter and jelly sandwich when I'm frying chicken for supper?" She scowled at him.

"Appetizer. I'll save plenty of room for the chicken."

Please don't put that same knife into the jelly, she thought right before he put the same knife into the jelly.

"Like I was saying, you're going to go to Moira's party and you're going to have a great time with your friends." Sean quickly glanced at her as she poked at the golden chicken crackling in the hot oil. "And David Markowski is *not* going to have a great time when I beat him at golf that Saturday."

"Golf? What are the kids going to do home alone while you're at the course all day?" Celia Kate slapped her hand on her hip.

"Well, as long as I hide the matches, they won't burn the place down." Sean scoffed. "Our children are sixteen, eleven, and nine, CK. You have got to cut the—"

"I'd be more worried about your throat than their cords." Celia Kate waved the steaming, oily fork at Sean.

He left the peanut butter and jelly jars open on the counter and walked away after saying, "I love you, but I'm kicking you out, woman. You're going to have three days of relaxation!"

The thought terrified her.

Chapter 7

ERIN SAT ON the edge of her unmade bed in her dimly lit bedroom, her fingers gliding over the cracked screen of her phone as she scrolled through her ex-husband's Facebook page. His new bride was blonde. Tucking her short, stark black hair behind her pierced ears, she thought, *I knew Phillip always had a thing for blondes.* Erin carefully examined a selfie of Phillip, his gorgeous wife, and her two young children posing against the postcard backdrop of Tybee Island's sandy beaches—a tight-knit family enjoying the warmth of the late-summer sun and each other.

As Erin continued to snoop through his profile, the next set of photos revealed the interior of Phillip and his platinum-headed bride's new home. It appeared that Phillip had purchased the brick house at the beginning of the construction phase, allowing Sister Golden Hair to choose her favorite paint colors, tile, and cabinetry. *How fascinating.*

Erin had never owned a new home, much less built one. She had always lived in poverty, raised in a holler in the Blue Ridge Mountains by parents who had various health issues and struggled financially. In his early twenties, Phillip was working on the railroad in her small North Carolina town when he noticed her, only eighteen at the time, at the diner where she had worked since she was thirteen to help her parents make ends meet. He took her away from that awful place and brought her down to Savannah, where she basked in his affection and provision. However, after three or four blissful months of marriage, Phillip changed. It was as if a storm had rolled in unexpectedly and wreaked havoc on everything in its path. After twelve years of storm damage, Erin finally walked away, but not unscathed. Erin's pride and joy—the *only* good thing she had ever received from Phillip Pepperell— was PJ.

It made Erin angry to think about Phillip and his wife enjoying a comfortable life in their lovely new home in a Savannah suburb while she and Phillip Jr. lived in a run-down apartment on the outskirts of town, where gunshots sometimes rang out and the flickering streetlights cast shadows across the cracked pavement. It made Erin angry to think the blonde Mrs. Pepperell was afforded the luxury of being a stay-at-home mother while Erin worked tirelessly at two jobs: as a clerk at a convenience store that had been robbed several times over the years and as a housekeeper on Allyson Island. It made her angry to think of Phillip being a good father to his stepchildren when he had no relationship with his own son.

Erin couldn't bear to think about Phillip any longer, so she irritably tossed her phone onto the bed while the image of her ex-husband's smiling, bearded face pressed into his wife's fair hair was still visible on the screen. She shuffled into the bathroom and looked at her tired reflection in the mirror. She was only thirty-eight, but the abuse she endured at Phillip's hands, combined with constant worry, multiple jobs, and lack of sleep, had taken a toll on her once-youthful appearance. Crow's-feet had formed around her dark eyes, and her once shiny and thick black hair appeared dull and thin. Each day that she went to work for Moira, she felt intimidated by her boss's flawless and seemingly timeless beauty, even though she was twelve years older than Erin.

As she splashed cool water on her face, Erin thought she would rather be paid to work at Moira's party than attend as a guest. While a weekend of pampering would be lovely, massages and Italian pastries wouldn't cover her rent and electric bill. The hatchback had recently started making a funny noise, and it wouldn't be long until it needed repairs. Where would that money come from?

Next, she put a dollop of moisturizer on her weary face that resembled her long-dead mother's because of the creases, dark circles, and overall fatigue of her skin. She continued to dwell on the anxiety of being at the party among Savannah's elite. What would she wear? Her clothes came from the clearance racks of the same store where she bought milk and bread. Her beat-up hatchback would stick out like a sore thumb parked next to European sedans. She would feel safer on a shift at the convenience store, behind the bars on the windows, than she would in a house full of socialites who would surely judge her from behind their long-stemmed crystal wineglasses.

She turned off the bathroom light and walked into the small kitchen, where the invitation sat on the chipped plastic counter. With an exasperated sigh, she tossed it into the garbage can, feeling a mixture of relief and disappointment. Erin then returned to her small bedroom, pulling the phone from the top of her thin beige comforter.

"Hey, Moira, I just found out I need to work at the Family Pantry during your birthday party weekend. The schedule just came out," she said, her voice laced with reluctance as she delivered her lie.

"Oh, I'm really disappointed to hear that," Mo replied. "I was looking forward to spending some quality time with you—completely off the clock, you know? You've been such a big help to me around here. I know you're—you are," Moira stammered, "juggling your other job and taking care of your son, so I wanted to find a way to show my appreciation to you. Did you check the itinerary on the back of the invitation? We'll be getting massages, Erin. Don't tell me you couldn't use a massage!" Moira squealed with childlike delight.

Well, of course worn-out and stressed Erin could use a massage. And she could use some good sleep, in a safe place far from drug deals on the corner and dangers of the night. The thought of a weekend away felt almost as intoxicating as what Moira was feeling at that moment—an opportunity to forget the mounting bills and even the cockroaches she spotted scuttling across her bedroom baseboard while she listened to Moira's drunken pleading. It would be a blessing to be too distracted to think of Phillip and Blondie laughing joyfully together on sun-soaked beaches. And it would be nice to pretend she was part of the privileged for once, even if she drove a sputtering jalopy and wore bargain-basement clothing. Moira persisted, painting vivid pictures of laughter and relaxation, and Erin finally relented.

After all, she deserved it.

Chapter 8

NELL STOOD IN her dark, rustic kitchen and carefully read the itinerary on the back of the elegant, heavyweight black invitation before she tossed it on top of the army recruitment brochure in the garbage can. She turned to her husband, Chip, sitting in the leather recliner in the adjoining hearth room, and said, "Wine, wine, and more wine."

"Nothing wrong with a glass of wine, Nelly," he replied without removing his eyes from the thick murder mystery novel in his hand. "Jesus turned the water into it at Cana, you know?"

"And I would have guzzled three jars before Saint Peter had to escort me out of the reception," she replied with sarcasm.

"You haven't had a drop in five years, Nell. You have self-control to make it through the other social affairs we attend. I know you can survive a weekend on Allyson Island." Chip turned the page of his book.

"It's not that I think I'm going to fall off the wagon. I'm past that. I know how to confidently stand by my convictions and ask the Lord for strength in times of temptation." Nell sighed as she stepped into the cozy hearth room, her eyes settling on the matching chair beside Chip's.

Alcohol addiction is often associated with images of quickly downing shots of tequila, chugging cases of beer, and getting into drunken fights in bars. However, Nell's relationship with alcohol was quite different. Growing up with an alcoholic father, she was acutely aware of the dangers of excessive drinking. Yet, as a good Catholic girl, she also viewed wine as an integral part of celebrations and something that could be beneficial for the soul.

Chip, Nell's college sweetheart, was a Southern Baptist, not a Catholic. Along with him came his Southern Baptist family, known for their casseroles, potlucks, and teetotaling lifestyle. Chip had a Methodist uncle who liked to share a joke: "You know why I don't go fishing with just one Baptist? He'll drink all my beer. If I take two, then he won't touch a drop." This joke contained some truth. Whenever Chip did have a drink, it was always in private—either in the hearth room or on the back patio during a summer evening—never in public, as he was concerned about causing a brother or sister to stumble into their own temptations.

After Chip and Nell got married, Nell managed to hide her enjoyment of wine while outside the home. However, she still had a few glasses during meals and before bed. It wasn't until years later that she realized the more she tried to conceal her drinking from her in-laws and church family, the more she craved it. Eventually she found herself consuming a bottle or two a day. Her drinking behavior led her to say and do things that were uncharacteristic for her, including posting silly ramblings on her social media accounts late at night. Many mornings, with a terrible headache and a steaming cup of coffee, she would discover the posts she had typed in the early hours and feel a sense of shame.

After deleting a confusing and deeply embarrassing rant about Tate's girlfriend at the time—a post that had received no likes despite being seen by hundreds and led to a scolding from her freshman son—Nell felt more exposed and humiliated than ever.

As she buried her throbbing head in her hands, she composed an apology to the young girl she had called a Jezebel and thought, *I can't keep doing this.*

Nell believed she could quit drinking cold turkey, but as the days went by, she quickly realized that breaking free from her habit was much harder than she had imagined. The harsh realization of her dependence on alcohol hit her like a ton of bricks, leaving her feeling vulnerable and scared that her family might fall apart because of it. Ironically, her fears about drinking only led her to drink more. Each hangover and reprimand from her husband and children about her behavior caused Nell to drown further in guilt.

"That is not merely guilt," her pastor told her as she and Chip sat in his office at church. "That is conviction, Nell. It isn't meant to condemn you or make you feel worthless. Conviction is meant to lead to repentance. Some people can enjoy wine at a wedding or another joyous occasion, but others must avoid it altogether. It sounds to me, Nell, that the Lord is telling you that you belong to the latter group."

"I know it's hurting me. I know it makes me act out of character and embarrasses my family. But in all honesty, I don't want to stop drinking," Nell confessed, unable to look at Chip sitting in the chair beside her. "I like it too much."

"Denying yourself and following Jesus is never easy," Pastor Floyd replied with love. "But you can rely on his strength in your times of weakness."

She wanted to follow Jesus because she believed his plan was better than hers. She loved him for restoring her parents' marriage after her father's drinking led to an affair. She watched God at work when her daddy got sober and rededicated his life to the church, serving until his last breath. When he suddenly died, her mother endured with the comfort that only the good Lord could provide. All the prayers God had answered for Nell and her family put into perspective that the least she could do was deny herself. So she finally did. And that was five years ago.

She regularly attended Celebrate Recovery meetings and counseling sessions with her pastor, and most importantly, she leaned on Jesus. In the beginning of her journey, she faced many challenges that were often difficult, but staying sober was worth it. The clarity of mind, absence of guilt, peace in her soul, and sense of God's presence were far more valuable than any fleeting moment of indulgence.

Despite all the gains she had made in her sobriety, she still didn't want to go to Moira's party, and she told Chip so.

Chip dog-eared the page, closed the book, and gave her a warm smile as she fell into the chair beside him. "And why not?"

"I'm not particularly fond of being around drunk people. Especially Moira."

"Don't worry about what Moira and her other guests are doing, and don't judge them either, Nelly. That is a matter between them and God."

"I really don't know why I was invited to her party. Mo and I haven't spoken in months. She's still angry with me for calling her out about all that drama at the Sunday school Christmas party that she hosted. I mean, we are Baptists. We don't have an open bar at church functions! And not only that, but she got hammered. Her rendition of 'Santa Baby' while standing on top of her coffee table was not an innocent performance, Chip! Marty slapped her husband for staring too hard. The whole evening was like a scene out of *Animal House*." Nell picked at her long nails coated in clear polish.

"*Animal House* is a stretch." Chip shook his balding head and set the book on the polished mahogany table beside his oversized chair. He turned to look at her with love and concern in his eyes. "Go and have a good time, Nelly. It's an opportunity for you to make amends with Moira. This invitation is her olive branch. Besides, you need a weekend away. It has been tough on you with Taylor moving out, and Tate will soon be joining the—"

Nell interrupted her husband, and anxiety was obvious in her voice. "I texted Jess and asked if she was going, but she's going to be out of town. I won't know anyone else there. It will just be Mo's friends from her hometown, her sisters-in-law, and a bunch of other lushes I've never met. I keep picturing a Sodom and Gomorrah situation."

Chip laughed. "*Animal House* and Sodom and Gomorrah?"

Nell scoffed.

"Go, Nelly." He grabbed the book from the table and opened it to the dog-eared page. "And represent Jesus well by showing Moira some patience and love."

With a frown, Nell murmured, "I'm afraid I won't."

She left Chip in the hearth room to continue reading his grisly story. She retrieved the invitation from the stainless-steel trash can, sighed, then secured it to the refrigerator with a magnet that read, "I can do all things through Christ who strengthens me."

Chapter 9

Two hours after leaving her house in Tunnel Hill, CK pulled her black SUV into Gemma's brick driveway in the Atlanta suburb and honked the horn once, twice, and then a long third time for added annoyance. For CK and Gemma, this kind of playful irritation was the foundation of their friendship, a bond born in sarcasm, teasing, and laughter.

Celia Kate spent every moment of the entire two-hour ride to Gemma's worrying about things back home. Sophie had called to say she wasn't sure if she could continue reading *Watership Down* by Richard Adams because she couldn't bear to read about one of the rabbits dying. CK couldn't remember if the protagonist, Hazel, was killed in the novel, so she encouraged Sophie to start *Little Women* instead. Tucker also called to ask where more nails were because he was working on his fort's roof. Surprisingly, Silas had yet to call his mother that morning.

CK honked the horn again, and, wearing a cute short-sleeved black knee-length dress with tall brown boots, Gemma stepped out of the side door of her white-brick home shaded by oaks. It was a beautiful, classic house—a farmhouse in the middle of the city—reflecting the black and white trend seen across the United States, thanks to Joanna Gaines. Gemma had no fewer than three barn doors in her home and a "Fresh Eggs" sign on the wall, though CK knew the eggs in Gemma's refrigerator were shipped from a large-scale egg farm to the superstore next to the strip mall.

Gemma stumbled toward CK's honking SUV, her breath coming in slight gasps as she struggled to pull an extra-large pink suitcase behind her, its wheels clattering on the brick pavers. A matching overnight bag swung from her arm, while in her other hand she clutched a stainless-steel cup and a grocery sack overflowing with what appeared to be an assortment of snacks. CK knew she was going to have to hold her tongue. Gemma had shared her latest doctor's report with her a few days ago—her bad cholesterol was high, her good cholesterol was nonexistent, and her blood pressure was teetering on hypertension; issues that could all be resolved with a healthy diet and exercise. But she wouldn't admonish her or be responsible for chipping away at any more of Gemma's self-esteem. That was Tyler's job.

As Gemma reached the vehicle, she opened the back door, its hinges creaking slightly, and started tossing her belongings into the space with haphazard motions.

"Why in Sam Hill do you keep honking the horn? You're going to get the HOA called on me! I'm already on thin ice with them because that delinquent Carolina is dating drives a monster truck with the loudest exhaust on earth. Every time he comes over it sounds like a freight train rolling through the neighborhood."

CK turned in the driver's seat and asked Gemma, "What do you possibly have in that enormous suitcase? We're going to Moira's for one weekend, not Seville for a month."

"My clothes are big, CK." Gemma huffed. "Big clothes need a big suitcase."

"And what about that other one?" she inquired, watching as Gemma slammed the back door and crawled into the passenger seat, her face still flushed from the effort of lugging the heavy bags. She forcefully placed the tumbler into the cup holder, and the ice cubes clinked together.

"In that other bag is everything I need to carry my weight well," Gemma replied with a cheeky grin, placing the grocery sack on the center console. "That should be enough food to tide me over for a few minutes."

CK gripped the steering wheel and looked at her friend. "I'm not listening to you make fun of yourself for the next three days. Stop putting yourself down or I'm leaving you here."

"Okay, okay." Gemma nodded and rifled through her snacks. "Look, we haven't even left the driveway and already my sugar is low."

"Gemma, I'm serious about this," CK said sternly. "I'm taking *you* on this trip, not Tyler, but already I hear stuff *he* would say coming out of *your* mouth."

"Only when donuts aren't going *in* my mouth." Gemma snickered.

"Gemma!" CK scolded before she threw her hands in the air.

Gemma laughed. "Okay, I'm sorry, CK. I am good enough. I am smart enough. And, doggone it, people like me."

CK first met Tyler Gardner in 1994 when he accompanied Gemma to their hangout in the grocery store parking lot, where high school kids gathered on truck tailgates after football games to talk and sing the Seattle grunge catalog. It didn't take long for Celia Kate to realize she wasn't going to be a fan of his. Gemma laughed and playfully swatted at his arm while CK and Moira exchanged looks of disgust at his degrading remarks about her weight. CK's mama used to say that a boy was mean to a girl because he liked her. While this might have been true for younger kids, Gemma believed it still applied—even at seventeen. But CK saw his actions for what they were: belittling and ridiculing.

She would never say it out loud, but a callous thought flitted through CK's mind when Gemma eagerly tore open a crinkly bag of chips and the sound of the crumpling package echoed in the car as she drove out of the neighborhood. *Bet you can't eat just one . . . bag.* The Tyler-esque jab immediately made CK wince and feel like a lousy friend.

It was plain to see that Gemma had put on more weight since their last get-together on the Fourth of July, when they had spent a carefree day at Lake Lanier, basking in the sun and splashing in the water. The only annoyance of the day was Tyler's drunken insults about Gemma's swim skirt, coupled with a bet he made with his daughter about whether his kindhearted wife would sink or float when she entered the cool water. More than once that afternoon Sean had to calm Celia Kate down.

"Hey, giving Tyler a piece of your mind would only make things worse. And if you say something to him, he's liable to say something back to you, and then I'll have to kill him and I really don't want to commit murder on my day off," Sean said to his wife after swimming over to where she lounged on a raft away from the others.

She'd taken his hand resting on the float and said, "Thank you for being a good husband."

———

WHILE GEMMA SAVORED the saltiness of the potato chips, she gazed out the passenger side window and quietly sighed in relief to be leaving Atlanta and Tyler and senior year madness behind. She was excited about the food and friendship that awaited her.

CK and Moira were the only two people with whom she could truly be herself without fear of ridicule. They loved her enough to let her live on her terms, and they never insulted her or even suggested that she lose an ounce of weight. She could eat all she wanted in their presence without fear of judgment.

"So what's new?" CK veered the SUV onto the interstate, and the GPS updated their estimated time of arrival to five hours and twelve minutes.

"Not much. Carolina and I had a pretty heated argument this morning."

Gemma and Tyler's only child, Carolina, didn't resemble her mother in the slightest. Tall and thin, she had been crowned Miss Pre-Teen Georgia a few years earlier. Carolina adored her mother but often teamed up with her dad to poke fun at her. "Mama, you're my big, safe, squishy place to land," she would say when she rested on her shoulder after a hard day. Or "Mama, I love you as big as your belly." Gemma would laugh at her daughter's comments, but they only made her more self-conscious.

Gemma continued, "Carolina really wants to go to the Virgin Islands for her senior trip—with Colton. Has she lost her mind? I'm not allowing my daughter to go off to a foreign country with her boyfriend, especially not at my expense!"

CK set the cruise control and replied, "I'm fairly certain that the Virgin Islands are not a foreign country, Gemma. They are an unincorporated territory of the United States."

"It might as well be Russia, CK. And she's not going!" Gemma shifted in the passenger seat.

"It blows my mind how much kids expect these days just for graduating high school. You and I didn't go on a senior trip."

"No, we sure didn't. Moira's daddy took her somewhere exotic like Seychelles, but you and I spent our summer after high school graduation at the Dairy Dream. We lived off chocolate shakes and chicken strip baskets," Gemma reminisced with a broad smile.

"Oh my goodness. I haven't thought about one of those peanut butter and chocolate shakes since Dairy Dream closed ten years ago. Remember they were so thick that we could turn the cup upside down and it wouldn't even drip out?" CK raised her eyebrows. "Man, that was some good ice cream."

"Virgin Islands," Gemma grumbled, looking out the passenger window at the trees whizzing by. "She won't be a virgin after spending the weekend alone with that raging hormone Colton Conway."

CK laughed. "What does Tyler think about it? Surely he isn't going to let his little girl run off on a vacation with her boyfriend."

Gemma let out a heavy sigh and furrowed her brow. "She hasn't talked to him about it yet. But as asinine as it sounds for a dad to let his daughter shack up with her boyfriend across the ocean, I'm sure she'll get his approval. All Carolina needs to do is bat those baby blues and stick out her bottom lip and Tyler will melt like butter at his baby girl's request. Then I'll have to fight with both."

"It seems like it's always you against them, Gemma. You're supposed to be a team," CK said as she glanced at her.

"On our team, they're the star players and I'm the big loser on the bench." Gemma popped another handful of chips into her mouth, then folded the bag closed. She pressed the cool metal tumbler to her lips and took a generous swig of tea sweetened with sugar, not aspartame, to wash away the salt lingering in her throat. "I'm putting my foot down this time, though."

Gemma dreaded the argument that was sure to follow when

her husband and daughter approached her, united in their ridiculous decision that Carolina should escape to the beach with Testosterone Timmy or whatever his name was. The very thought of them ganging up on her made her want to tear open the bag of starchy chips again. After all, food had always provided Gemma with the comfort she needed. Especially her mama's food.

Linda Howell got to work in the kitchen to whip up a homemade chicken pot pie after Gemma returned home from the water park with her church youth group, crying that some strangers had followed her around the park all day to make fun of her. Another time, when Gemma came home from school feeling embarrassed because her custom-made cheerleading uniform was a slightly different shade of burgundy than the other girls', Linda consoled her with a chocolate meringue pie. If Gemma were to call her mother and tell her Tyler and her granddaughter were bullying her again, she would insist Gemma make the short drive to their home in Alpharetta for a fried chicken dinner, along with enough strawberry cake to take back home in a Tupperware container for a midnight snack.

They rode in comfortable silence for a few minutes, both lost in their own thoughts.

A text message alert suddenly appeared on the screen on CK's dashboard. It was from Silas, asking his mother where the cereal was.

"I was wondering why I hadn't heard from him yet this morning. It's because he just woke up," CK said before she pressed a button on her steering wheel and spoke her reply: "It's in the pantry on the second shelf."

Almost immediately, Silas sent another text that read, I checked. It isn't there. Where else could it be?

Gemma watched a roaring semitruck out the window and

secretly rolled her eyes at Silas's dependence on his mama before, once more, CK pressed the button and spoke into the car's speaker: "Check the cupboard next to the refrigerator."

A moment passed before Silas replied, It's not there either.

CK pressed the button on her steering wheel again and Gemma shouted, "CK! Good grief! That is enough!"

"What?"

"Are you really going to keep texting your teenage son different places to search for the cereal? Should we turn the car around and go back to Tunnel Hill so you can find the box of Fruity Pops for your baby?" Gemma asked, frustrated.

"I have never fed my kids Fruity Pops," CK retorted sharply. "Do you have any idea how much dye and chemicals are in those things? Kids would be safer slurping a bowl of weed killer."

"Well, whatever organic, whole-grain, dye-free, non-GMO cereal you choose to buy, I'm confident Silas can find it. And if he can't, he's not going to sit there and starve, is he? He can figure it out, CK."

"Can he, though?" Celia Kate let out a sigh.

"If you let him, he can," Gemma said before she pressed the tumbler of sugary tea to her lips and took a slow sip.

CK clicked her blinker and merged around a slow sedan being driven by an older woman who could barely see over the steering wheel. "I do too much for my kids, I know. Silas especially. But I refuse to see any harm in helping the kid find his Coconut Puffs."

"Not the Coconut Puffs." Gemma groaned and rolled her eyes.

"Yeah, and they are made with *real* coconut." CK gripped the wheel. "I'm not going to defend my parenting style to you for the next five hours. If I wanted to do that, I could have stayed home with Sean. You worry about your kid going to the Virgin Islands and

I'll worry about mine not knowing how to iron his shirts because I have always done it for him, okay?"

Gemma knew CK well enough to know that her lashing out meant she was freaking out about leaving her family for a few days. She reached over and rested her hand on her best friend's shoulder.

"I trust you left instructions for Silas, Sophie, and Tucker for school? Numbers for the police, fire department, and poison control?" Gemma asked while CK cut her eyes at her. "Seriously, Celia Kate, they'll be just fine. Silas will probably find the Coconut Puffs in some crazy, unexpected place like the broom closet. They'll have breakfast, get their Friday work done, and Chipper Jones will munch on a can of tuna. Sean will come home to happy, healthy kids and play air hockey with them. Everything's going to be just fine, all right?"

"I don't think I left the poison control number for them," CK said, looking worried as Gemma gave her shoulder a pinch before pulling her hand away.

Chapter 10

IT WAS 3:30 p.m. on Friday, September 20, and Moira Allyson walked through each room of her home for one final inspection. The afternoon sun streamed through the floor-to-ceiling windows of the main living area, and a warm glow danced across the polished hardwood floors. In the dining room, Moira stopped to admire the elegant dining table that had been passed down from Jeffrey's grandfather—a stunning mahogany trestle that gleamed faintly, the edges scratched from years of elbows and wineglasses.

It started raining, seemingly out of nowhere, the day the newly-weds moved into the row house on Chatham Square. She remembered the slick brick steps, the way her boots squeaked, the smell of wet magnolia leaves.

"This table has been in my family for three generations," Jeffrey had said, gripping one end like a soldier going into battle. "We're not leaving it in the back of the truck."

They wrestled with it themselves, soaked to the skin, bumping walls and doorframes and each other. At one point, Moira had dropped her end, swearing, laughing, wiping rain out of her eyes with the sleeve of her sweatshirt.

"It will never fit, Jeffrey!" she exclaimed.

But when it finally settled into place—wedged tightly into the narrow room like a ship in a bottle—he stepped back, hands on his hips, and said, "Look at that. Like a glove."

"Like OJ's glove," she answered.

He smiled at her with that soft, crooked smile she could still see perfectly, even now.

They ate takeout that night: Indian food, samosas, and warm naan straight from the cartons, seated across from each other like royalty at the mahogany trestle table. Just them and the echo of rain on the windows.

She snapped back to the present and eyed the center of the table; the vibrant floral arrangement she had made featured a colorful array of limelight hydrangea blooms, pink azalea blossoms, and stems of resurrection ferns, all from her property. The fine white china, arranged meticulously around the table, sparkled in the sunlight.

Moira loved to cook, but this weekend she decided to relax and let her favorite Italian chef, Antonio, and his assistant, Renata, take charge of the meals. They were scheduled to arrive by four thirty to begin preparing dinner and fresh breakfast pastries for the weekend. The menu for Friday evening featured spicy shrimp fra diavolo served over polenta, alongside an arugula salad and garlic herb bread. Guests were expected to arrive at five, with drinks served first, followed by dinner at six thirty.

While Moira continued to check her home, making sure nothing was out of place, she thought about her guest list. Only four women were expected. Her youngest brother's wife, Penny, was battling breast cancer and was too fatigued to fly in from Houston, even though she was doing well overall and was expected to make a full recovery. Her friend Jess would be at a cousin's wedding in Charlotte. Both were understandable and valid reasons for not being able to attend. And it was no surprise that MerryLee had texted

Moira to decline—probably before she made it back to her house from her mailbox. But at least she was honest and said she just didn't want to come.

On the other hand, the excuses given by her sorority sisters Carla and Jenna, as well as her sister-in-law Tabitha, were laughable. Who in their right mind would pass up a weekend of great food and good conversation to do yard work, detail the car, or hang new drapes? They might as well have declined because they had to wash their hair.

Before even receiving their RSVPs, Moira knew she could count on her childhood friends, CK and Gemma, to make the drive halfway across the state of Georgia to celebrate with her, even if it was hard for worrywart CK to leave Sean and her kids, and for Gemma to suspend her busy schedule filled with real estate showings and senior-year preparations. They'd always been there for Moira when she needed them.

Moira traced a manicured finger across the foyer table in the living room to check for dust and thought about how happy she was that Erin was coming for the weekend. When they made casual chitchat while Erin swept the floors and wiped down the kitchen countertops, Moira couldn't help but notice that the late-thirty-something carried some sadness in her dark eyes. Moira hoped this weekend off would be an opportunity for them to get to know each other better and even for Erin's burden, whatever it was, to be lightened.

Satisfied with the aesthetic and cleanliness of her gorgeous waterside home, Moira Allyson stood at the center of the two-story foyer, hands on her slender hips, and looked out the front window and down the shady drive. One of her white cats, Dove, interrupted her gaze by weaving between her ankles before she looked up at her with bright green eyes.

"I trust you and your sister will stay out of the kitchen. I would be humiliated if your hair ends up in the cuisine," she said to the cat, who seemed unfazed by her request.

She picked up her friend from the floor, and the cat went limp in her arms like a rag doll. While she stroked the long fur on the top of Dove's head, she thought of Nell's acceptance of the invite and felt a sense of disappointment. Since their falling-out last Christmas, they occasionally exchanged "thinking of you" texts and suggested meeting up for coffee, but they never did. They reminisced through text about the unforgettable Braves game they attended together, where Chip accidentally dumped an extra-large order of nachos onto Jeffrey's head after tripping in the aisle, leaving everyone in stitches, and getting drenched in rain at the azalea festival. When Moira extended the birthday invitation to Nell, she was feeling nostalgic, but she regretted her decision the moment she dropped the black envelope into the blue box outside the post office.

Moira pushed thoughts of Nell out of her mind, placed Dove back on the floor, and headed to the bar in the butler's pantry to prepare a drink. As she sipped her stout cocktail, she reflected on the upcoming weekend, which not only promised relaxation and enjoyment but also offered a chance to show appreciation for the friends who had supported her during the toughest period of her life. These were the friends who continued to text and call even when she didn't respond. Although she had distanced herself from them over the past two and a half years, she had begun to realize how much she missed the laughter and connections they once shared.

Moira felt the heavy cloud of depression that had loomed over her for so long begin to lift as she imagined the indulgent meals prepared by Antonio and Renata and the relaxation by the pool. The golden September sun would warm their skin, while the ocean breeze provided a refreshing coolness. She was ready to shake off the heavy sadness of her widowhood and celebrate a new year—celebrate a comeback.

———

ONE WARM DAY last spring, Erin was sent to Moira's home by Coastal Cleaning Co. and was struck by Mo's classic beauty and elegant clothing as soon as the front door of the waterfront mansion opened. For the next several weeks, Erin arrived right on time and thoroughly cleaned Moira's home and helped with tasks like picking up packages at the post office and running other errands. On Erin's fourth visit to Allyson Island, Moira persuaded her to leave Coastal Cleaning Co. and work exclusively for her. Erin quickly agreed because the pay was competitive, the hours were flexible enough to allow her to take a second job at the convenience store, and the work itself was easy because although the house was large, it was without children to create clutter or a husband to leave dirty laundry on the floor and glass rings on the coffee table. She only had to tidy up after Moira Allyson, the sophisticated widow in need of a friend.

As Erin put away dishes and dusted the frames that held photos of Moira's happier days, Moira engaged her in conversation. However, their discussions rarely ventured into deep or emotional territory. Moira never broke down in tears over her husband, nor did Erin express her own grief. Though they never openly addressed it, Erin could see the sadness in the former beauty queen's eyes when she finished off a bottle of wine. Erin never dared to question Moira's choices, pry into her life, or ask why she seemed to spend more time in her living room with her two cats than participating in Savannah's social circle. Erin simply did what was asked of her and deposited her paycheck. Perhaps that was why she was invited to the birthday weekend—she was a listening ear instead of a talking mouth.

Erin was the first guest to arrive at Moira Allyson's coastal mansion on Friday afternoon. She parked her eighteen-year-old silver hatchback at the rear of the property, where she usually did, beneath the mossy oak next to the side portico and a white catering van with a chef's hat painted on the side. As soon as she slid her brown sandal onto the cobblestone driveway, the savory smell of tomato and spices wafting from the kitchen caught her attention.

She stood up and straightened the blouse she had owned since her marriage to Phillip. Once a deep navy color, it had faded over the years, but she hoped it looked okay with the jeans she had purchased from the clearance rack. Her jewelry—off a card of costume earrings for $4.88—came from the same store where she bought her groceries. Her entire outfit likely cost less than Moira's left shoe.

Erin grabbed the sage-green duffel bag filled with clothing from the car's back seat. She'd had a difficult time deciding what clothes to pack for dinner, a boat ride, a massage, brunch, and so on. However, she felt she had done her best with what she had to choose from.

As Erin approached the back door, she noticed that Spanish moss had fallen from one of the aged live oaks and gathered in a pile. She made a mental note to retrieve the broom when she got inside and sweep it away. Standing at the door and rocking from one foot to the other, she felt uncertain about what to do. If it were work, she would let herself in, but this time she was a guest, not the hired help. Should she knock? Should she have gone to the front door instead?

"May I help you?" a dark-featured man with beautiful deep-set eyes called through the open kitchen window next to the back door.

"She's a guest, Antonio!" Erin heard Moira declare just before the back door swung open and she appeared, wearing a form-fitting black scoop-neck shirt and tan wide-legged pants cinched with a sash belt. "What in the world are you doing back here at the service entrance? You're a guest, Erin. Get out of the worker frame of mind!"

Erin guessed she wouldn't be sweeping up the pile of moss after all.

Moira then pulled Erin close to her, over the threshold and into the kitchen, and Erin inhaled the flowery scent of her perfume, or maybe that was grenadine. When they pulled away, Erin felt vulnerable, as if her cheap jeans and old shirt were blatantly out of place. She blushed for a moment, tucking her black bob behind her ear, until Moira added, "You look lovely!"

Moira surely recognized that Erin's clothes were inexpensive, but her compliment sounded sincere.

"Well, come on in!" Moira said as she closed the door. She then motioned for Erin to follow her through the kitchen, where Antonio and a woman were bustling about, speaking in Italian. Erin trailed behind her, passing through the dining room and arriving at the front of the home. "I assume you don't need me to show you to your room, do you?" Moira chuckled, gesturing toward the staircase in the foyer. "It's the blue one."

"Oh, it's my favorite!" Erin exclaimed.

When she walked through the bedroom door, Erin smiled at the French-country blue and white toile print that wrapped the walls. The centerpiece of the room was the stunning antique four-poster bed covered in a plush white eyelet comforter and ocean-blue accent pillows. Soft natural light spilled through the plantation shutters and created shadows on the wide-planked wooden floor. The view out the window was of the wide tributary that surrounded the home on three sides and lush greenery. Mature palm and palmetto trees dotted the lawn here and there, while the oak tree branches were wrapped with delicate moss and resurrection ferns crept up the trunks.

Erin stepped away from the window and peeked into the adjoining bathroom that she'd cleaned many times. It was small but elegant—like a spa retreat—with gleaming white marble countertops and tiles and blue accents that complemented the bedroom decor.

Erin often let her imagination wander while she dusted and vacuumed this beautiful house. She dreamed about what it would be like to call it her own—to close her eyes at the end of the day and truly rest, free from danger and financial worries and bad memories and concern for the future, in this very room. While she unzipped the duffel bag that she had tossed onto the plush comforter, she exhaled with gratitude.

While Erin was hanging her inexpensive, simple sundresses in the closet, an alarm chimed throughout the home, signaling that a vehicle had entered the driveway gate. She glanced at the pendulum clock on the distressed white nightstand and noticed it was just three minutes until five o'clock. A wave of anxiety washed over her at the thought of making her descent down the grand staircase, facing the scrutinizing gaze of high society while wearing her cheap clothing, faux diamond studs, and dollar store makeup. Taking a deep breath, Erin looked around the beautiful room one last time and wished she could hide beneath the down comforter until Sunday afternoon.

Chapter 11

CELIA KATE'S BLACK SUV moved through the tall and sturdy driveway gate, made from detailed wrought iron that shone in the sunlight. It had elegant scrolls and palm designs, and in the center, the name "Allyson Island" was beautifully engraved in a flowing script with decorative details around it. The rich black color of the iron stood out against the bright green grass and other plants.

Centuries-old live oaks draped with Spanish moss lined the winding driveway, leading to a tall, white clapboard home. The charming low-country house, situated on the banks of the Ogeechee River and its salt marshes, featured transom windows and grand steps that ascended to a wraparound porch. The property really was a private island, as it was surrounded by water: the river to the north, a tributary to the west and south, and the confluence of the stream and the main river to the east.

Moira swung open the transomed Jacobean door to see her longtime friends with arms full of luggage and travel bags. CK looked disheveled, with her tortoiseshell sunglasses crooked on her face and a pillow cradled in the crook of her arm. Gemma shifted a bag of snacks from one hand to the other. Their familiar lighthearted squabbling crossed the threshold and filled the front foyer.

"You're here!" Moira exclaimed, her voice rising above their sarcastic banter. She stepped aside, holding the heavy door wide open to welcome them farther into the house. As soon as they stepped onto the fern-green Persian rug in the entryway, they burst into laughter and happy squeals, exchanging enthusiastic hugs. This was always how it had been with the three of them—no matter how much time had passed since their last visit, they seamlessly picked up right where they had left off.

Erin had been slowly making her way down the staircase and didn't want to interrupt the moment the two women and Moira were sharing. She paused when one of them noticed her and smiled invitingly. Moira gestured for Erin to join them. When she finally reached the bottom of the stairs, Moira introduced her not as the housekeeper but as a friend.

Even though they were friendly and welcoming, Erin couldn't shake her usual feeling of self-consciousness. Moira's larger friend, Gemma, who had a pretty face, radiated wealth in her cute dress and sparkling jewelry. The tall, slender friend's outfit—tapered athletic pants, a flowy pink T-shirt, and expensive sneakers—was a far cry from the inexpensive workout gear found at superstore chains. CK's outfit appeared to be specifically designed for serious runners; it was both comfortable and stylish.

"What is that fabulous smell?" Gemma sniffed the air and then looked at Erin. "As you can see"—she gestured to her figure as if she were Vanna White presenting a puzzle on *Wheel of Fortune*—"I love to eat."

Erin was uncertain if she should laugh at the self-deprecating joke, and she noticed the annoyed looks that Moira and CK gave Gemma after her remark. Gemma must have been the type to ease awkward tension by poking fun at herself. Perhaps Erin should make a joke about her jeans costing less than a dozen eggs.

"Antonio is whipping up something absolutely spectacular," Moira announced like the hostess of a cooking show and clasped her manicured hands together. "I have decided to take a complete break. I'm going to relax all weekend and not lift a finger in the kitchen."

CK reached into the paisley-print bag slung over her shoulder and pulled out a rectangular box wrapped beautifully in black-and-gold-striped paper. "This is for you," she said, holding the gift out to Moira. "I know you said no gifts, but we don't follow the rules. You know that."

Erin watched the exchange and felt embarrassed. She had obeyed Moira's request and come empty-handed, and now it seemed so foolish. What was she thinking? And what could she have even afforded to buy for Moira Allyson? A cardstock of plastic studs didn't belong in the jewelry box that housed diamonds and emeralds worth her entire year's salary.

"You really shouldn't have. I'll wait to open it on Sunday, then," Moira said, smiling warmly as she leaned in to give CK a gentle kiss on the cheek and then turned to Gemma to do the same.

The three old friends began gossiping about people Erin didn't know, and she wondered if the entire weekend would be like this. Would she be the only outsider not in on the inside jokes? She nervously gnawed on her short thumbnail painted messily by her own hand and realized that maybe she had made a mistake coming here.

Erin's mama, who was often ill and needed tending to by Erin, always said her daughter had a servant's heart. Her mother had also taught her that it was sometimes okay to be served, just like in the story of Mary and Martha in the Bible; it was perfectly fine to take a moment to be still and have her own well filled. As Erin continued to chew on her thumbnail, Moira invited her into the conversation. Erin recognized Moira's intentions of inclusion and appreciated the gesture, but it also made her feel pitied. Then she was angry with herself because she constantly worried what others thought of her, like a middle schooler. All she wanted was to turn off her mind and relax.

"Who wants a glass of wine?" Moira asked.

"I do!" Erin nearly shouted, craving something to calm her nerves and self-doubt.

They followed Moira to the wet bar in the butler's pantry, where she poured each of them a glass of chardonnay in sparkling crystal wineglasses. Erin watched the bubbles float to the top and realized it was a far cry from the box of pink stuff she had on her birthday. The four ladies clinked their glasses, and CK asked, "So who else are we waiting on?"

"My friend Nell from Oglethorpe is on her way," Moira replied while slowly walking toward the living room; her friends followed. "You and Gemma remember her, don't you?"

"Oh yes, the pretty redhead from your church. I really enjoyed getting to know her when we stayed with you after the funeral. She had such a sweet spirit," CK remembered while Moira nodded and sipped from the glass.

Moira then went on to explain the reasons the other guests couldn't come.

"Well, Moira, I'm sure sorry Jenna couldn't hold off putting out mums until next weekend," Gemma said with sarcasm.

"It's really okay," Moira said. "We get together plenty, and I'm always on the go, volunteering or having dinner at the country club. A small, intimate gathering with you all is exactly what I need this weekend. Let me show you to your rooms, okay?"

Throughout her explanation, Moira avoided looking at Erin, knowing that Erin knew she was lying about keeping busy. The truth was, since Jeffrey's passing, the thought of attending social gatherings without her college sweetheart by her side had become unbearable for Moira. As a result, she had distanced herself from her once-bustling calendar and active social life. Rather than dancing in ballrooms and waving an auction paddle, she opted to mail in charitable donations and spend her time beneath her favorite tree with Dove and Pearl. There, she would sip wine and watch boats float by.

"Well, I'm not going to lie. I'm relieved MerryLee won't be here," Gemma confessed as they approached the stairwell. "I forgot to pack my migraine medicine. I couldn't imagine having to listen to her drone on for three days without it. I'd end up down in the basement in a corner, rocking in the fetal position."

Moira laughed and turned to Erin as they climbed the stairs. "MerryLee is my least favorite sister-in-law because she's downright rude and doesn't know when to stop talking. I only invited her out of love for her husband, my brother." She took another swig from her glass. "Since the crowd will be small this weekend, you two don't have to share the guest room that sleeps four. You're welcome to take your own private rooms."

"Are you kidding? I wouldn't dare miss an opportunity to keep CK awake all night with my snoring!" Gemma poked her tall friend's shoulder when they reached the landing. "We're bunking together. Right, roomie?"

CK sighed in annoyance. "Lucky for me, I *did* pack my migraine medicine."

With Erin following close behind the trio, Moira showed CK and Gemma to the seafoam-green room they would share, with two sets of white wooden bunk beds blanketed in pink and white plaid. The pretty, feminine room overlooked the back garden, a turquoise infinity pool, and the calm, dark water of the Ogeechee River. Two large windows were raised, allowing salty breezes to flow inside while the white linen curtain panels danced in the wind.

CK leaned against the window frame, enjoying the beautiful view as she slowly sipped her wine. She tried to push away the worrisome thoughts and worst-case scenarios about what might happen back home while she was away.

Mo interrupted the anxieties that were running through CK's mind and suggested that they sit on the porch while they waited for Nell to arrive. With their glasses in hand, the four ladies followed Moira back down the staircase and through her extravagant, well-decorated home, eventually stepping onto an outdoor cobblestone sitting area off the main living room. They settled onto a comfortable L-shaped settee made of white wicker, topped with black-and-white-striped cushions, and gazed through a row of pampas grass at the confluence, where the tributary that surrounded the house joined the Ogeechee River.

"There's just something special about being on the coast," Gemma said as she slowly inhaled the warm ocean air. The others nodded in agreement and sat quietly for a few seconds to soak in the peacefulness of their surroundings.

Moira interrupted the silence.

"Girls, I'm a little nervous about Nell coming this weekend," she confessed while crossing the legs of her tan pants.

"Oh, spill the beans!" Gemma eagerly leaned forward, her eyes shining with the idea of juicy gossip. She was ready to devour every word.

"What in the world about that sweet lady could make you nervous?" asked CK. "And the prayers that woman prayed? My goodness, they brought me to tears every time."

"I was brought to tears by the food she kept bringing over," Gemma added. "What was that cheesy concoction? Pepper jack hash brown casserole? Lord, have mercy." She shook her bouncy brown hair at the satisfying recollection.

"Yes, she's a good person, and a good cook"—Moira darted her eyes at Gemma—"but she's a little goody-goody for my taste. She's super religious, and the last time we saw one another, she lectured me, a grown woman, about drinking. I just don't want you all to feel uncomfortable around her because she's a teetotaler."

"What are we, seventeen, Mo? Is this an after-school special where we're going to bully her for not sneaking into the liquor cabinet with us?" CK laughed and playfully rolled her eyes while she leaned back into the wicker. "Mo, I honestly don't care if another adult drinks or not."

"I know all that, girls," Mo rushed to clarify, "but she just rubs me the wrong way. She seems so judgmental. She's a buzzkill."

"Then why did you invite her?" Gemma asked.

"I don't really know. She was a good friend to me when Jeffrey died, and we— I just didn't think it through, I guess. I was surprised she accepted the invitation." Moira took another drink. "I just don't want any of you to feel like you can't loosen up around her."

Gemma let out a hearty laugh and swirled her glass. "You get a little *too* loose at times, Mo."

"I resent that," Moira shot back defensively while Erin watched the interaction with wide, amused eyes.

Suddenly CK and Gemma burst into a duet, singing the chorus of a Pat Benatar hit. After finishing, Gemma turned to Erin, her expression animated as she remembered, "Two summers ago, we spent the weekend here with Mo. We woke up at 3:00 a.m. to Moira drunker than a skunk, and she was singing completely off-key through the intercom. I was nearly startled from my sleep straight into the arms of Jesus."

Mo giggled and dangled her crossed leg back and forth. "I thought that was a fun night."

"Getting you back to bed was no fun," CK added. "You ruined my house shoes." She looked at Erin and continued, "Mo was in mid-sentence, and the spinach and artichoke dip she had made came up—"

"Okay, that's enough," Moira interrupted, dismissing them with a wave of her hand. She finished the last gulp of wine while the sun dipped lower in the sky and cast a golden glow over them.

Erin wasn't surprised by the conversation because Moira was often on her second or third drink of the evening when Erin finished her work. She was unsure what happened after she was gone, with Moira alone in the house, but some mornings Moira would still be sprawled out in bed, dead to the world, when she arrived. On other occasions, the usually immaculate home would show signs of a long night: broken glass littering the floor or even a wastebasket filled with the contents of Moira's stomach. She and her employer never discussed it, and Erin never intended to.

The loud chime of the doorbell echoed through the open

French doors leading to the cobblestone porch where they were sitting.

"Well, that must be Judgy McJudgerson," Moira groaned.

"She's a perfectly lovely woman, Mo. Be nice," CK replied.

The bell rang once more, and Erin felt a strong urge to jump up and answer it. Moira seemed to sense this as she quickly said, "Stay put. I'll get the door." With that, she disappeared, leaving the three women sitting on the patio in the September breeze.

IN THE FOYER, Nell and Moira stood face-to-face for the first time since an inebriated Moira had hiccupped into a red cup with Christmas trees on it and thanked Nell and Chip for bringing brownies to the party. Their reunion now was somewhat awkward as they exchanged a quick formal hug, and Nell told Moira she appreciated the invitation.

"I was a little bit surprised, to be honest. I mean, after our last conversation." Nell cleared her throat and set her white suitcase at her feet.

"Water under the bridge," Moira said dismissively, waving her hand as if to brush the past aside. Then, with a raised eyebrow and a tone dripping with condescension, she added that the other guests were on the porch enjoying cocktails before dinner and asked, "Is that all right with you?"

Nell held back the impulse to walk out, get into her sedan, and drive back home. Instead she replied, "Are you asking me if it's all right because you're concerned for my well-being or because you're concerned for your well-being?"

"I don't quite—" Moira began.

"Are you worried that I might be tempted to drink, or are you worried that I would judge you for drinking and make you feel uncomfortable in some way? So my well-being or yours?"

Moira narrowed her eyes at the woman in her foyer who, like Job's friends, had sat in silence with Moira as she mourned Jeffrey during the first year after his passing. However, unlike Job's friends, when Nell finally spoke to Moira, she offered encouraging words Moira needed to hear. Their friendship deepened during that dark time and remained strong over the next two years. Even when Nell gently suggested that Moira might be drinking too much, Moira didn't take offense. It wasn't until Moira decided to serve wine at the Christmas party that Nell's attitude turned judgmental and critical.

Even though she knew that Nell had struggled with alcohol addiction in the past, Moira thought it was innocent enough to serve cabernet sauvignon to the Sunday school class. She simply wanted a glass of wine to help her cope as she navigated the holidays without her husband, and since it was her house, she felt entitled to serve it. The grown-ups at the party had every right to turn it down, and many did without a fuss.

So what if Moira had a few too many glasses? So did Nikki, Charley, and Dana, and they were good Christian women. While they didn't join Mo on the coffee table to sing "Santa Baby," what harm was there in cutting loose? After all, if anyone deserved to have a good time, it was a widow who would wake up on Christmas morning in an empty bed.

The day after the lively party, Nell called Moira. Words like *sin* and *accountability* were thrown around in a harsh and hostile tone. The way Nell scolded her, you'd have thought Moira had robbed a liquor store at gunpoint on her way to volunteer at vacation Bible school. After ten minutes of being berated like a child, Moira angrily slammed her phone to the table and poured herself a whiskey and club soda. She vowed then to cut that critical Nell Rehman out of her life, even if that meant not returning to the church that had been so good to her.

Surely Nell knew that Mo was going to serve alcohol during her birthday weekend. Antonio would oversee pairing the right wines with the meals, and mimosas would be provided for brunch while champagne was set to accompany massages. Besides that, there was a fully stocked bar in the butler's pantry, which would be open to her friends throughout the weekend. If Nell chose to be overly condescending and judgmental about it, she was free to leave. After all, it was Mo's house, Mo's party, and her husband was dead.

Moira smiled. "Let's just try to have a good time, okay?"

"Of course," Nell said with a nod.

BACK ON THE porch, Gemma was peering at Erin over her half-full glass before she asked, "So, Erin, do you live in town? You have kids?"

Erin nodded. "My son and I live in town about twenty minutes west of here."

"Oh, how old is your son?" CK asked and mentally reminded herself to text Silas to set his alarm for the morning. If she didn't make sure he was awake, he was liable to sleep until noon, and he needed to log on to the college website as soon as the applications became available.

"My boy, PJ, will be turning twenty in a few months and is currently taking classes at the technical college," Erin replied, feeling slightly embarrassed that her child was not attending an SEC school.

"That is smart," Gemma said, nodding in approval. "My daughter is a senior in high school this year, and she wants to go to a four-year university for a degree in fashion design. Honestly, can you imagine spending fifteen thousand dollars a semester on that? I wish she'd think about something more practical. We really need more skilled trade workers in our society than we need fashion designers. I can always find cute clothes, but the last dental assistant I met was so rough that my gums bled for three days!"

CK chimed in. "I absolutely agree. My oldest son, Silas, wants to study graphic design. He's only a junior in high school, but he's already built a fantastic website for his little sister, Sophie, who makes greeting cards. I've often wondered if he even needs a formal degree to succeed in that field. It seems like he's learning a lot on his own just by tinkering around on the computer."

"You just don't want him to leave home and go to school," Gemma teased CK and then looked at Erin. "She can't cut the cord."

Celia Kate rolled her eyes, even though she couldn't deny that she had resisted the overwhelming urge to call home at least fifteen times since arriving at Mo's house. She had sent a group text to Silas and Sean to tell them that she had made it to Savannah safely, and neither had replied. Had they not responded because they were busy prying the dead cat out of a coyote's mouth or because the house had burned to the ground with them trapped inside?

Curious, Gemma asked Erin, "So how do you know Mo? She didn't mention it."

Erin felt uncomfortable as she shifted on the plush cushion on the wicker settee and answered, "I started working for Moira after Mrs. Joanie retired. I'm her housekeeper." Erin searched for judgment in their demeanor; perhaps that was part of her defensive nature. However, they both seemed indifferent to the fact that she was a maid.

"Wait. What happened to Mrs. Joanie? She worked for Moira for years, didn't she?" Gemma asked, glancing at CK for confirmation.

CK bobbed her shoulders and replied, "Oh yeah. I'd forgotten that Mo told me she retired. Do you know what she's up to, Erin?"

"Yes, she moved down to Fort Lauderdale to be closer to her children and grandchildren. That's when I started working for Moira," Erin explained while rolling the stem of the empty wineglass between her fingers.

"CK talks to Moira more than I do. I only get random texts now and then. The last time we were here was the weekend she harassed us with a Pat Benatar tribute," Gemma reminisced again with a smile creeping across her face. She set her now-empty glass down on the matching wicker table beside the settee, and her expression turned serious. "Since you spend so much time with her, tell us. Is Mo doing okay, Erin?"

Erin wasn't sure how to respond to that question. She didn't want to gossip about her boss, but she felt that Moira's closest friends should know she was quite reclusive. Maybe they should know she polished off a bottle of wine, sometimes vodka, every day. Her heart pattered as she contemplated how to respond, and she felt relieved when Moira and a slender redhead in a flattering and casual emerald maxi dress appeared at the French doors and stepped outside.

Moira walked with the woman toward Gemma and CK. "Girls, you remember my friend Nell."

"Of course," they replied in unison, and Gemma reached out to grab Nell's delicate hand adorned with long burgundy nails.

"It's so good to see you again, ladies," Nell softly said to them both while squeezing Gemma's hand. "You look lovely as always."

"And this"—Moira gestured toward Erin—"is my friend Erin Pepperell."

"Hello there," Nell said, greeting Erin cordially before sitting in the crook of the L-shaped couch. She noticed the empty glasses sitting before her on the table but made sure not to stare at them for too long.

CK jumped in to make Nell feel welcomed. "So how are your kids doing, Nell? If I remember correctly, you have twins, is that right?"

Nell settled onto the sofa and smiled at the question. "You have a great memory. Yes, I do. Tate and Taylor. My daughter, Taylor, is a sophomore at UGA this year."

"Just like my Bradford," Moira interjected. "Taylor is a beautiful girl. Strawberry-blonde hair and big green eyes. I told Bradford to keep an eye out for her."

Nell thought to herself, *Heavens, no. Bradford Allyson is one of the wildest bulldogs on campus!* Then she continued, "As for my son, Tate, he's currently working with his dad at our family-owned drugstore. He's still trying to figure things out."

"Who isn't?" Gemma chuckled while jogging her shoulders up and down.

Nell sighed in discontent and continued, "He's considering joining the military."

"Well, isn't that wonderful?" Moira added while holding up a hand to shield the sun that was slowly setting in her line of sight.

"Yeah, but how do you feel about that, Nell?" asked CK. "I come from a long line of military men. My mother was a nervous wreck when my brother joined the National Guard. I couldn't imagine my child being on the front lines."

"You can't imagine your child being on the sidelines," Gemma remarked as she looked to Celia Kate. "That's why you didn't let Silas play football."

"It's not that I didn't *let* him," CK replied. "I just didn't push him. By the time middle school rolled around, all my kids had lost interest in sports, and I accepted that. You know I was an athlete in high school, Gemma. I understand the dangers of sports. I had two concussions, a torn ACL, and knee surgery before my senior year, remember? Still, I would have loved nothing more than to watch my kids play basketball."

"Tate broke his leg in middle school football and never played again. I wish he'd never set foot on a field. He wasn't even that passionate about it, but Chip was insistent that he play. Would have saved him a lot of pain and us a lot of medical bills if we'd let him sit that season out like he wanted to." Nell tossed her long auburn hair over her freckled shoulder. "And, yes, CK, I'm honestly a nervous wreck about him joining the army. I know I'm supposed to trust the Lord with him, but it's proving hard. Every time he mentions being all he can be, I feel sick to my stomach."

"My son thought about the military for a while too," Erin offered as she pulled her black hair behind her ear. "But he decided kind of last minute to go to trade school. He's interested in auto mechanics."

Nell smiled while running her hands across the wrinkles that had formed on the lap of her green dress. "Well, pass his number along. I'd like a good, honest mechanic. The last guy I went to really ripped me off. He ran one of those diagnostic checks and said my car was going to blow up before I pulled it out of the parking lot if I didn't pay to have this and that replaced. It was quite the swindle. The world would benefit from some honest mechanics."

CK said, "We need trade workers. If you ask me, the entire education system is a scam. From kindergarten to—" CK began, but Gemma interrupted.

"CK homeschools."

Celia Kate's dark eyes narrowed at Gemma, and she said in a sure voice, "I most certainly do, and I'm proud of it."

Gemma held up her hand in a calming gesture. "Oh dear, don't get yourself riled up. Have another glass of wine," she suggested while nodding to the empty glass dangling from CK's hand.

"Don't take those two seriously. They will bicker all weekend, but it's the foundation of their friendship. I've only ever seen them throw punches once," Moira said to Nell and Erin.

"Yeah, and I won." Gemma pounded her fist into her palm.

"I can get on board with another glass of wine!" Moira jumped from the wicker chair in her black woven sandals. "Nell, it was rude of me not to ask if you want some water or ginger ale or something."

"Water will be just fine," Nell answered with a nod.

"I think I'll have water as well, Moira." CK rubbed her temple. "This is the first drink I've had in months, and I already have a headache."

"A headache after only *one* glass of wine?" Moira teased while walking toward the French doors. "Goodness, you've turned into a lightweight."

Celia Kate called after her, "I'm not a lightweight, Moira. I'm forty-nine, just like you, in case you didn't notice. Except you'll be fifty on Sunday."

Mo playfully stuck out her tongue at CK. "Age is just a number. Mick Jagger is eighty and he still has a good time."

"If you want to look like Mick Jagger at eighty, then be my guest." CK winked while the others chuckled.

"Ladies." Antonio appeared at the French doors leading into the house. "Dinner is served."

"Oh, right on time, Antonio!" Gemma exclaimed.

Chapter 12

M OIRA AND HER friends entered the elegant dining room just as the autumn sun was setting over the marsh beyond the blackwater river. Shades of orange and pink streamed through the floor-to-ceiling windows and illuminated the room with a warm glow. The sparkling white china set a beautiful backdrop for their spicy meal of savory shrimp in tomato sauce. Ice water and sweet tea were already poured into the silver-rimmed goblets on the table, and a freshly opened bottle of pinot grigio had been placed at the center near Moira's lovely flower arrangement.

"You never let me down, Mo," Gemma said, eyes wide at the delicious meal before her while she unwrapped her silverware from the linen napkin.

"Would you all mind if I prayed over our meal?" Nell offered and they all nodded. Nell said a quick but heartfelt prayer of thanks for the food and the friendship.

Erin felt awkward at such a fancy table setting and was unsure which fork to use or where to place her elbows. She carefully watched the other guests as they unfolded the fine napkins and put them in their laps. She did the same, thinking the napkin with mitered corners probably cost more than her jeans and blouse combined. She hoped she wouldn't knock over a glass or drop her silverware on the floor.

While everyone else remarked on how savory and spicy the shrimp was, Moira poured another glass of wine for herself, Erin, and Gemma.

"I am so glad to have all of you here and am looking forward to our day tomorrow," Mo said with a bright smile as she looked around the table. "It's going to be a full one."

"Run us through the schedule." CK dipped the buttery garlic bread in the tomato sauce that was pooled on her plate.

"I figured you didn't want to be up too early, so we'll have coffee at nine or so, followed by a walk along the shore. Brunch will be served at ten fifteen and—"

"Brunch!" Gemma enthusiastically interrupted. "Nell, you should have made that pepper jack hash brown dish you brought over after Jeffrey's funeral. I swear that casserole had a lasting impact on me."

Nell laughed. "Well, I sure would have brought one if I'd known you were so fond of it. My family loves it too. I make it at least once a week. Remind me to give you the recipe before the weekend is over, okay?"

"May I continue?" Moira asked, sounding annoyed, while Gemma batted her eyes and motioned for her to keep talking. "Then we will have some relaxing time by the pool, followed by massages in the pool house courtesy of Kaylee, who works at one of Savannah's finest spas."

"That all sounds heavenly," Nell said while gathering shards of fresh arugula on her fork.

Moira continued with a coy smile, "And tomorrow night I can't wait for our sunset cruise and dinner on the catamaran."

"Wow," slipped from Erin's mouth.

Gemma, intrigued, asked, "Where in the world did you get this boat, Mo? It's not yours, is it?"

"It belongs to Martin Naysmith. He was a good friend of Jeffrey's. I'm sure you met him at the funeral," Mo responded while wiping the corners of her mouth with the delicate linen. "He used to host the most fantastic New Year's Eve parties on it, and we'd sail out into the open water and watch fireworks on the shore. I phoned him up and asked for access to it this weekend, and he was more than happy to oblige. He's even sending his nephew to captain it for us."

As the portions on the plates became smaller, the five ladies enthusiastically chatted about the weekend, and the conversation naturally shifted to their spouses back home. Gemma talked highly of Tyler to Nell and Erin, who didn't know him from Adam. She boasted about his recent job promotion in insurance sales and didn't notice CK and Moira exchange sarcastic glances as she painted their marriage as a Hallmark movie. CK spoke of her husband, Sean, with complete honesty and a hint of sarcasm in her tone as she joked that she might return to a home that resembled a frat house on Sunday afternoon. Nell described her loyal pharmacist, Chip, softly and gently, without a smidge of teasing or resentment. Erin imagined the kind, loving men the other ladies shared their lives with and felt a twinge of jealousy. Nosey Gemma asked if Erin was in a relationship.

"Oh, we divorced years ago. Irreconcilable differences, you know? He's remarried now." Erin poked at the remainder of shrimp on her china and changed the subject. "So have you all been keeping watch on the tropical storm brewing in the Caribbean? I heard it might make landfall next week."

"If it stays the course, I don't think it's going to come as far inland as Gemma and me," CK answered. "We might get a little drizzle, but from the predictions I've seen, it's going to head from

Nicaragua to Nassau and then up to Jacksonville, Savannah, Charlotte, and then swing back out to sea."

"If it does hit Savannah, my husband, son, and I will be at Oglethorpe. It's a designated shelter. Mo, Erin, you're more than welcome to come to the church to ride it out," Nell offered.

"Oglethorpe Church on Pooler Avenue?" Erin inquired and Nell nodded. "I may do that. Thank you. The last time we had a hurricane I spent the night in the basement of the civic center with a poodle that had diarrhea and barked incessantly."

The group laughed.

"I'm sure I'll be fine here. I know how to batten down the hatches. The cats and I will survive. We've been through plenty of storms together." Moira drank the last gulp from the goblet and motioned for CK to pass the half-empty bottle of pinot to her.

"Where are those little furballs?" Gemma asked, pushing her empty plate away. It clinked against a sweating crystal glass of water.

"Probably curled up in my room, sound asleep," Mo responded with a playful grin. "They'll come alive just as we're all settling down for the night. You will hear them, I'm sure, scurrying around the house."

Gemma raised an eyebrow. "They better not scurry anywhere near me," she said, pointing a playful finger at Mo. "And they had better not try to steal my breath while I'm sleeping either. Whiskered demons."

CK let out a bustling laugh and tossed her napkin onto the table while leaning back in the sturdy mahogany chair. She looked at Nell and Erin and said, "Gemma hates cats, as you can tell. I love to hurl my little guy, Chipper Jones, into her lap when she least expects it. She jumped up from my couch so quickly one time that she tripped and fell into the wall."

"And busted right through it like the Kool-Aid Man!" Gemma imitated a drummer's rim shot at her joke.

No, she didn't, CK, annoyed at yet another one of Gemma's self-deprecating comments, mouthed to the group.

"Tell her, Erin. Tell Gemma what sweethearts Dove and Pearl are," Mo insisted while pointing at Erin.

Erin shrugged and said, "I don't like cats very much either, but Dove and Pearl are sweet. They're affectionate, and they don't weave between my legs trying to trip me up. Honestly, I rarely even see them."

"That may be true, but I don't care. I'm still locking our door tonight, CK." Gemma crossed her arms with determination. "Cats are homicidal maniacs. I've never owned a dog that brought a dead rabbit in the house or tried to steal my breath while I slept. Only cats do that kind of villainous mess."

The group laughed together, their voices blending with the sound of jingling glasses. Moira offered more wine to her guests, but they all declined. With a disappointed scoff, she poured some more into her own glass. The golden liquid sparkled under the clear crystals hanging from the vintage brass chandelier.

CK exchanged a knowing glance with Gemma. Moira had already drunk far too much that evening, especially since it was not yet seven o'clock.

Antonio and his assistant, the strikingly beautiful Italian woman named Renata, with dark hair elegantly pinned in a bun, entered with black trays topped with fancy etched cups filled with the evening's dessert.

"Chocolate panna cotta," Antonio announced in his delicious, thick accent, and the women responded with enthusiastic smiles and gasps of approval. He and Renata placed the cups of the rich chocolate custard before them, and Gemma clasped her hands together.

"Heavenly!" Gemma exclaimed, her voice filled with delight as she was the first to scoop the sparkling, polished spoon into the creamy confection. She closed her eyes in bliss while she appreciated the sweet flavor. "This ain't Heathcliff Huxtable's pudding."

The dining room fell quiet as the women all dug into the decadent chocolate dessert, until Erin broke the silence and asked Nell somewhat bashfully, "If I do need to come to your church's hurricane shelter next week, would it be okay if I bring my son?"

"Absolutely!" Nell responded enthusiastically, her smile wide and inviting. "He is most welcome too. We'll exchange numbers so we can keep in touch, okay?"

"That sounds great. I appreciate it." Erin nodded at the genuinely kind invitation from a woman wearing what appeared to be real emerald earrings.

"And of course, we'd love to have you both visit even when a hurricane isn't bearing down. There's always some activity or Bible study going on for the ladies of the church." Nell took another bite of the rich chocolate. "Tate is active in our college-aged ministry and would be glad to show your son around." Nell nodded her auburn head.

"Here we go," Moira said, her words slightly slurred from the wine. "Do you earn a commission from the pastor every time you bring in new blood?"

Nell's smile at Erin faded. She looked down at her dessert as her expression shifted to one of hurt.

"That was uncalled for, Mo!" CK exclaimed firmly. "I'm sorry she said that, Nell."

Mo felt her face flush with embarrassment. Where had that nasty response come from? She bit her bottom lip and looked away.

The congregation at Oglethorpe Church had certainly been the hands and feet of Jesus when Jeffrey passed. They covered Moira with love and compassion by bringing her home-cooked meals and offering heartfelt prayers. Yet despite their support, she stopped attending the church after Nell displayed typical Christian judgment after the Sunday school Christmas party. Since she had quit going to Oglethorpe, Moira often recalled the pastor's words that he regularly repeated from the pulpit: *"You're only as close to Jesus as you choose to be."* After nearly a year without stepping foot in the church or even opening her Bible and talking with the God of the universe, those words resonated with her now, making her aware that, at this moment, her relationship with Jesus felt distant and cold. She felt guilty as she imagined her parents, devout churchgoers in their lifetime, disapproving of her choice to turn her back on her faith. She could almost hear them rolling over in their graves.

Albert and Louise Wallace were known in Tunnel Hill as fine Christian folk, deeply respected for their unwavering faith. After dinner each evening, while still seated at the table in their grand dining room, Albert read from the King James Bible. Moira's maternal grandfather, Dayton, had devoted over fifty years of his life to serving as a pastor in Chattanooga, nurturing the spiritual growth of countless individuals, so she had been raised with strong moral values and a steadfast belief in God. Still, no matter how much she prayed, she hadn't felt God's presence in quite a long time. There were nights while lying in silence in the spacious king-sized bed that Moira was overwhelmed with loneliness and despair, as if the darkness of widowhood had wrapped itself around her like a heavy blanket.

But on one particularly difficult night this past summer, Moira was lying beneath the cool covers and crying out to God, begging him not to turn a deaf ear to her—much like a desperate David did in the book of Psalms—and something extraordinary happened. A flash of light illuminated the pitch-black room. Not a flashlight, not a flicker, but a warm, vibrant glow that she could not explain. Only for two seconds, maybe three. And with it, a sense of relief, of peace, of being enveloped in love. That was God. It had to be.

Despite the profound experience, Moira didn't return to church or even open the Bible. She recognized that pursuing God was like drinking enough water—she knew it was good for her and essential to her well-being. Still, for no clear reason—perhaps just laziness, stubbornness, or even anger over having to say goodbye to Jeffrey so soon—she didn't do it.

She finally muttered, "You're right, Celia Kate. I'm sorry, Nell."

"Thank you," Nell replied quickly and quietly, dipping her spoon back into the cup of velvety chocolate.

"Oglethorpe is a great church. I went there for a few years." Mo turned to Erin. "The congregation is made up of very loving people. I really don't know why I said what I did."

"Because you're drunk," Gemma said, looking Mo directly in the eyes.

CK, who was sitting beside Gemma, nudged her arm and caused a dollop of chocolate to tumble from Gemma's spoon back into the glass.

"What?" she said to CK while raising her eyebrows. "She is."

"Gemma, that's enough," CK said, pursing her lips.

"I'm certainly not drunk after just two glasses of wine," Mo said with a hearty laugh before stifling a burp that bubbled up her throat.

"Try four, sister," Gemma corrected her.

"Okay, four then," Mo conceded with a sigh, her eyes rolling in annoyance. "Can we please drop it now?" She dabbed her mouth with her napkin in an attempt to compose herself. "If everyone has finished with dinner, it's time for movie night!" She clapped her hands together excitedly, eager to shift the focus from church and her alcohol intake and onto the rest of the evening's plans.

GEMMA AND CK grabbed the luggage they had left in the foyer and went up to their shared pink and green room to change out of their clothes and into pajamas for movie night. Behind the closed door, they quietly gossiped.

"I knew MerryLee wouldn't come. I mean, it's not a secret that she's not a fan of Moira. But what do you think is the real reason Jenna, Carla, and Tabitha didn't show? You think Moira said or did something to them? They've always been close." CK removed the gold hoops from her ears and jingled them in her hand.

Gemma tossed her clothes out of the large pink suitcase and onto the paisley print chair in the corner of the room. "She's probably pushed them away, the same way she did with Nell. And me. I never hear from Mo unless I reach out to her first, and sometimes she doesn't even reply. It seems you and the maid are the only two people Moira ever talks to anymore."

"Well, she doesn't talk to me *that* much. We just text now and again about our gardens or when one of us is watching *Gilmore*

Girls reruns." Celia Kate walked to the en suite bathroom, turned on the overhead light, and placed her jewelry on the white marble vanity.

"I don't think she's telling the truth about being busy all the time. She never posts on social media." Gemma sat on the pink-and-white-plaid quilt on one of the bottom bunk beds and took off her tall brown boots. "Where are the pictures of her tagged at events and galas and throwing around Jeffrey's money? She's been a socialite for as long as she's lived here, regularly in the newspaper and society magazines. I googled her name earlier this evening and the most recent mention of her was when that memorial fountain in honor of Jeffrey was placed at the country club a few months after he died."

CK walked out of the bathroom that was decorated in rose-gold accents, then tossed her suitcase onto the opposite bunk and unzipped it before Gemma continued, "Something isn't right. I'm going to ask Erin what's really going on around here."

It was Gemma's turn to go into the bathroom, and so she did, with cheetah-print pajamas in her hand. "CK, what if Moira is in the depths of depression? What if she needs some kind of help?"

"And what if you're just nosey, Gemma?"

"You're the nosey one, wondering why her other friends didn't show up this weekend. And I know I'm nosey. I always have been. But I'm also genuinely concerned about my friend."

CK could hear Gemma changing into the satin short-sleeved top and long bottoms in the bathroom. She must have caught a glimpse of herself in the mirror because CK also heard a snide comment about her stomach. By the time Gemma walked out, Celia Kate had put on her buttery soft long-sleeved pajamas. Gemma said, "I really like her. That Erin, I mean. I wonder what *her* story is."

"Again, you're being nosey." CK folded the athletic wear she'd been wearing all day and tucked it neatly into her suitcase.

"Yeah"—Gemma nodded—"but aren't you curious? She must not have much money. Her clothes, you know?"

CK shot a dissatisfied look at her friend.

"I don't mean to sound judgmental. Tyler and I certainly went through some lean years. Don't you remember when I was eating five packs of ramen a day and still nearly starved to death?"

"Shut up," CK said without taking her eyes off her suitcase.

"I'm just saying that Erin looks like she's, well, like she's poor."

"So what if she is, Gemma?" CK sat back on the bottom bunk and slipped her feet into a pair of pale purple terry-cloth thong slippers.

"So nothing. I'm just interested in her. There's something mysterious about her." Gemma shrugged and rifled through her crowded carry-on bag, emerging with her own pair of house shoes, also cheetah print.

CK gasped. "Oh! What about Moira's comment to Nell about Oglethorpe?"

Gemma responded by shaking her head in disappointment.

CK continued, "I'm no psychiatrist, but it's obvious that she lashed out at Nell because of her own guilty conscience about not attending church anymore. When Jeffrey died, that church was good *to* her and good *for* her. She knows that. What she said to Nell was completely rude and inappropriate. I wanted to come up out of that chair and pop her in the jaw."

"Why did she quit going to church anyway?" Gemma asked.

"She told me she just didn't belong there anymore. She's never given me a specific reason, and I didn't press her about it."

"And what about downing that much chardonnay and pinot in

an hour? Good grief. I wouldn't be able to stand up straight. Her tolerance must be awful high," Gemma remarked. "When she got so wasted the last time we were here, I didn't think anything of it. You know, I simply thought of it as a long-overdue weekend for Mo to let loose. The three of us have done that plenty of times over the years on our beach trips and at class reunions. It's never been an issue. But if she's drinking a bottle or two all the time, her Check Liver light must be on. Erin knows for sure. That's something else for me to ask her. Is Mo depressed and is she drinking because she's depressed, which is probably making her more depressed?"

Gemma continued to talk, but CK tuned her out and grabbed her phone from the chest of drawers. She texted Silas to remind him to set his alarm bright and early.

Gemma noticed her friend typing on her phone but had already spoken to Carolina earlier and wasn't at all interested in checking in with Tyler before bed. He would probably only ask how much she had eaten since leaving the house. Besides, it was Friday night, and Gemma knew that meant Tyler was most likely busy enjoying himself in downtown Atlanta without her.

IN THE BEDROOM across the hall, Nell sat on a tufted white stool at the foot of the sleigh bed covered in a velvety black comforter. She held the phone to her ear with one hand and picked at a loose thread in the hem of her blue-and-white-striped pajama shorts with the other.

Chip was talking on the other end of the phone while she reminisced about the first time she met Moira, which was when she and her husband, Jeffrey, began attending Oglethorpe Church about a year before he passed away from a massive heart attack. They became acquainted in Sunday school and started spending time together outside of church. The two couples hit it off well, as they had much in common. Chip and Jeffrey shared a mutual interest in stocks, bonds, golf, and fishing, while Nell and Moira enjoyed discussing their children, exercising, and savoring good Brazilian coffee.

After Jeffrey died, it didn't take long for Nell to recognize that her newly widowed friend was seeking solace from a bottle rather than God. On several occasions, Nell gently expressed her concerns, but Moira dismissed them and remained in denial. It wasn't until the morning after the Sunday school Christmas party that Nell's gentle correction escalated into a serious confrontation, and a wedge was driven between the two. Moira stopped attending church altogether and cut off all communication with Nell.

"I'm no genius," Chip's deep voice said over the line, "but she lashed out at you that way because, yes, she's had too much to drink and because she's trying to justify not attending church anymore. That comment had nothing to do with you and everything to do with Moira."

"As soon as I stepped foot into this house, she told me she was just having a drink on the patio before dinner. And, Chip, she said it in such an arrogant tone, almost like she wanted me to know that what I said to her last Christmas had no influence on her whatsoever. I almost walked back to the car right then. I should have. I could make up some excuse tomorrow to leave. I could say—"

"I think you should stick it out unless you think it's a stumbling block to your sobriety by being there," Chip interrupted.

"Tell me, how did you feel watching them drink during dinner tonight? Did it make you uncomfortable?"

"There's no temptation, Chip." Nell shook her head. "Being around these ladies having cocktails is no different from that book club I go to every few months. One day at a time, right? I succeeded today and I'll succeed the rest of the weekend. It's just that I'm finding it very hard to represent Jesus well by loving Moira. If I'm honest, I can't stand the sight of her. Not because she's got a buzz, but because she's just so smug."

"What about the other guests? Getting along with them?" Chip asked.

"Yeah." Nell cradled the phone between her ear and shoulder and pumped a few dollops of lotion into her hand from a bottle sticking out of her suitcase. "CK and Gemma, Moira's childhood friends, are here. I got to know them after Jeffrey died. They are both very kind and seem to be lots of fun. They also seem nearly as annoyed with Moira as I am. Her housekeeper is a younger woman named Erin, and she is a guest also. I'm not sure what the story is with her and Moira. She's the one I was talking to about church when Moira said what she did about making a commission."

Chip said, "Stick it out and have a good time, Nelly. Maybe the opportunity to make amends with Moira will present itself. If not, enjoy her friends and the food anyway."

"I'll do my best." Nell massaged the vanilla-scented lotion into her dry skin. "Is everything okay there?"

"Tate and I grilled some steaks and Taylor just texted me a few minutes ago. She's safe and sound in her dorm watching television."

"I already know," Nell replied.

"Quit tracking our every move and relax and go watch a movie. Focus on the positive and not the negative, okay?"

"Yeah, I'll try. Pray for me, okay?"

"Always, Nelly."

⌣

ERIN RIFLED THROUGH the duffel bag sitting on top of the white eyelet bedding in the blue toile room, overthinking her choice of pajamas. She hadn't expected anyone to see her in them this weekend. All she'd brought to sleep in was a ragged black Pearl Jam T-shirt and gray cotton shorts that she'd owned for over a decade. She looked at the worn but comfortable clothing in her hands and considered faking an illness to stay in her room for the evening. How would she look in this garb when everyone else would probably be dressed in elegant silk gowns with feathery collars and high-heeled slippers?

And then she rolled her eyes at her ridiculous thoughts, remembering how sweet and personable each woman had been to her throughout the evening. Not one of them had looked her up and down or grimaced at her faded blouse or well-worn shoes. These were mature, welcoming women, not snobby high schoolers. While she changed into her cozy sleep clothes, she made a promise to let down her guard. These women didn't care that she was poor, just like she didn't care that Gemma was self-deprecating, CK and Nell both worried incessantly over their kids, and Moira was a lush. They all had obvious hang-ups, and that was okay.

⌣

MOIRA STOOD BESIDE the brick fireplace in her spacious bedroom, which was decorated in shades of cream and khaki, and poured herself another glass of wine. The cool autumn wind rustling through the palm trees carried the briny scent of the sea and marsh through the open doors of the balcony. She was already dressed in her expensive pastel pink pajamas, accessorized with gold hoop earrings, and her blonde hair was neatly pulled back from her face and secured with a gold barrette. Her makeup remained flawless, and her pedicure was concealed by soft pink slippers topped with a pom of feathers.

She stepped out of the French doors and onto the small balcony with its plank flooring and haint blue ceiling. She rested her elbows on the wooden railing and admired the early autumn moonlight dancing on the water, casting a gentle glow over the cluster of chairs beneath her and the tree that had been Jeffrey's favorite on the property. For months after his death, she had avoided that spot, but now, during the late afternoons, she found solace there with her cats, who curiously observed the birds flapping overhead and the redbreasts and crappie splashing in the water. Instead of sitting by the water and resting her hand in Jeffrey's on the arm of a wooden chair, she now held a glass.

She pushed the memories of them beneath the live oak out of her mind and focused instead on how relaxed, carefree, and maybe a little silly she felt at that moment. This was her favorite feeling—one she wished could be permanent. Shifting her gaze around the dark backyard, she took another sip of golden wine and recalled her comment to Nell at the dinner table.

It was a crude remark—one that would undoubtedly cause Moira's mother, whose sense of etiquette rivaled that of Emily Post, to turn seven shades of red with embarrassment. Moira didn't genuinely believe what she had said about Nell treating her religion like a pyramid scheme. It was just that Nell's demeanor seemed so pious, holier-than-thou, rigid, and judgmental. Although it was a petty comment, Moira felt a fleeting sense of satisfaction when she thought she had managed to cut Nell Rehman down to size.

Speaking of cutting one down to size, Moira was disappointed to hear Gemma still putting herself down—a habit she had developed from the man who was supposed to honor her, put her on a pedestal, and treat her like a princess. Tyler was aware that Moira wasn't fond of him. Almost a decade earlier, they had all attended the wedding of a mutual friend in their hometown. Throughout that lovely spring day at Lake Conasauga, Moira held her tongue while Tyler continually mocked Gemma about her appearance. While waiting for the newlyweds to exit the church, Tyler snidely told Gemma not to eat the rice in her hand and winked at Moira. In response, Moira threw her handful of rice in his face and yelled at him in front of all the guests. It was a loud, embarrassing scene, and Gemma defended Tyler afterward. She didn't speak to Moira for several weeks. When they eventually made amends, Gemma insisted that she didn't want to hear a single negative word about her husband again. Since that incident, Moira kept her opinions about the despicable Tyler Gardner to herself.

At that wedding ten years ago, CK had defended Moira the same way she had defended Nell at the dinner table only half an hour earlier. CK, always the defender, the protector. Judging by the way she talked about her kids and was continually sending them text messages, it was evident she was maybe a bit too overprotective.

When Moira's sons, Bradford and Brent, were Silas's age, it was not uncommon for them to be left home alone while Moira and Jeffrey took weeklong trips to the Caribbean or had overnight stays in Atlanta. Moira wondered if Celia Kate's helicopter parenting would lead Silas to go wild once he was out from under his mother's control. With that thought, she downed the last of the liquid in her glass.

Moira walked back into her bedroom and placed the empty goblet on the tan bedside table. She then checked her reflection in the ornate bronze floor-length mirror that leaned against her wall. She adored the silky pajama set she was wearing—a gift from her beloved. She had chosen the pajamas at a boutique in Beverly Hills and suspected they probably cost more than Erin's weekly salary. Then she started to wonder if Erin had felt out of place among the group. Moira would hate to think that any of her guests were uncomfortable.

Moira had long known, by the car Erin drove and her cracked phone and even her address, that she wasn't well-to-do. And Moira had never ridiculed her for that. Mr. and Mrs. Albert Wallace had taught all four of their children to treat everyone equally, from the CEO to the custodian. So Moira didn't look down on Erin. But she did wonder if she could help her out.

What this group needed was another round of drinks. A couple of whiskey and sodas would knock Nell down a peg, make Gemma comfortable in her own skin, calm CK's anxiety, and help Erin feel included. Steadying herself in her pink slippers, Moira admired her beauty one more time before leaving her bedroom.

Chapter 13

THE THEATER ON the ground floor, located next to Moira's gym, was a midsized dark space without windows. Ten black recliners were arranged in a semicircle in front of a large projector screen on the long wall. At the back of the room was a small kitchenette with a black countertop that displayed a red and white popcorn machine, as well as a large woven basket filled with a variety of candies.

Samantha Baker's family struggled to get out the door on time in the opening scene of *Sixteen Candles* while the party of five settled into their leather recliners with bowls of fresh buttery popcorn and their choice of sugary candy. Everyone but Moira grabbed a bottle of water or a can of cold soda from the mini fridge. Instead, she sipped chardonnay with soda water and a squeeze of lemon from a silver tumbler she'd purchased at the gift shop at one of her favorite places on earth: Wormsloe Historic Site.

CK noticed that Mo drank from the insulated cup after every few bites of popcorn, which piqued her curiosity as to what Moira was downing.

When CK's phone vibrated in the recliner's cup holder, she frantically reached for it, expecting a text from Sean saying that Chipper Jones had keeled over from feline leukemia. Instead, it was from Gemma, and it said, She must have the tolerance of a frat boy.

The group was quietly engrossed in the movie for the first twenty minutes until Nell got up to head to the bathroom.

"I'm not it this time!" Gemma exclaimed with pride. "I'm not the first one to leave the movie to go to the bathroom. Where's my medal?"

"I thought I would be the first one to get up," CK added. "I remember when I could drive down to the Gulf Coast on summer vacation without pulling over once. Now I'm stopped at a gas station before we even get out of the county."

Nell stopped at the theater door and said, "I walk down our road and back every morning, and a few days ago, I couldn't hold it until I got back to the house. I had to dart down into a ditch. And wouldn't you know, on a red-clay Georgia back road that rarely gets traffic, two trucks came barreling by at that very moment!"

Nell disappeared out the door and the group continued to laugh at her story, except for Moira, who was annoyed at the attention being lavished on the Goody Two-shoes.

CK popped a few peanut butter candies into her mouth before saying, "I remember my mother telling me that she should have worn a diaper to my basketball games because as soon as she jumped up to cheer, that was it." CK smiled at the thought. "That seems so long ago, but here I am now, just like my mother, with hot flashes, reading glasses, and a useless bladder."

"Notice Erin hasn't said a word because she's still in her thirties. You just wait, kid." Moira winked at Erin sitting quietly in her recliner.

"Yeah, y'all are scaring me a little bit." Erin laughed and ate a handful of sour candies.

"It's all downhill after forty." CK pointed her thumb downward and rolled her eyes.

Nell reentered the theater and picked right back up where she'd left off by saying, "And all that walking I do every morning doesn't even count for anything because my metabolism isn't what it used to be." She sat back in the chair and covered her legs with a white chenille throw blanket. "There was a time when I could eat whatever I wanted if I walked two miles a day. But that is not the case anymore. I swear I could walk to Miami and back and only burn ten calories. But Chip? He wanted to lose a few pounds, so all he did was cut sugar from his coffee, and suddenly he was back to his college weight."

Moira smirked quietly and allowed herself to feel vain for a moment because she still had the metabolism of her younger self. Whether cycling, walking, or swimming laps in the pool, she made sure to stay active for at least an hour each day. This moderate exercise allowed her to indulge in all the delicious, fatty foods and glasses of wine she wanted without worrying about her weight.

Gemma saw an opportunity to poke fun at herself and said, "Nell, my metabolism is as useless as a screen door on a submarine." She laughed and dug into the popcorn bowl resting in her lap. "And speaking of submarines, I'm about the size of one, aren't I?"

The mood in the room suddenly changed from light and humorous to thick with tension.

"There you go again. Stop, Gemma," CK said seriously.

"Oh, Celia Kate, you know it's true. You all do." Gemma's smile faded as the kernels rolled to the bottom of her plastic bowl with a soft patter.

"Gemma, you are beautiful, and you know it," Mo declared with a drunken slur. "You are so beautiful to me. Can't you see? You're everything I hoped for. Everything I . . ." Her singing trailed off when no one laughed at her attempt to lighten the atmosphere.

"I carry my weight well." Gemma nodded at the screen and changed the subject. "Jake Ryan looks like Tyler back in high school, doesn't he, CK? Mo?"

"I don't see it." Moira hiccupped before taking another drink from the stainless-steel cup.

"You don't see the resemblance, Mo? Oh, I certainly do," CK said, agreeing with Gemma. "Tyler used to look a lot like Jake Ryan. But I never thought Jake Ryan was attractive. Maybe it's his caterpillar eyebrows or that big, goofy hair. Either way, he's not my cup of tea."

Gemma was distracted by the peanut M&M that had fallen into her pajama top, but she still heard the insult Celia Kate directed at her husband.

SAM AND JAKE shared a kiss over the glowing birthday cake in the final scene of the movie, and a loud snore escaped from Moira's open mouth. Her neatly secured hair had come loose, and messy strands framed her sleeping face. One of her house shoes had slipped off her pedicured foot, while the other dangled from her toes. As the final credits rolled on the screen, Nell was the first to stand up and reach for a heavy sherpa blanket on one of the empty chairs. She carefully moved the empty popcorn bucket and chocolate candy box from Moira's chest and covered her.

"Do you think we should just leave her down here?" Nell asked Gemma, CK, and Erin.

"Sure, she'll be fine," Erin said. "Sometimes she falls asleep in here while watching old home movies."

CK let out a sad moan. "You mean, like, movies of Jeffrey and the kids?"

Erin nodded. "And her wedding. She watches it quite a bit."

"Bless her soul," Nell remarked, her voice tinged with sympathy.

Moira's guests left her sleeping soundly in the dark theater and moved through the house, turning off lights and locking doors. Once they finished securing the downstairs, they walked up the staircase and gathered in the hallway outside their respective rooms.

"I'm concerned about Mo, Erin. How much is she really drinking?" CK asked while leaning against the doorframe to her and Gemma's bedroom.

Because she knew that these women were Moira's closest friends and truly cared for her, Erin explained that Moira usually opened a bottle of wine or vodka before she left for the day. She recalled times when she arrived at work to find broken wineglasses or evidence that Moira had hurriedly grabbed a trash can. She also told them Moira rarely left the house anymore, sometimes not for days or even weeks. Erin had become her connection to the outside world, taking the cats to the groomer, grocery shopping, and even scheduling a nail technician to come to the house every other week for manicures and pedicures.

"Moira Allyson, an alcoholic recluse?" Gemma said with disbelief. "I know she hasn't been posting things online, but still, this blows my mind. She's always been the extrovert, the socialite."

"I had no idea," CK confessed, a look of surprise covering her tired face. "She and I talk on the phone or text every few weeks, and she's never let on that she was lonely or depressed or holed up in the house. Like Gemma said, Mo has always been such a social butterfly. When Jeffrey died, I figured she'd throw herself into as much charity work and volunteering as possible to keep her occupied."

"I think she did in the beginning," Nell added. "But it wasn't too long after he died when I noticed she was more reliant on alcohol than she was on God, the church, her friends, and charity work to help her through her grief."

They all expressed their discontent and worry for Moira.

Nell continued, "I don't guess she told you all about our little tiff, did she?"

"She mentioned something, but not in much detail," CK said.

"Last Christmas I confronted her about her drinking. I did it in love, I promise. I was stern with her, but I was also very careful not to sound critical or condemning. After all, I struggled with the same addiction for years. I know how quickly it can get out of control."

"Oh, Nell, I didn't know that either," CK said while she ran a hand through her long ponytail.

Gemma guiltily gnawed on her lip and added, "I hope tonight, us drinking, you know . . . I hope that hasn't been uncomfortable or awkward for you."

"Yeah, Nell, I'm sorry if—" Erin began.

"Oh no," Nell assured them. "The Lord helps me overcome temptation day by day. Sometimes hour by hour. But I'm fine, really. I wouldn't have come this weekend if it was a problem."

"So how did she take it? When you talked to her last Christmas?" CK asked.

"She cut me off. She quit coming to Oglethorpe. I felt so guilty about that. I still feel guilty at times. I certainly don't want to be the reason she pulls away from her faith." Nell looked downcast.

"Don't you dare think that way," Celia Kate said, comforting Nell. "You spoke the truth to Mo, and I trust you delivered it with love. You have such a kind and forgiving spirit, Nell, which draws people to you instead of pushing them away. You aren't responsible for how Moira feels, nor are you responsible for her decision to leave the church."

Nell smiled in appreciation at CK. "Thank you."

Gemma added, "I agree with CK. If Mo pushed you away, it's because what you said made her feel uncomfortable. Being confronted with the truth often does that."

Beautiful Moira was completely unaware of the conversation taking place upstairs in her home as she slept soundly in the movie theater. Gravelly snores escaped her open mouth, and a warm stream of drool pooled in the crease of her neck. Meanwhile, those she considered her dearest friends whispered in the dimly lit upstairs hallway about her alleged alcohol problem. If Moira had known they were critiquing her choices under her own roof, she would have certainly confronted them and kicked them out, sending them back to their boring, mundane lives.

Chapter 14

THE NEXT MORNING Nell was awakened by her phone alarm chiming at eight o'clock. She had slept well and felt refreshed. Stretching beneath the plush black blanket piped with white, she looked out the large window. Through the top of a palm tree in her view, she noticed the sky was dark with clouds. How might this affect Moira's plans for their morning walk along the shore, pool time, massages, and dinner on the catamaran?

She walked into the small adjoining bathroom, its walls adorned with palm leaf wallpaper reminiscent of Blanche Devereaux's bedroom from *The Golden Girls*. After washing her face, she found herself wondering how Moira was feeling after drinking so much. Moira had not just fallen asleep in the theater; she had passed out on the first night of her own birthday celebration. Nell quickly reined in her thoughts, steering them away from any hint of condescension.

"God, I'm not saying a word to her. You can handle it," she said out loud as she pulled her toothbrush and toothpaste from her flowery toiletry bag on the bathroom counter. "You are the one who can convict her and change her. You don't need me."

God hadn't necessarily needed Chip Rehman either, but he used him to show Nell the error of her ways. Like Moira, Nell was defensive and accused her husband of being dramatic and holier-than-thou for disapproving of her choices. Over time, however, her heart softened, and she came to understand that her husband's words came from a place of concern, not criticism. God had used him to communicate with Nell. Perhaps he wanted to use Nell to reach out to Moira again. It had not gone very well back in December, but maybe it was time for her to take another swing at it.

"Okay, maybe. I trust you, God, to tell me what to say, if anything."

Nell found it difficult to trust anyone—herself, Chip at the beginning of their relationship, and even the Lord and his divine plan. To her, trusting meant relinquishing control, which made her uncomfortable. As the oldest of three children, she had to take charge when her father's drinking and affair brought chaos to their family. Nell was only a teen then, but she felt responsible for comforting her mother, caring for her younger siblings, and maintaining peace and hope within their home.

As an adult, Nell tried to control her house, the schedules, the appointments, the extracurricular activities that her twins were involved in. And drinking had provided relaxation from the burden of needing to be in charge. Nevertheless, after becoming sober and drawing closer to God, Nell realized she didn't have to manipulate everything. The need to be in charge was a false belief she had created—a purpose she had assigned to herself. One of the most beautiful aspects of her relationship with Jesus was the act of surrender. It was liberating for her to acknowledge that she couldn't manage everything on her own. Finding rest at his feet was exactly what she needed.

Knowing all that, she still faced moments when she struggled to trust. It was simply part of her human nature, a struggle inherent to being flesh and blood. She spent hours lying in her dark bedroom and worrying about her children's safety, the possibility of backsliding, and even about her friend Moira. She tended to stew in panic for a while until the Lord gently reminded her that she wasn't in control—and that she didn't need to be. Peace would eventually wash over her whenever she whispered, "I trust you, Lord."

Nell spent the next thirty minutes in the palm-print guest bathroom talking to God, then getting ready for the morning walk along the Ogeechee. She laced up her green and white tennis shoes and checked her phone to see where her children were early that Saturday morning. Both were safe and sound in their beds, and she thanked God for it.

CK AND ERIN sat at the round wrought iron table on the back patio, holding hot cups of coffee. They gazed at the calm water beyond the manicured lawn, which was dotted with oak and palm trees and patches of blooming pampas grass. The same pampas grass plumes were in fresh flower arrangements throughout the home.

"Cloudy today, isn't it?" CK broke the silence as a cool breeze wafted through the green canopy above them. Bits of moss fell onto the cobblestone patio and tumbled into the mulched flower beds filled with begonias in shades of pink and red.

Erin tightened the strings of her gray hoodie and used the toe of her worn tennis shoe to pull the tapered leg of her sweatpants down over her exposed ankle. "It's a little chilly for me," she admitted.

"You'll warm up once we get moving," CK said as she picked up her phone from the table and sent another text to Silas. "My son Silas texted earlier that he was awake and was about to log onto the college's website. I hope he didn't just roll over and go back to sleep."

"What's he got to do this morning? You mentioned it last night, but . . ." Erin's voice trailed off.

CK sat back in the cool iron chair. "Cumberland State began accepting applications this morning. He's only a junior, but the earlier he applies, the better his chances for admission. I'm most concerned about some of the questions on the application— essay-type questions about his goals and challenges he has had to overcome. That kind of thing. I really wish I were there to help him through it, because he isn't the best writer."

"I'm sure he will be fine," Erin assured her. "What if he doesn't get into Cumberland? Any second choices?"

CK took a sip of the steaming coffee flavored with hazelnut creamer. "He's only ever mentioned Cumberland State. It's just forty-five minutes from home. He would commute, continue living with us, and save money. I honestly don't know what plan B would be. I guess we still have plenty of time to figure that out."

CK was quiet for a moment and then said, "My husband, Sean, wants him to go as far away from home as he can. He's not opposed to us sending him off to a big city in another state. 'He needs life experience. Cut the cord,'" CK said, imitating her husband's deep, serious tone. "I get it. I really do. But I just—" She let out a deep sigh and shifted her gaze from the calm water to Erin, searching for understanding. "How do we let go of them when the time comes? Gemma seems ready to push her child out the door without a second thought, and I simply can't wrap my head around it. How did Mo and Nell manage to do this? It feels so unnatural, doesn't it? After dedicating eighteen years to raising a child and preparing their lunches, bandaging their scrapes, and holding them when storms roll in, I mean, how do we just abandon all that and release them into the world? What if your boy decided to leave, Erin? How would you deal?"

Erin pulled her feet up onto the iron chair, tucking them beneath her as she cradled her coffee mug tightly in both hands. "PJ is all I have. It's just been the two of us for the last nineteen years. Not literally, because I was married to his dad for twelve of those years, but that marriage was far from happy, and PJ and I only had each other to depend on. We weren't the picture-perfect family frolicking around on the sandy shores of Tybee Island on a Saturday." She glanced over at CK from beneath the gray hood of her sweatshirt. "His dad abused me both physically and mentally."

"Erin, I'm sorry to hear that," CK offered.

Just a few months into Erin's marriage, minor irritations—such as having a stressful day at work or being stuck in traffic—triggered Phillip's volatile temper. For the next twelve years, Erin found herself walking on eggshells, living in a constant state of fear and uncertainty. It was perhaps too soon for the new Mrs. Pepperell to witness that cruel side of him. She likely wasn't aware that Phillip had left Erin without a penny and that his nineteen-year-old son did not have a relationship with him due to the mental and physical abuse he had inflicted on his mother.

Erin continued, "There have been many times when PJ stepped in and came to my defense, not just as my son, but as my only protector. When the time comes for him to leave the nest, it will be very difficult for me. But, CK, I'll be honest. It's not me holding on to him; it's PJ who clings to me. He's filled with anxiety whenever I mention his next steps in life. Even while I'm at my second job at the convenience store, he makes it a point to check on me constantly. He's texted me ten times since I have been here. *He's* the one who can't cut the cord."

"Oh, Erin, you must think I'm such an idiot," Celia Kate said, shaking her head in embarrassment.

"Of course not," Erin gently reassured her. "I understand where you're coming from. I love PJ more than anything in this world. He's my greatest blessing. But he's got to find his own way. I hate that he's always worried about me. I want him to embrace life fully—to explore the world, find love, get married, have kids of his own. Those dreams mean everything to me, but here he is, focused on making sure his mama is okay, putting my needs above his own. So when you ask me how I would feel if my boy chose to leave home, I'll tell you honestly. I would be relieved. It would mean that I had done my job, that I raised him to be strong and independent." Erin reached over, her hand lightly tapping CK's knee covered in trendy joggers. "I don't know you that well, but I trust you've done your job and your boy will be just fine. And you will be too."

"You haven't said much so far this weekend," CK said, "but I hope that changes, because you have a lot of wisdom."

Erin smiled appreciatively at her new friend before they were interrupted by the sound of Gemma and Nell talking while exiting through the patio doors. Gemma had a cup of orange juice in one hand and an éclair in the other.

"Did you see these beauties in the glass container on the kitchen counter? Antonio must have put them out for us last night—chocolate and strawberry," Gemma said as she popped a bite into her mouth and then wiped the crumbs from her navy Atlanta Braves sweatshirt.

"Has anyone seen Mo this morning?" Nell asked, steam rising

from the white mug in her hand. She settled into one of the empty chairs at the iron table while the sunlight filtered through a heavy cloud and cast patterns across the ornate tabletop.

Gemma replied between bites, "I haven't seen her this morning. Either one of her cats stole her breath while she was asleep, or she must still be passed out in the theater. Do you want me to go get her?"

"Leave her be." CK waved Gemma's suggestion away with her hand.

"Well, she's the one who insisted we all be out here for a brisk walk at 9:00 a.m. sharp. I could still be curled up in bed, enjoying my sleep on this Saturday morning," Gemma pointed out before yawning.

"I'll go and wake her if that's okay with you, CK?" Erin volunteered from beneath the hood of her sweatshirt. "I've done it before."

"Fine by me," CK answered.

Erin walked through the living room and down the long hallway until she reached the partly closed door of the movie room. She quietly pushed it open, and light from the hallway spilled into the dark theater, giving her just enough visibility to enter. She reached over to the wall and flipped on the light switch before she approached her sleeping friend.

"Moira? Moira?" Erin said in a soft voice while she gently tapped her shoulder.

Moira was curled up on her side in the oversized recliner, her head resting on the arm of the chair. Dove and Pearl were pressed against her back and gently purred.

As Mo gradually opened her heavy eyelids, still caked with dark shadow and smudged liner, the bright glow of the recessed lights momentarily blinded her.

When she finally focused on Erin kneeling over her, panic washed over her face. She shot upright in the recliner, causing both cats to jolt from the chair. Almost immediately, a sharp throb shot through her head, prompting her to groan and grip her forehead with her sweaty fingers.

"What time is it?" she asked, her voice scratchy and her mouth dry.

"It's about nine fifteen. Everyone is already on the patio, dressed and ready for our morning walk along the water. Do you want us to go ahead without you?" Erin quietly offered.

"Oh, good grief," Moira replied, then she nodded hesitantly, strands of hair tumbling around her face. "Yes, go ahead. I don't want you all to wait any longer for me to get ready. I'll see you back here in a little while, yeah?"

"Okay." Erin turned to walk out of the theater when Moira stopped her.

"Erin, I need you to do me a favor. Please?" Moira reached out her hand, desperation in her tone. "Don't tell them that I was still asleep. Tell them that, uh . . ." She paused and licked her dry lips. "Tell them that you found me on the phone with one of the boys. I think—Bradford, yeah, Bradford is having girl trouble again this morning. And I told you all to go ahead while I help him sort it out on the phone."

"Moira, I really don't want to lie," Erin said, her brows furrowing and her head shaking as she considered her boss's request.

"Erin, you know Nell already thinks I drink too much. She will undoubtedly hold this over my head for the rest of the weekend," Moira insisted, her voice rising slightly. "Even though I'm not hungover—not at all. I mean, I slept so long because it's just so dark down here in the theater. I know that and you know that, but Nell will still insist that I slept so long because I drank last night. I can't give her that satisfaction." She paused and then repeated slowly and insistently, "I am on the phone with my son, and I'm going to shower and see you back here in about an hour, okay? Then we'll have brunch, pool time, massages, and a whole lot of other fun things lined up."

After a moment of silence, Erin reluctantly agreed and left Moira alone. Just as the door was about to click shut behind her, Erin heard Moira groan and sink back into the leather chair. She walked out to the patio and delivered Moira's lie. CK, Gemma, and Nell didn't dispute what Erin told them, but the looks on their faces led Erin to believe they knew it was a farce.

WHILE WAITING FOR hot water to reach her shower, Moira, feeling nauseated and trying to ignore the throbbing pain in her head, watched from her balcony as her guests walked across the dewy grass in her backyard. They passed beneath the massive tree with its furrowed trunk and went by the group of Adirondack chairs before disappearing down the sandy path that meandered between the waters of the Ogeechee River on one side and clusters of spartina grass and live oaks on the other. Across the river, the tea-colored water mixed with flourishing salt marshes filled with grass, sedges, and rushes.

She wished she could join them. Walking that path in the mornings was her tradition, a part of her exercise routine that kept her metabolism working strong. However, she wasn't going to feel guilty about it. She hadn't drunk too much the night before; she had only overslept because the theater was dark. Just like when she fell asleep watching herself and Jeffrey dance to

Etta James at their wedding reception. It was dark, quiet, and comfortable. No, she wouldn't feel guilty for having a little fun and being a bit silly on her birthday weekend. She wouldn't give Nell Rehman that satisfaction.

———

NELL SPENT MUCH of her childhood not far from here in the low country. As she walked the path with Erin, Gemma, and CK, she felt a wave of nostalgia wash over her. She reminisced with the other ladies about how she often stalked tailing juvenile redfish with her father in the marshes and winding waterways, where he spent much of his time drinking. For a while after she got sober, it was difficult for her to separate the beauty of the low country from her memories of alcohol. Wine had long been a part of weddings and her bedtime routine, while a nice bourbon had kept her warm on the boat or during autumn nights on the beach. Now she was finally free of that association and could enjoy God's beautiful landscape without aid.

"Are there alligators out here?" CK asked, a hint of worry plain on her face as she took in her surroundings with anxious eyes.

"If there are, I'd say Al E. Gator has his sights set on me. I'd be his ideal meal—breakfast, lunch, and dinner all rolled into one!" Gemma chuckled, her laughter ringing out across the salt marsh, harmonizing with the whispers of the wind and the rhythmic lapping of the dark water against the grassy shoreline.

"Al E. Gator would rather have fish and herons, Gemma," Nell reassured her and lightly nudged her arm. "May I ask you a question?"

Gemma was curious. "I suppose so."

"Why are you so hard on yourself?" Nell inquired gently, her eyes meeting Gemma's with sincerity before Gemma shoved her manicured hands into the pockets of her windbreaker.

"Preach, Nell," CK enthusiastically agreed and held up a hand in praise.

"I don't mean to overstep," Nell clarified while her red ponytail slapped the shoulder of her silver jacket. "I just can't help but notice how you often belittle yourself."

"She's been demeaning herself for as long as I can remember," CK offered.

"Okay, zip it," Gemma shot back while rolling her eyes at CK. Then she turned her gaze back to the expansive salt marsh. "I just say what everyone is thinking. I'm the elephant in the room, pun intended. And frankly, I don't like to leave the elephant in the room unaddressed. It feels so much better to confront things directly. Get it out in the open, you know?"

"Maybe," Nell said, "but you're such a beautiful lady, Gemma. I hope you recognize that."

Erin and Celia Kate audibly agreed.

As they continued along the winding trail, canopied with bright greenery, CK's long dark hair swung behind her with each stride. "Nell, she's just repeating what she hears every day."

"There it is." Gemma stopped and planted her white tennis shoes firmly on the silty ground as she turned to face her friend of nearly forty years. "I know how much you dislike my husband, but I don't want to keep hearing about it, okay?" Her tone was serious and defensive, and a scowl covered her face.

The atmosphere shifted suddenly, becoming somber and tense. Nell and Erin, who had been walking a little behind Gemma and CK, exchanged bewildered looks. They redirected their attention to the stunning antebellum home belonging to Moira's neighbor.

"Well, my goodness! Would you look at those grand columns," Nell said to Erin, trying to change the subject. "Do you know who lives there, Erin?"

"I think it's a senator, but I'm—"

CK interrupted Erin, saying, "It's hard for me to hold my tongue, Gemma, because I know how verbally abusive Tyler is to you. All the self-deprecating jokes you make, the ones that come so easily to you, he inspires them. He encourages the negative way you see yourself. He talks better to his hunting dogs than he does to you."

Gemma narrowed her eyes at CK and began to defend him. "My husband is not verbally abusive, CK. He doesn't mean anything by it—"

CK cut her off, her voice rising slightly with frustration. "What infuriates me even more than his comments about you is how quickly you jump to his defense. I swear, it's like you are brainwashed! You deserve better, Gemma."

Celia Kate quickened her pace, continuing down the path and leaving the rest of them behind. Gemma dug the heel of her shoe into the soft, warm sand. Nell and Erin remained next to her.

"Gemma, I'm so sorry," Nell began, gently placing a comforting hand on Gemma's shoulder. "I had no idea I would open that can of worms. I really—"

"No," Gemma replied while brushing her dark bangs away from her sweaty forehead with the flick of her wrist. "It's okay."

"My ex-husband was always putting me down," Erin admitted, her tone reflecting the pain of her past. She shoved her hands into her hoodie's pockets after a sudden gust of crisp morning air swarmed them, causing a shiver to run down her spine.

"Tyler doesn't *always* put me down," Gemma said to reassure herself. "It's true that he makes fun of my weight. But he really doesn't mean anything by it. He's just a kidder. A funny guy, you know? You tease the one you love, right?"

Even though Gemma defended him, she couldn't help but remember that while she was packing for the weekend on Allyson Island, he had stood in her closet and tugged on hanging shirts and dresses. "Look at this thing!" He pulled a white sundress off the hanger and laughed. "I could cover my boat with it. I mean, how many yards of material is this, Gemma? This is a whole roll!" And when he caught a glimpse of her getting into the shower before bed that night, he didn't even smile when he called her a "disgusting pig."

As Gemma, Erin, and Nell slowly resumed their walk, Celia Kate continued to distance herself from the group, her steps quickening. Gemma watched her best friend get farther away and chewed on her bottom lip.

"Maybe she's right. I don't know why I keep defending him. It's just habit, I guess. I've defended him since I met him thirty-one years ago," Gemma admitted, her voice barely above a whisper. She looked out at the beautiful marshland, where elegant herons flew gracefully against the gray sky. Each movement was a testimony to their freedom. The beauty of her surroundings certainly did not match her inner struggle.

"Anyway, enough about me and my fat-shaming husband," Gemma said with a chuckle, brushing off the topic. "May I ask you a question now, Erin?"

Erin felt a rush of nervousness as the attention shifted entirely to her. "Well, yeah," she replied, her heart quickening a little.

"I know you are loyal to Mo, not only as a friend, but also

because you work for her, and I don't want to make you feel uncomfortable with what I'm about to ask. So if you don't want to answer, I get it. I really do. I just have a nagging concern for Mo after watching her drink like a fish yesterday."

Erin's stomach tightened. "Okay, what's your question?"

"Was she really tied up with Bradford on the phone this morning, or was she too hungover to join us?" Gemma asked.

Nell was especially eager to hear Erin's response and leaned in closer, her eyes scanning Erin's pale face for any hint of the truth.

"You're right, Gemma. I don't feel comfortable answering that," Erin finally admitted, her voice barely above a whisper. "If you're concerned about her, you should ask her. I don't mean to sound rude, but it isn't my place."

"I respect that." Gemma nodded in understanding. "Maybe you can answer this for me, then?"

"Yeah?" Erin's heart fluttered.

"The cats killed her in her sleep, didn't they?"

Erin and Nell giggled.

Although Nell respected Erin's decision to decline answering, she felt that the refusal spoke volumes.

⁓

THE TRIO FINALLY met up with CK, who was standing where the loamy path ended at a grove of bald cypress trees that had not yet shed their needles. She kicked her sneaker at one of the many surrounding cypress knees—scraped, cone-shaped mounds that jutted up from the roots of the trees—and looked across the dark water to the boggy shore on the other side. A breeze stirred the gray clouds above them as they stood quietly watching a wood stork, with its hefty, football-shaped body perched on slender legs, wading in the shallow water before them.

Erin pulled her phone from her pocket to take a picture of the serene view and said, "I have never been this far down the trail before. It's just beautiful."

"I would like to put a hammock right here," CK said, gesturing between the gray trunks of two cypress trees. "Let the wind lull me to sleep like a baby."

"I have been blessed to travel a lot," Nell shared. "I've been out west, to Europe, and to the Caribbean, but this is my favorite place. The brackish water, the cordgrass, the egrets, the smell of salt—I don't even mind the scent of the pluff mud so much." She laughed. "The low country is home, and there's no place like it."

"Thankfully we don't smell that pluff mud today." Erin winced at the thought of the sulfurous scent.

"You've mentioned the low country a few times, Nell. What's that mean?" Gemma asked.

Nell cleared her throat as if she were about to give a school lesson and said, "My mother's family comes from the Low Country, so I know all about this. Now, that's the Low Country with a capital *L* and *C*, and it's the coastal part of South Carolina that includes Beaufort, Colleton, Hampton, and Jasper counties. Depending on who you're asking, it might cover some nearby counties too, but it definitely doesn't include us up here in Savannah—only the area north of the Savannah River. Now, the whole area from South Carolina to Georgia is called the low country, but that's with a lowercase *l* and *c*, because it's at sea level or even lower. If we ever get hit by a hurricane like the ones back in the early 1890s, it's likely that this whole place would get flooded again."

The ladies nodded at the cultural lesson, and Gemma said,

"Whether it's capitalized or not, I could go for a low-country boil right now."

"Should we head back? Maybe Moira is waiting for us," CK said as she pulled her phone from the pocket of her joggers. She checked the notification volume to ensure it was set to high, just in case one of her kids or Sean needed her. The volume was still up, just as it had been the last time she checked ten minutes earlier.

"Can we talk first?" Gemma asked.

CK shrugged nonchalantly in response.

"Erin and I will head back," Nell said, nodding to Erin before tapping her elbow. With that, they left CK and Gemma alone beneath the light green canopy of the cypress trees.

"CK." Gemma cleared her throat and crossed her arms over her Atlanta Braves sweatshirt. "I appreciate how protective you are of me; you always have been. You came to my rescue when I was bullied on the playground, and I still have the card you made for me when I didn't make the middle school cheerleading squad. It's like your role in our friendship has always been to stand up for me."

"You make it sound like you're defenseless," CK said. "There have been times when you have done the same for me. Remember the creepy guy who kept hitting on me at the Bush concert? You scared him off."

Gemma flexed her arm like a bodybuilder and said, "We protect each other. Look, I understand why you don't like Tyler. I know you've never liked him, and believe me, I know he can be a bit crude. But he's my husband, CK, and I wish you would respect that."

Celia Kate looked at her dearest friend on earth and said, "I wish he would respect you."

Gemma sighed and gazed back out across the Ogeechee, admitting, "You're right. He doesn't respect me; sometimes he is downright cruel. I know, I've known, that I deserve better."

CK, pleasantly surprised by Gemma's realization, placed her arm around Gemma's shoulders. "Thank the Lord you finally recognize it. Now what are you going to do about it?"

Gemma pulled away, wiping her tear-filled eyes. "I'm not going to do anything about it right now. I agree with you that my husband is mean. Let's leave it at that, okay?"

"But, Gemma, you cannot allow him to—"

"I'm not divorcing my husband just because he calls me fat and isn't attracted to me, CK. The truth is, I am fat, aren't I? Can we please drop the subject? I want to enjoy the rest of the weekend. Dwelling on the fact that my husband finds me repulsive is not how I want to spend my time. So once again, can we agree to drop it?"

CK didn't want to let it go. She was a fixer, and she was determined to address the issue right there on the riverbank in the September breeze. Reluctantly, she nodded in concession, and they began the walk back to Allyson Island.

Chapter 15

MOIRA STOOD AT the kitchen counter, blowing into her mug of steaming black coffee and gazing out the window at the dark sky that threatened rain. Her Jeffrey loved rain. When storms rolled through the marsh, he spent his time on the back porch, watching the clouds and breathing in the damp, clean air.

In fact, Moira and Jeffrey met on a dreary night at a fraternity party at the University of Georgia. Moira wanted to stay inside, away from the water and humidity that made her hair frizz. However, that night during the fall semester of '92, her roommate, Carla, convinced her to go out. Carla said they needed to "do something stupid and glittery," which meant putting on a crop top, applying too much eyeliner, and pretending, if only for a few hours, that the ache in Moira's chest didn't exist. That ache was there because her father had died of lung cancer only three months earlier.

The party was loud, crowded, and chaotic, and nearly everyone held a red Solo cup filled with cheap beer. Someone had rigged up Christmas lights over the kegs, and the speakers blasted Alice in Chains. Moira stood near the stairs, arms crossed, trying to decide how long she had to stay before leaving wouldn't seem rude.

That was when she saw Jeffrey Allyson.

He was wearing a worn Bulldogs T-shirt and was huddled in the kitchen with a couple of guys she didn't recognize, laughing easily and loudly. He was tall, dark-haired, and radiated a confidence that was not cocky but warm and magnetic. His dark eyes were filled with humor and something deeper beneath the surface, something that, almost painfully, reminded her of her father. He saw her watching and tipped his head like he knew he'd caught her thinking about him, and he walked right over.

"You look miserable," he said, smiling. "You want a drink or a door?"

Moira blinked and tucked her blonde hair behind her ear. "What?"

"I'm fluent in freshman, and you have the look of someone who is already regretting life choices."

She cracked the faintest smile. "You're not wrong."

"Come on," he said, already turning. "It's stopped raining, and it's quieter out here."

He led her out back, down the creaking steps to a little porch overlooking a patchy yard. It was much quieter and cooler. The cicadas were still buzzing, and someone was throwing a football in the dark.

They sat in mismatched lawn chairs and talked for hours about music, classes, and where she was from. He shared stories about fishing inshore near Tybee every summer with his father and how he could tie a fly with his eyes closed. When she mentioned that her dad had passed away that summer, her voice trembled. Jeffrey didn't flinch or rush in with awkward sympathy. Instead, he looked at her with something quiet and certain in his face and said, "I would have loved to shake the hand of the man who raised you."

That was the moment she fell in love with him.

He reminded her of her father in ways she hadn't realized she was longing for—tall, steady, funny, and always ready with a story or a sarcastic remark. He had the same ability to make her feel seen and important, as if she were the sun in the room. In some ways, he picked up where her dad had left off, almost without knowing it. He didn't replace him, but, like Albert Wallace, he made Moira feel spoiled, cherished, and reassured. By the time they parted that night, she had his flannel around her shoulders and his number inked in messy script on her forearm. She didn't sleep for a minute.

Jeffrey graduated the following spring, but he and Moira dated exclusively throughout the rest of her years at the University of Georgia. Although Moira received her BS in business, she never intended to use it. The only degree she truly desired was an MRS. Despite her intelligence and potential for success in the business world, Moira's primary ambition was to marry into wealth and live a life of leisure. She wanted nothing more than to dedicate herself to her Jeffrey, raise their children, and manage the household, a choice she made without a single regret.

After they married, Moira's diploma was displayed along with Jeffrey's achievements and degrees on the office wall in the charming blue antique row house they shared in Savannah's historic Chatham Square. Jeffrey's years at UGA were worth it only because he met Moira there while frivolously spending his father's money, hanging out with his fraternity brothers, and failing classes. As James Allyson's only child, Jeffrey didn't need to worry about grades and degrees because he was always destined to assume control of his family's asphalt shingle factory. Just as Moira was blessed with striking beauty from the good genes of her mother, Jeffrey inherited business savvy from his father.

After eight years of marriage, the Allyson family, now including two toddlers, moved from their row house to the eight-thousand-square-foot home they designed on a coastal sanctuary that perfectly represented low-country living.

The energetic and handsome brown-haired Allyson boys, Brent and Bradford, grew up fishing and sailing from Tybee Island to Skidaway Island and back. Even as her children became older and more independent, Moira was often busy with various charities, clubs, and community functions, and she was always expected to look radiant on Jeffrey's arm at his business events. Although they were wealthy enough to afford a chef and a gardener, Moira loved cooking elaborate meals and tending to the acres of flower beds on their property. Her unused degree hung on the wall, and that was okay because she had her boys and she had her Jeffrey.

Bradford was the first to leave home to pursue yet another useless degree at UGA. Jeffrey had already decided that his oldest son would eventually take over the family's shingle company. Brent had different aspirations: he was accepted into Vanderbilt University's premed program. Moira wasn't surprised by his choice. Given Brent's childhood, when he cared for ospreys with broken wings and watched *ER* while other kids were glued to *Clifford the Big Red Dog*, it was clear he was destined to dedicate himself to helping others. The younger dark-haired Allyson boy often joked that he wasn't meant to work with shingles unless they were the chicken pox variety.

While sipping her hot coffee, Moira continued to stare out the window at the spot beneath the live oak by the water's edge, the place she and Jeffrey cherished. With their children nearly grown, Moira and Jeffrey deeply valued their time together. They spent hours under that tree, discussing their future or simply enjoying moments of comfortable silence.

The thoughts of her beloved were interrupted when her friends came into view, walking alongside the narrow tributary at the east side of the plush yard. Erin was laughing at something Nell was saying, and Moira was happy to see her relaxed and enjoying herself, even if it meant a friendship was blossoming between her and the captain of the pleasure police. Moira felt a sting of guilt for her unfair thought about Nell and turned her attention to Gemma and CK, who were quietly following behind with stoic expressions. Because of their silence, Moira assumed they had been arguing and wondered what the issue was this time.

The hot shower and headache powder she had taken still hadn't alleviated the pounding in her head. As her friends approached the house, she rubbed her temples and walked over to the mirrored backsplash in the bar area off the kitchen to check her appearance. She was wearing a black button-down cover-up over her classic black one-piece bathing suit, which featured ruffled trim along the V-neck. Her makeup was light, but it concealed the puffiness beneath her bloodshot eyes, and her hair was casually pulled back into a loose ponytail. She puckered her lips, glistening with gloss, and turned around just in time to see her friends entering through the kitchen door. She blocked out the sharp pain in her head and greeted them with a big smile.

"Girls, please forgive me for not joining you all this morning," she said, gripping her coffee mug tightly. The large diamond wedding ring she still wore clinked softly against the ceramic handle.

"Is everything okay with Bradford?" CK asked as she pulled off her windbreaker and set it on the counter. "Erin said he was having a lovers' quarrel?"

Moira nodded, dismissing the question with a wave of her hand. "Oh yes. Just typical Bradford drama this morning. If it's not one thing, then it's another with that boy," she replied with a hint of exasperation in her tone. She could feel the awkwardness between her and Erin, who knew she was lying, so she quickly changed the conversation while glancing out the window to the overcast sky. "I certainly hope our day isn't ruined by rain."

"I checked the radar earlier," Gemma chimed in. "It looks like we might get a light sprinkle within the next hour or so, but it should clear up by lunchtime."

"Well, that's good news," Moira said, relieved. "The massage therapist, Kaylee, will be here right at noon to set up. She's young, but she's the best at what she does. You girls will love her."

As she spoke, Moira's wedding ring caught the gray light from the kitchen window, sending small glimmers dancing across the kitchen.

CK reached over and turned Moira's left hand toward her. "I had forgotten how stunning your ring is," she remarked, her eyes wide with admiration.

"Nearly three years and I just can't bring myself to take it off yet," Moira replied, her fingers brushing over the shimmering solitaire, lost for a moment in the memories tied to it. "That's crazy, isn't it?"

"That isn't crazy at all, Mo. You leave it on as long as you like," Celia Kate answered. "Jeffrey certainly had wonderful taste, didn't he?"

"And he was as handsome as they come," Gemma added with a grin. "Really dashing, you know? Like one of those classic actors from the '50s. I always thought he would look great in a fedora. Cary Grant–type charm."

Nell added, "I didn't know him nearly as long as you ladies

did, but I was always amazed at how well he remembered names. When someone visited church, he knew them the next time he saw them, right down to their spouse's and kids' names. He always made people feel welcomed, known. He certainly was personable."

"I asked him about that one time," CK said. "Sean and I and our kids went with him and Moira and their boys to Edisto Island one weekend, and I was so impressed with how he remembered all of the staff's names at the resort where we stayed. He told me it was an old Dale Carnegie trick."

Moira smiled. "He was constantly turning names into pictures." She imitated her husband's deep voice as she said, "His name is Alfred. That reminds me of Alfredo sauce. So every time I see him, I picture him in a kitchen, surrounded by pots and pans, stirring Alfredo sauce. That's him. That's Alfred."

They laughed as Gemma and CK shared another story about the generous donation Jeffrey made to Tunnel Hill High School after a fire destroyed several classrooms. He contributed to the school simply because it was attended by the love of his life. He was a kind and giving person with a big heart.

Moira felt warm and soothed at the compliments about her one true love, but then a wave of sadness crossed her face.

"Mo, did we say something to—" CK started.

"No," Moira replied quickly, though her smile remained dim. "It's nice to hear all these good things about Jeffrey, but I can only take so much before it gets a bit overwhelming. It's bittersweet, you know?" She gave CK's hand a gentle pat. "Anyway, how about you all change into your bathing suits, and we'll meet by the pool?"

~

GEMMA WAS IN the bathroom that she and CK were sharing for the weekend, and she was trying on the last of three bathing suits she had bought online. She wasn't happy with how she looked in the full-length mirror on the back of the door and let out a frustrated huff as she turned from side to side.

"I should have starved myself last week," she whispered to herself.

Gemma was on a diet more than not. Keto seemed the most effective, as she swapped mashed potatoes for cauliflower and eliminated every slice of bread and grain of rice. She sometimes shed ten or twenty pounds, even forty before COVID-19. She knew Tyler loved her more when she was thinner. He treated her differently, often splurging on flowers and jewelry (but never candy). However, she gained it all back during the pandemic while bored and confined to the house. She turned to food, feeling stressed with work and frustrated by Tyler's passive-aggressive remarks.

Eating was her coping mechanism; she didn't need a psychiatrist to tell her that. In fact, she was so worried about having to wear a bathing suit on her trip to Allyson Island that she made the quick drive to her parents' house in Alpharetta for a pan of her mother's blonde brownies.

"This thing looks like it is painted on!" Gemma yelled through the bathroom door to CK, who was sprawled on the bed, keeping an eye on the live camera feed from her house. Chipper Jones was prancing around the backyard as she watched anxiously, fearing that a rabid raccoon might claw his eyes out or a starved coyote might jump out from the woods beside the trampoline and grab him.

Gemma flung the bathroom door open, panted, and marched

over to her open suitcase on the paisley chaise lounge in the corner of the room. Celia Kate paid her no mind and was determined not to take her eyes off the stealthy cat that was stalking something in the flower bed by the well spigot.

"Hello? Are you ignoring me?" Gemma groaned as she rummaged through her suitcase. "Are you going to hold a grudge against me for the rest of the weekend because of our little argument this morning?"

"No," CK replied matter-of-factly without taking her eyes off the live footage of her backyard. "What are you going on about?"

"I'm wearing this ridiculous swim dress—literally a dress that hangs down to my knees—and it still doesn't provide enough coverage," Gemma exclaimed, putting her hands on her hips as she turned to CK. "Look at me! I'm just one backstroke away from having a Janet Jackson wardrobe malfunction."

CK rolled her eyes and tried not to laugh. "The swimsuit looks fine," she said while quickly glancing at the black tankini top and the pink and white stripes on the skirt.

"What kind of a moron designs a swimsuit this large with horizontal stripes?" Gemma complained as CK turned her attention back to her phone screen. "Are you listening to me or are you still watching your house?"

Celia Kate nodded and said, "I'm doing both."

Gemma continued digging through the pile of clothing. "Well, what have you concluded from your surveillance? Is the house still standing?"

CK got up from the bed and slid on her blue rubber flip-flops that perfectly matched the blue and white seersucker cover-up she was wearing. "Yeah, everything's fine. Silas told me that he logged in right on time this morning and finished the application without any problems. Sophie is at a friend's house, and Sean took Tucker golfing. Chipper Jones is chasing a mouse in the flower bed. Everything is great."

"Why do you sound kind of annoyed then?" Gemma asked while retrieving a long black linen cover-up from her suitcase. She stretched and pulled it over her dark head.

CK let out a deep sigh. "I'm just mad at myself for always worrying over nothing."

"You certainly don't have to worry about cellulite, do you?" Gemma eyed her tall, thin friend. Her physique proved that she was once an athlete, even after having three kids.

"I have cellulite," CK said before pinching a small fold of skin on her outer thigh.

Gemma laughed, shaking her head. "Well, if that's what you call cellulite, then I must have what they call cell-u-lot. I can't even look at you," she playfully teased before she tossed her orange and yellow towel over her shoulder. "Come on, let's go."

WHEN CK AND Gemma arrived at the pool, Moira was already lounging in one of eight matching teak pool chairs next to the rectangle of aquamarine water. The sky was still a blanket of gray, but a glimmer of brightness appeared in the far west, which relieved Moira.

Gemma, however, was hoping it would storm so they could go back inside, change into sweatpants, wrap themselves in blankets, pig out, and watch *Dawson's Creek* reruns.

"You just missed my friend Harry, the great blue heron. He visits me all the time," Moira exclaimed. "He was right over there." She pointed to a rock formation and a cascading fountain at the deep end of the pool, surrounded by several small palmetto trees.

"What do those devil cats think about your bird buddy? I bet they'd love to get their homicidal paws on him," Gemma said before tossing the towel on the lounger next to Moira. She felt self-conscious when her thin friend looked up at her from beneath expensive square sunglasses.

"Dove and Pearl are lovers, not fighters." Moira chuckled.

"Still, I bet they'd love a heron sandwich," Gemma said.

"I saw several big seabirds on our walk this morning," CK said. "It's so beautiful out here, Mo. You must smile as soon as you wake up each day because you live in paradise." CK sat on her matching wooden lounger and squeezed some sunscreen into her palm. She rubbed the white lotion into her dark-complected arms and then gestured at the stunning flower beds and terracotta pots in the backyard, which were bursting with color from the annuals. "Paradise."

"Do you have a gardener to help with all of this?" Gemma asked as she leaned back cautiously in her chair, hoping it would support her weight without creaking or groaning.

"Nope," Moira replied with a proud grin. "You girls know I love gardening. I can't imagine paying someone to do something I enjoy so much."

"What about that hydrangea you asked me about a few weeks ago? Did you transplant it? Or are you going to wait?"

"I took your advice and I'm going to wait until winter. But it has outgrown its space in the front garden. It's crowding out my weigela."

Before reclining back into her chair, CK made a point to do her usual check that her phone's ringtone was set to a loud volume, just in case anyone from home decided to call. She placed the device next to her leg on the comfortable lounger, where she could easily reach it.

"Mo, CK and Erin said that Mrs. Joanie retired," Gemma said. "I had no idea. She was with you for how long?"

"Oh yes," Moira said with disappointment. "Joanie moved down to Fort Lauderdale to be closer to her kids and grandkids. She had been with me and Jeffrey since the boys were little. I still talk to her on the phone every few weeks. She isn't in the best health." Moira leaned over to pick up a clear glass that shimmered with a bright orange liquid. She took a sip from the elegant fluted glass, savoring the refreshing taste. "Oh, I'm sorry! Did you girls want a mimosa?" she asked, glancing between them with a friendly smile.

"No, thanks. I don't usually have champagne before lunch," CK answered with a touch of sarcasm and raised one eyebrow above her tortoiseshell sunglasses.

"You know what? I will take one," Gemma said with a bit of mischief. "It's the weekend, after all."

Moira hopped up from her chair, moving smoothly to the covered porch where a pitcher of mimosas was sitting on the outside bar, surrounded by several clear, sparkling glasses.

CK gave Gemma a stern look. "What are you doing? We just talked last night about how much Moira is drinking. Besides, Nell is a recovering alcoholic."

Gemma was unbothered by the judgmental look on CK's face and waved it away with her hand. "I'm fat and my husband is mean. I'm entitled to live a little, aren't I?"

CK answered with her signature eye roll and a sigh.

"Besides, Nell said she has a handle on it, and I know when to quit."

"I just don't think you should encourage Mo and play the part of drinking buddy when she clearly has a problem," CK quietly disputed.

Gemma stuck her tongue out at CK before she rested her head on the soft cream cushion on the teak lounger. Moments later, Moira returned, balancing a freshly filled glass for Gemma in one hand and a green and white ceramic bowl filled to the brim with trail mix in the other.

"This trail mix is really good for you," Moira declared enthusiastically as she set the bowl on a small glass table next to Gemma's chair. "It's packed with omega-3s, very filling, and low in carbs," she continued, proud of offering the healthy snack option.

"Sounds great," Gemma responded dryly, her tone dripping with mockery as she took the mimosa from Moira.

"When Joanie retired," Moira said, settling back in her comfy lawn chair while a sliver of the sun finally snuck from behind a cloud, "I called up a local cleaning service, and they sent Erin. Honestly, I was impressed right away. She was super thorough and didn't let any corner go untouched. You girls know how OCD I am about cleanliness. It felt amazing to see clean baseboards again! Joanie hasn't been able to bend down to clean a baseboard since the late 1900s."

Moira took a moment to look out at the garden, admiring the beautiful blooming flowers, some of which would wilt when cooler temperatures finally made their appearance.

"But the next person they sent was just not up to par," she said, shaking her head a little before sipping from the glass again. "I requested that Erin come back. I liked her so much that I offered her a job to work just for me, and luckily, she said yes."

CK replied, "She really is a sweet girl. I enjoyed talking with her this morning."

Moira's voice softened as she continued, "I don't really need her three days a week, but I get the impression that she needs me. It's obvious by her clothes and her car that money is tight for her. I was unsure where she lived until I found her address to send her the invitation for this weekend, and her place is in a really rough part of town. I like being able to help her out. I know very little about her personal life, but something tells me there's a lot more to her story than she lets on. I just want to help her get back on her feet. Besides, it's nice having someone around the house to talk to. I mean, I talk to Dove and Pearl, but they don't answer. I mean, sometimes they don't." Moira laughed.

"They probably do answer you because they're possessed," Gemma commented. "Anyway, Erin mentioned during our walk this morning that she and her ex-husband didn't have the greatest relationship." Gemma absentmindedly ran her finger around the rim of her glass.

"She hasn't really opened up to me about much at all, but I suspected as much. I do know she's juggling a second job at the Family Pantry convenience store just to make ends meet, and that her son is also working hard to help with the bills."

Moira's tone conveyed genuine concern, not pity. She was well-known in Savannah for her kindness and generosity; she frequently donated to various charities and, before Jeffrey passed away, dedicated much of her time volunteering at the local soup kitchen and other nonprofit organizations.

Erin stepped onto the patio, and the conversation suddenly halted. She immediately assumed they had been talking negatively about her, which made her feel insecure. An awkwardness washed over her as she walked toward the vacant lawn chair, aware that everyone was staring at her in the aqua-blue tankini with white dots that she had bought from the superstore.

"What a cute suit," CK said right away. "I have loved polka dots since I was a kid. My mom painted huge pastel polka dots all over my walls when I was little."

"Thanks," Erin said.

"What does your tattoo mean?" Gemma nodded to the black-inked flower on the front of Erin's shoulder.

Erin tossed her towel onto the chair next to CK and answered, "I got the daffodil tattoo after my husband, Phillip, and I divorced. Daffodils represent new beginnings." She distractedly touched her shoulder.

"You don't mention him often, Erin," Moira said. "How are things between you two now?"

Erin groaned with contempt and sat in the lawn chair. "Things aren't good between us. In fact, they never have been."

A glowing ray of sun finally emerged from behind the clouds and cast warmth on their exposed skin.

"There it is!" Moira shouted with excitement. "Welcome, friend!"

"Your husband, Erin?" Gemma nodded the mimosa glass toward her, nosey to hear more. "You were saying?"

Erin massaged a dollop of thick sunscreen that smelled of coconut onto her arm and continued, "He was, well, I told you all on the walk this morning that he was emotionally and physically abusive for the twelve years we were married. I finally got the courage to leave him about seven years ago. He'd always told me he'd make my life miserable if I left, but my life was already miserable, so I got out."

CK, Gemma, and Moira offered sympathetic looks as Erin shared her story.

"He's newly remarried now with two young stepchildren. It's only a matter of time before they discover how cruel Phillip really is," she said while adjusting her round wire sunglasses. "He was the breadwinner throughout our marriage. He wouldn't allow me to work. He said my place was in the home. So when I left, I had to find work. He wouldn't pay child support or alimony, and I don't have the funds to cover the court costs to dispute it. So I do what I can."

"Does your son ever see his dad?" Gemma asked.

"Oh, not at all. Phillip never physically harmed PJ, but the emotional damage he caused was enough for PJ to cut him out of his life entirely. He is certainly protective of his mama," Erin replied.

CK leaned across her lounge chair and gently squeezed Erin's hand, recalling their morning conversation on the patio.

"Leaving him was hard, but no harder than living with him," Erin said while glancing at Gemma, hoping she would consider those words.

At that moment, Nell stepped out the back door in a cute sage-green tankini that really suited her auburn hair and freckled olive skin. She was holding a big floppy straw hat that went perfectly with her strappy leather sandals. A tattoo with some Hebrew letters peeked out on her shoulder, which immediately caught Erin's eye.

"Sorry I'm late, ladies," Nell exclaimed when she joined the group by the pool. "Taylor called. I can't miss a call from my college kid."

"Never!" Moira chimed in, sneaking a glance at Erin.

"How's your daughter doing?" Gemma asked, finishing off the last of her orange juice and champagne.

Nell answered while adjusting her towel on the lounger beside her, "She's doing well. She and some friends are heading to the Georgia versus Auburn game this afternoon. Moira, is Bradford going to be there?"

"I have no clue. That boy doesn't tell me anything." Mo pouted while Nell noticed the empty champagne flute sitting on the table next to her lounger.

CK leaned up in her lounge chair and looked at Moira. "He didn't say anything about the game when you spoke to him this morning?"

"Oh," Moira replied, a bit flustered. "We got so caught up talking about his girl drama that we totally forgot to discuss the game. I'm sure he'll be there. He never misses one."

Yeah, he never misses a chance to chug beer at a tailgate party, Nell thought. Then she felt guilty for thinking something so judgmental about a kid, so she silently prayed, *Sorry, Lord.*

"What does your tattoo mean?" Erin asked as she tapped Nell on the shoulder.

She tilted her chin down and replied, "It's Hebrew and means 'Yahweh,' which translates to 'I Am' or 'He Is.' I got it after I got sober as a symbol of my dedication to Christ." Nell smiled at the thought of her sweet relationship with God and his Son. "I see you have a tattoo as well. Daffodils?"

Erin then explained the meaning of her tattoo to Nell.

Nell responded, "Both of our tattoos represent new beginnings. Saint Paul said in Philippians: 'Forgetting what is behind and straining toward what is ahead, I press on toward the goal to win the prize for which God has called me heavenward in Christ Jesus.'"

"I like that," Erin said. "So tell me how you overcame your addiction. I've never had an issue with drugs or alcohol, but a lot of my family, cousins up in North Carolina, struggle with it."

Nell started telling Erin her testimony, her voice filled with excitement and enthusiasm. She spoke about the dark times in her life when alcohol consumed her and the desperate moments when she thought she would never escape its grip. With a smile, she recalled how God rescued her and how she leaned on his strength to overcome her addiction.

It wasn't an easy journey, but she emphasized how important prayer was, along with the support of her family and church community, which helped her get her life back on track. Nell was very grateful that her faith allowed her to turn down the many temptations she faced at weddings, country club parties, and even this weekend.

Nell radiated joy when she spoke about Oglethorpe Church and how the community there gave her a sense of purpose and belonging that she had never felt before. Because of their encouragement, she felt a strong call to share her testimony and the victory she found through her faith, which she did during the Celebrate Recovery meetings held by her church on Sunday nights.

Erin listened intently to Nell, her mind swirling with thoughts and memories. Her parents believed in a higher power and occasionally mentioned God, which was where she first heard the story of Martha, the servant who was too busy to spend time with Jesus—a tale that had always stuck with her. However, religion was not a central focus in her family; it served more as a backdrop in their lives. Phillip, on the other hand, was staunchly atheist and had little patience for discussions about God or faith.

She recalled one of the many terrifying nights during her marriage to Phillip. In a moment of sheer desperation, as Phillip struck her, she had cried out to God for help. Instead of stopping, Phillip became even more infuriated by her plea, and his punches landed even harder. That moment left her both physically and emotionally scarred. It also pushed her farther away from believing in a loving and caring deity who was looking out for her.

But as Erin listened to Nell, something began to change within her. This sweet, soft-spoken woman talked about Jesus as though he was a very real presence in her life. There was an unmistakable light in Nell's eyes, and a genuine peace and joy that Erin found intriguing. Nell described Jesus not as a distant historical figure but as a living companion who guided her every day.

Erin wondered how it was possible for someone to have such unwavering faith in something unseen. How could Nell talk about Jesus with such familiarity and love, as if he was a close friend likely to show up poolside at any moment? The way Nell described her relationship with him made it seem so tangible and accessible. It was the opposite of the cold, distant God Erin had encountered in her childhood. And the conversation she was having with Nell contrasted sharply with any talk she ever had with Phillip.

Perhaps this faith Nell spoke of could offer Erin some healing and peace in her own broken life. For the first time in a long while, Erin felt a glimmer of hope. Maybe there was something greater out there, something that could heal her troubled soul. Something money couldn't buy.

Nell had shared her love of the Lord with enough people to know when they were uninterested and she should stop talking, but with Erin, she could sense that her interest was blossoming into a quiet longing, a desire to explore the same path of faith that had so profoundly transformed Nell. "You know, Erin, God is the great provider. I can see in hindsight the many ways he has provided for me."

Provision was exactly what Erin Pepperell needed.

CELIA KATE, GEMMA, and Moira were caught up in their own conversation, their laughter and animated gestures reflecting the decades of memories they shared. While Mo and Gemma refilled their mimosa glasses, they reminisced about their high school days when life was simpler and their biggest concerns were exams and winning the Friday night football game.

CK, who still lived in their hometown, shifted the conversation to the present, filling in Moira and Gemma on the latest small-town scandals.

"You won't believe what's been happening lately; it's like a soap opera! Do you remember Mrs. Henderson, the elementary school secretary? Well, she has been stealing lunch money from the cafeteria cash register for years. Apparently that's what paid for Mr. Henderson's casket a few years back. It's the talk of the town."

"There's no way!" Moira exclaimed while nearly spilling her drink. "Not Mrs. Henderson. She was always so prim and proper, with her starched dresses and her hair neatly pulled back in a bun. She reminded me of my mother."

CK nodded emphatically. "And listen to this. Kathryn Marcum's daughter, the one who's a popular TikTok influencer with all the makeup tutorials, shoplifted from Talbot's Pharmacy. The police arrived, and she was busted with three tubes of concealer and a contouring stick in her bra."

"That's wild," Gemma said before popping a handful of the bland nuts and omegas into her mouth.

"I'm not done. Another kid was in the pharmacy when it happened and recorded the whole thing. He posted it on TikTok, and now there's a whole drama unfolding. It's *trending*; I think that's what the kids call it."

"Gosh, aren't you glad we didn't have phones when we were that age?" Moira asked.

Gemma nodded in agreement. "I certainly am. I don't know what the statute of limitations is on—"

"Oh, and listen to this, Moira," CK exclaimed, waving her hands wildly. "I already told Gemma about this, but you remember Todd Chambers, right?"

Gemma added, "He graduated a few years before us. He drove that Camaro he had painted that awful lime green."

They paused while Mo nodded in acknowledgment.

"Well," Celia Kate continued, "he was hired as the head football coach at the high school last year. That idiot went to a party at one of his players' houses and got arrested for DUI on the way home! I couldn't go to the salon or the grocery store for months without hearing about it."

"That Todd Chambers was always bad news," Moira said before sipping her third mimosa. She leaned back in her chair and smiled. "That one-horse town always did have a way of keeping things interesting. I almost miss it."

"I sure don't," Gemma said. "I haven't been back since Mom and Dad left and moved to Alpharetta."

"I think it would be fun if you both come back for a visit. We can go get ice cream and cruise the strip like the good old days," Celia Kate suggested.

"Yeah, and nearly puke at the smell coming from the dog food factory," Gemma added with a snarl.

"You get used to it." CK defended her speck on the map. "You know, the only reason I let you get away with slamming Tunnel Hill is because you lived there for eighteen years, Gemma. I would never let an outsider talk about our town that way. Sean was born and raised only one county over, and he made the mistake of criticizing Tunnel Hill one time, when he said that his Catoosa County grew better tomatoes than my Whitfield County."

While CK argued for the pros of their hometown and Gemma pointed out the cons, Moira began to feel warm and flustered from both the sun and the champagne. Her stance earlier that morning, while her head pounded and her stomach churned, had been defensive. But now she realized that her excessive drinking the night before probably had been a mistake. The more she thought about asking Erin to lie to the others for her about being hungover, the more immature and silly she felt. It was reminiscent of a high school student attempting to avoid getting into trouble with her parents.

She didn't want a repeat of the previous night, so to cool off and sober up, Moira stood from her lounger and slowly waded into the shallow end of the pool until she was immersed to her waist. The chilly water provided the relief she desperately needed.

Moira expected her friends to join her in the water, but they didn't. Instead, the four of them continued talking and laughing with one another on the pool deck as the bright sun shone down on them. Moira struggled to catch the details of their conversation over the sound of water splashing off the rock feature into the aquamarine pool. She could tell it must have been a good story since Gemma's face glowed with excitement as she animatedly spoke, her hands moving energetically to emphasize her points. CK shook her head and smiled while Nell and Erin reclined in their lounge chairs, clearly captivated by the tale.

Moira watched as her friends enjoyed one another's company, trying to shake off the feeling of being left out. She waded along the sun shelf, then sat on the warm slate stone that edged the pool, dipping her pedicured toes back into the cool water. She focused on the turquoise ripples, watching them expand outward with each gentle kick of her feet, and tried to ignore the cloudiness of impairment and the loneliness that surrounded her.

Moira didn't need anyone, especially Nell Rehman, to tell her how ironic it was that she drank to escape the pain of losing her husband, even though drinking only made her feel more depressed and alone. This weekend, in part, was meant to motivate her to socialize, but at that moment, all she wanted to do was revert to her routine of curling up on her living room couch with Dove and Pearl and a few more drinks until she became unaware of her heartache.

That heartache began on a cool spring day two and a half years earlier, when Moira struggled to understand what Jeffrey's frantic secretary was saying when she called to inform her that Jeffrey had been found slumped over his desk at Allyson Supply. Dead? Not her tall, thin Jeffrey, with his dark eyes and rugged good looks.

It was true that Jeffrey didn't exercise much, and he occasionally enjoyed a cigar and a glass of brandy. Among his closest friends, there was even a joke that he preferred red meat for dessert. Jeffrey's father had died of a heart condition at the age of sixty-three, and his grandfather had passed away at sixty-five. The family business seemed to be handed down quicker with each generation, creating a tragic cycle: a father, a heart attack, and then the legacy passed on to the son. Because of this, Moira encouraged her two sons, who were in their late teens and early twenties, to start taking baby aspirin, eat healthily, and exercise regularly. Despite the family history, Jeffrey's death came as a shock to Moira.

It still felt unfathomable as she took another drink and considered sinking to the bottom of the deep end of the pool.

Chapter 16

KAYLEE REYNOLDS HAD been a massage therapist for only a few months at one of Savannah's most elegant spas when Moira Allyson booked an appointment with her because Moira's regular masseuse of nearly a decade, Danielle, had moved to South Carolina to care for her ailing mother. Kaylee felt a bit nervous about working with Moira; there was something intimidating about her. Perhaps it was her wealth or the confident way she carried herself. However, Danielle had reassured Kaylee that Moira was easy to get along with and always tipped well.

Within two minutes of meeting Kaylee, Moira made her massage preferences very clear—she did not want a deep tissue massage. She then recounted an experience from years ago with a woman who had been so rough with Moira that she could have pressed charges for assault. Kaylee, with her hands shaking, felt nervous about meeting Moira's expectations. However, judging by her client's relaxed state and the fact that she fell asleep within the first ten minutes of the massage, Kaylee assumed she had done a good job. Although she did wonder if the champagne Moira had consumed in the spa's waiting room contributed to her calm demeanor. Regardless, Kaylee felt relieved when she heard Moira snoring.

During their second meeting, Moira talked about the plans for her birthday party in September and asked if Kaylee would be interested in providing massages for her guests. Kaylee was pleased to have the opportunity to make some extra money and excited to get a chance to see where her elegant client lived.

Kaylee arrived right on time, and when she stepped inside the pool house to set up, she was greeted by the subtle, even pleasant mixture of salt air and chlorine. The walls of the cozy lounge area, furnished with plush pastel-colored seating, were adorned with vibrant, water-themed decor—framed pictures of the serene coastal scene right out the door and a large watercolor of a blue heron. A few green potted plants added extra life to the inviting space. Large windows along one wall provided a lovely view of the low country while also allowing plenty of natural light to fill the room, creating an airy, open feel. To one side was a compact kitchenette with a long butcher-block countertop, a black matte sink, a microwave, and a mini fridge with a see-through door showing refreshing beverages. There was a well-organized shelf in the corner filled with pool essentials—rolled towels, sunscreen, floaties, goggles, and brightly colored pool noodles.

Through a set of double French doors, there was a small bedroom with a queen-sized bed and matching teak furniture, along with a small en suite bathroom—all decorated in beautiful nautical colors. A row of windows beside the bed provided a stunning view of the Georgia blackwater and marsh, with reeds and grass swaying gently in the breeze. Kaylee imagined waking up to such a breathtaking sight every morning. Living in this small, cozy pool house would be several steps up from her apartment in the bustling city.

As Kaylee transformed the pool house into a tranquil spa by

drawing the curtains, lighting candles, heating oils on the kitch-enette counter, and playing relaxing music blended with wind chimes through her portable speaker, she thought about Moira's generosity of giving to others on her birthday. Moira must have spent so much time and money on this weekend and these friend-ships. She wondered if her friends appreciated all the effort Moira was putting into the weekend. The thought that they might not made Kaylee feel sad. She snapped photos of the beautifully ar-ranged space to advertise on social media. After all, private parties were a great opportunity for her to make some extra money.

Moira insisted on getting her massage last, allowing her friends to enjoy the relaxation and pampering first. So at precisely 1:00 p.m., a tall, thin redhead entered the pool house, her freckled face glowing with a touch of sun and excitement, and introduced her-self as Nell. She wore a soft, white terry-cloth robe, which had her initials classically monogrammed in black on the lapel—a thoughtful gift Kaylee had seen Moira present to all her friends while Kaylee was preparing the pool house—over her bathing suit.

Kaylee spoke kindly over the soft music, gesturing to the mas-sage table she had set up between the kitchenette and the sitting area. "Welcome, Mrs. Nell. I'm Kaylee, and I'll be giving you your massage today. Do you have any areas of concern?"

Kaylee took Nell's new robe and draped it over the khaki sofa in the sitting room. While assisting Nell onto the table on her stomach, Kaylee's long blonde ponytail cascaded over the shoul-der of her black scrub top. Nell mentioned having a slipped disc in her lower right back, a common issue for Kaylee's clients, of-ten resulting from daily wear and tear, bad posture, or slumped shoulders.

As Kaylee worked on her back, Nell basked in the relaxation. With her head resting in the hole of the massage table and her gaze fixed on the warm stone floor, she closed her drowsy eyes. She attempted to quiet her racing thoughts—worries about Taylor, Tate, and even Moira. But her mind wouldn't quiet. *Focus, Nell,* she reminded herself. *Focus on the music. Focus on the massage.*

So she intently centered her mind on the pressure being applied to her calves, which made her think of Taylor's complaint a few weeks ago about her legs hurting from having to walk to her last class on the opposite side of campus. This made her worry about the possibility of her daughter walking back to her dorm in the dark once the sun started setting earlier. She shook those thoughts out of her head and focused on the ambient music playing softly from the speaker, which reminded her of the wind chimes hanging from the crepe myrtle in her backyard. She noted how that tree hadn't bloomed well this season and was showing signs of disease; it disheartened her because it was such a lovely addition to her lawn.

No, do not focus on anything. Turn off your mind.

However, her thoughts continued to swirl. So she began to pray. *"Come to me, all you who are weary and burdened, and I will give you rest,"* she recited silently, envisioning herself at the feet of Jesus, free of any cares or worries. Soon she drifted off into a peaceful, deep sleep.

GEMMA HAD THANKED Moira for the luxurious monogrammed robe, but when she tried to pull it over her bathing suit, she struggled. Moira hadn't asked for her size; she must have just guessed. Unfortunately, her guess was wrong. Gemma didn't want to look to see what size it was; she didn't want to know. Did robes even come in sizes? How in the world was it possible for a bathrobe to be too tight?

Now she was expected to wear only a bathing suit in front of a young girl she didn't know. This Kaylee seemed fit, likely able to run marathons; perhaps she even competed in triathlons. As Kaylee looked at Gemma's softer body, Gemma couldn't help but feel she would be harshly judged. Would the table hold her weight? What did she weigh now? She hadn't stepped onto a scale in a while, and just like with the size of the robe, she didn't want to know.

"Do you have any areas of concern, Mrs. Gemma?" Kaylee extended her hand to help Gemma onto the table.

"Yeah, is it going to hold me?" Gemma asked, gesturing toward the table.

Kaylee tilted her head in confusion. "Ma'am?"

"I mean, is this table going to support me, Kaylee, or am I going to end up on the floor needing an ambulance instead of a massage?"

Kaylee chuckled and assured Gemma, "No, ma'am. It will hold."

Gemma began to lift her leg but stopped short. "I don't need to sign a waiver or anything first?"

Kaylee could sense that this woman's sarcasm came from a place of self-doubt. "Ma'am, I assure you that you are going to be fine. Lie down and relax."

Should Kaylee say more? Should she mention that she didn't judge? That she had worked with women much larger than Gemma? Would that sound offensive rather than complimentary? Unsure of how to respond, she decided to keep her mouth shut.

Gemma nervously climbed onto the table, hearing it creak under her weight. Thankfully, it held firm. She sighed and exhaled deeply, just as Kaylee had instructed, feeling the hot oil and gentle hands working on her tense neck. Gemma couldn't help but think that finding the muscle beneath the layers of fat would be no small feat.

Yet somehow Kaylee did just that, and Gemma quickly drifted off to sleep without caring about her body or her husband.

"I KNOW IT isn't typical to have a phone during a massage because the goal of all this is to disconnect from the outside world and enjoy the relaxation, but unfortunately, that's impossible for me. It's mandatory that I keep it nearby. I have to be reachable at all times," Celia Kate told Kaylee as she sat on the table and gripped the phone in her hand.

"I understand. Work?" Kaylee asked.

"Yeah, sure. Work," she answered while positiniong her head into the pillow. "Now, I have an old basketball injury. I tore my ACL during my junior year of high school. It's been thirty years, but my leg still gives me trouble sometimes. I guess arthritis has set in. Really work that muscle, Kaylee. I'm not tender or squeamish."

As Kaylee pressed her thumbs into CK's neck, working out the knots and tension, CK held the phone below the table and stared through the hole in the pillow at the security camera footage displayed on the six-inch screen. She saw Sean's truck parked in the driveway, with the boat hitched to it from his morning fishing trip to Lake Conasauga. Sophie's bicycle was also in the driveway, but Sophie was nowhere to be seen. The bicycle was not on its kickstand; it had been carelessly dropped onto the pavement, as if someone had forcefully pulled her off it. A wave of panic surged through CK. Had Sophie been kidnapped?

No, stop, Celia Kate! she told herself firmly. *Everyone is fine. Everything is fine. The kids are fine. Sean is fine. The cat is fine.*

She took a deep breath, trying to calm the rising tide of anxiety. She reminded herself that Sean was home, and he would have called if something was wrong. Sophie was probably just inside, having abandoned her bike in a hurry to sit at the kitchen table and work on greeting cards.

Kaylee, sensing CK's tension, paused for a moment. "Is everything okay?" she asked softly.

"Yes, everything's fine. Just a little distracted is all."

Kaylee continued the massage with a bit more pressure, hoping to ease Celia Kate's worries.

CK closed her eyes, trying to let go of the intrusive thoughts. She visualized each muscle relaxing, each knot releasing, as she repeated her mantra: *Everyone is fine. Everything is fine.*

The minutes ticked by, and slowly CK felt her body begin to unwind. She focused on the soothing pressure of Kaylee's hands, the gentle music playing in the background, and the faint mixture of lavender and chlorine hovering in the air. The tension in her neck and shoulders eased, and her breathing became more even. She knew she had to trust that everything was okay at home, to remember that she could not control every part of her family's life, no matter how much she wanted to.

CK knew what gave birth to her anxiety. It stemmed from the death of her grandmother, Sue, with whom she had been incredibly close. She vividly remembered the moment Vice Principal Wadley interrupted a sophomore season basketball practice, calling her name with a look of concern on his face. The image of her sweet mother, sitting in a red plastic chair in her coach's office with mascara stains on her rosy cheeks, would forever be etched in her mind. It was in a moment when she felt safe, when her guard was down—except for the defenses she maintained on the court—that tragedy found her.

Five years ago, the most devastating news came to CK in the middle of peaceful sleep. She was startled awake by a phone call from her frantic father, who told her that her mother was struggling to breathe and that an ambulance was on the way. He urged CK to come quickly. In an instant, she went from a state of calm to one of panic. Just a few hours later, as she paced the waiting room of Tunnel Hill Hospital in her pajamas, she learned that her mother, her best friend, had died.

Now, as she lay on the massage table, completely vulnerable, it felt like the perfect time for tragedy to strike again. There was no way she could be without her phone. There was no way she would ever fully relax this side of heaven.

—

ERIN WAS THIRTY-EIGHT years old and had never experienced a massage. Embarrassed, she didn't dare mention this to anyone, including the massage therapist. Unsure of what to expect, she entered the dimly lit, serene pool house with a swirl of thoughts in her mind. Would she be expected to take off all her clothes? What would she talk about during the session, or would there be complete silence? What should she do with her head and hands? The idea of a stranger touching her made her feel uncomfortable.

After Kaylee explained what to do, Erin lay down on the table, rigid and tense.

"Just take a deep breath and relax," the young woman advised her. "You're really tight."

So this was what it was like to pay someone to pamper you, to help relieve your stress? Who had extra money for this? Or even for cleaning their house? Who had extra cash lying around to spend on wants instead of needs? When she was married to Phillip, they only went on a few weekend trips here and there, but nothing extravagant. They stayed in two-star hotels, not five. There was often mold in the ice machine, and she occasionally spotted a roach darting across the stained floor. She certainly wouldn't want to use a black light on those covers. She and Phillip drove used cars and wore secondhand clothes. If she dared to buy something that Phillip didn't approve of, she would certainly pay for it.

Now, though, Phillip was doing well for himself. His construction business had grown, and he had been contracted to build some fast-food restaurants in Savannah. It seemed his new wife wouldn't be driving around in rusted, beaten-up hatchbacks or digging in crates at the thrift shop that smelled of sweat and cigarette smoke. The very thought of her horrible ex-husband being rewarded in some way made anger and resentment bubble up within Erin. So she pushed those feelings away and focused on the moment.

Finally, her body and stress melted under Kaylee's hands, and Erin pretended she had struck gold too. Look at her! She was spending a whole weekend on Allyson Island as a guest, not an employee. Massage included.

———

KAYLEE'S SOFT VOICE was tinged with concern as she asked, "I'm sorry I have to ask, but I have to know, Ms. Moira, how much alcohol have you had today? Massage can intensify the effects of intoxication. Are you feeling dizzy at all?"

"Nonsense, Kaylee," Moira replied, waving her hand dismissively, a tipsy smile spreading across her tanned face. "I've had four or five drinks throughout the day. It's nearly four o'clock. I've eaten a bowl of nuts, half a pineapple, and a chicken salad croissant. I'm perfectly fine." Clumsily and unsteadily, she climbed onto the massage table.

Kaylee felt a tug of reluctance at the back of her mind. She didn't want to refuse Moira because it was her party after all—she was the paying client, entitled to the pampering she requested. Sighing quietly, Kaylee decided to keep her technique gentle and soothing; perhaps Moira would drift off into a deep sleep, unaware that she was receiving an almost nonexistent massage, with barely any pressure applied.

As Moira placed her head into the cushioned hole of the chair, she felt a bit lightheaded and swimmy. Her stomach twisted a little, but nothing too serious. She wasn't drunk, for heaven's sake, just a little off-balance. She planned to drink plenty of water when the massage was done. That would certainly help her feel better, along with a hot shower to energize her before dinner on the boat that evening.

Kaylee pressed into her calf, and Moira thought about the weekend thus far. It was nice for her home to be filled with laughter again. She was especially thankful to be reunited with CK and Gemma. She made a mental note to pull out her wedding album before they left tomorrow afternoon, so they could think back on that beautiful spring weekend when she and Jeffrey exchanged vows. As she recalled the day at Tunnell Hill First Baptist, she remembered how lovely Gemma and CK had looked in their cornflower-blue bridesmaid dresses with puffy sleeves, a signature of the 1990s. The thought of revisiting that joyful, sunny day through pictures made her smile at the floor beneath her. However, with the sweetness came bitterness, similar to what she felt while watching their wedding video.

As the first widow in her friend group, Moira found it painful to listen to others talk about their marriages. Their discussions only reminded her of what she no longer had. Moira remembered how devastated her mother was after her father passed away. Mrs. Louise Wallace never remarried, and a shadow of sorrow seemed to follow her throughout her life. Moira feared this might be her fate as well.

When news of Jeffrey's death spread throughout the community, texts and social media messages from single men—even some from married ones—began to appear. They gave their condolences, but there was an underlying tone of interest that made Moira uncomfortable. The very thought of being romantically involved with anyone other than Jeffrey Allyson repulsed her. Perhaps in time, she thought, but thus far, she had no interest in dating.

She imagined the conversations her friends might be having about her. *"Poor Moira, she seems so depressed. Why didn't anyone else show up this weekend? Will she ever date again? What about her drinking? Should we be concerned? What a mess she's become since Jeffrey died!"* She pictured them lounging around the pool, relaxed after their massages and pampering—all courtesy of Moira. They were likely looking out across the scenic backyard, gossiping about her at that very moment, biting the hand that had fed them all weekend. And maybe there was some truth to their words. But she didn't have the energy, concern, or care to address it—not right now.

As Kaylee worked on Moira's lower back, her skilled hands kneading away the tightness, Moira's thoughts continued to wander. The rhythmic pressure and soothing ambience of the room lulled her into a state of drowsiness. The soft music, the smell of lavender, and the gentle hum of the massage table's heater created a cocoon of comfort around her.

She felt a deep sense of comfort like this with Jeffrey, whether it was in his arms or simply being in his presence. She remembered their spontaneous road trips, how they would dance in the kitchen to their favorite songs, and the quiet moments spent in the Adirondack chairs just enjoying each other's company. His smile, his embrace, and those cherished memories were a balm to her soul. However, they also brought a wave of sadness, just as photos and videos and conversations of him did. She missed him so much that it hurt.

Moira soon felt herself drifting into a deep sleep. Her breathing slowed, and her body relaxed to the point where one of her arms slid off the edge of the table and dangled toward the floor. In her dream, she and Jeffrey walked hand in hand along the silt path that curled beside the blackwater, their bare feet leaving soft imprints in the wet sand. The marsh grasses whispered in the breeze, and overhead, the sky was painted in beautiful shades of twilight—lavender and gold, rose and deep velvet blue. Jeffrey looked just as she remembered him. He wasn't older; he was unchanged. Sun-browned skin, wind-tousled hair, eyes that always seemed to know what she was going to say before she said it.

He squeezed her hand a little tighter, like he could feel the ache she carried. And when he finally turned to look at her, there was nothing in his expression but love. That quiet, all-encompassing kind that wrapped around her.

"Are you okay, Mo?" he asked softly.

She opened her mouth, but no words came out. The sad truth was caught in her throat. He brushed a strand of hair from her face and smiled in his warm, familiar way. In that dream, she experienced a sense of peace and contentment that had been absent from her life for two and a half years.

Chapter 17

AFTER THEIR MASSAGES, the women showered and dressed for dinner on the boat. While waiting for Moira to come downstairs, her birthday party guests gathered on the extra-long tufted sofa in the elegant living room. They chatted about the massages they had enjoyed earlier that afternoon. Erin, Nell, and Gemma could hardly catch their breath from laughing as Celia Kate recounted the time she went to a spa right after having a large Mexican lunch and couldn't control her flatulence.

They frequently checked their watches or phones as they awaited their six o'clock boat boarding time. Nell stood up from the couch and walked to the mahogany baby grand piano in the corner of the beige-colored room. She sat down and played a mediocre rendition of "Für Elise." Gemma followed her and picked up a ginger snap from the tin of Byrd's Famous Cookies that was sitting on a table beside the piano. She then glanced at herself in a large beveled mirror hanging above a white antique dresser. The small belt she had cinched at the waist of her long floral dress nearly disappeared into a crease at her stomach. She rolled her eyes at her reflection and popped another cookie into her mouth.

"It's nearly six," Celia Kate said while standing from the couch. "I'm going to go see what's keeping Moira."

"A cat is probably holding her hostage," Gemma called.

"Or a bottle," Celia Kate mumbled under her breath.

She climbed the stairs and found Moira in her bathroom, her makeup carefully applied and the soft white robe still wrapped around her shoulders. Sitting on a beautifully crafted wooden stool at her antique vanity cluttered with beauty products and brushes, she looked to be lost in thought. Despite the day of relaxation, Moira appeared fatigued and in need of a good sleep.

"What in the world is going on with you?" CK taunted her friend while stepping into the bathroom and crossing her arms over the chest of her pastel-pink V-neck dress. "We need to be going, don't we? It's nearly six."

Moira cleared her raspy throat and said, "I don't know what's wrong." She glanced down at her hands resting in her lap. "Something I've eaten today just didn't sit right with me. I think it was the pralines. Or maybe it's because I haven't exercised today. I just don't feel very well . . ." The last words slipped out in a whisper, accompanied by a weak smile. "See the coffee maker over there?" She pointed to a sleek machine resting on a separate vanity across the room. "Could you make me a small cup while I get dressed?"

CK was worried about her friend.

"Of course, Mo," she replied, turning her attention to the coffee maker. She couldn't help but notice Jeffrey's vanity. His watch, with a dark leather band, rested on the counter, and his toothbrush was neatly placed in its holder. A shaving kit sat on the other side of the sink, suggesting that Jeffrey had used the bathroom just that morning. This sight left CK feeling melancholic.

She tried to think what life would be like without Sean, but it was hard to envision such a future. The very idea stirred a deep sense of loss in her heart, one that felt almost suffocating. As the painful possibility of living without him began to overwhelm her, she purposefully redirected her attention to the makeup on Moira's vanity, grasping for anything that could distract her from the agony of that notion.

Moira shuffled into the expansive walk-in closet adjoining the bathroom, the louvered door swinging shut behind her with a soft whisper. As CK inserted a coffee pod into the machine, she stared at her reflection in the bathroom mirror, still shuddering at the idea of widowhood, and she smoothed down a wayward strand of dark hair that had escaped from her sleek ponytail. "What's *really* going on, Moira?" she called out, uncertain if her friend could hear her through the closet door.

Moira called from inside the closet, her voice muffled by the hanging clothes, "I told you, Celia Kate. The pralines and pineapple and—"

CK interrupted her, saying, "Nothing to do with the mimosas and mint juleps you've been pouring all day?"

Moira heard Celia Kate, but she didn't respond. A few quiet minutes passed before she stepped out of the closet in a stunning long-sleeved silk mini dress that hugged her figure, the dark fabric contrasting with her light hair.

"Well?" Celia Kate asked.

"Please don't start with me about the mimosas. Not now," she urged as she walked past CK to the brightly lit makeup mirror and released her long blonde hair from its messy bun and let it cascade down her shoulders. "I'm simply celebrating the last day of my forties. I just need a little coffee and I'll be fine, okay?" She sounded annoyed.

CK, leaning against the wall with her arms crossed over her pink dress, raised an eyebrow. "It isn't always like this, then?"

"Well, of course not!" Moira exclaimed, irritated, while she ran a brush through her tangled hair. "I'm getting really tired of these accusations that I'm an alcoholic."

A moment of silence passed before CK finally asked, "Well, are you?"

"CK." Moira met her longtime friend's hazel eyes in the mirror. "I resent that question. Are you as worried about Gemma's weight as you are about my drinking?"

"This isn't about Gemma—" CK began to protest, but Moira stopped her.

"She's a heart attack waiting to happen, Celia Kate. Can you imagine her triglyceride levels? Her cholesterol? And yet the only worry I've heard from anyone this weekend is about how many glasses of wine I have had."

"I am worried about Gemma, actually," CK replied, her tone steady as she watched Moira style her hair. "I know she isn't healthy physically. And she's not that great mentally either, I'm sure. I assume Tyler has been cruel as usual about her most recent weight gain."

"Maybe we should organize an intervention while we're all together?" Moira proposed, her brow furrowed with concern. "We need to talk to her about her health and the state of her marriage."

"I want to help her, but I don't think now is the right time for that, Moira. On your birthday weekend? Really?" CK shook her head.

"You're right. But the time is coming when we need to hold her accountable for her choices. We don't have to be ugly about it. We can address her overeating in a loving way. I know it will be painful for her to hear, but sometimes the truth is the hardest pill to swallow." Moira continued to fiddle with her blonde locks.

CK chuckled at the hypocrisy in Moira's speech.

Moira failed to grasp why she found it amusing.

"I'll be waiting downstairs with the rest of your guests, Mo," CK said as she started to walk out the door. Before leaving, she glanced at the coffee maker that was sputtering the last few drops of brown liquid. "It looks like your 5:58 p.m. cup of coffee is ready."

THE AGGRAVATED LOOK on CK's face when she entered the living room must have alerted the others, because Nell called out, "She's sobering up again, isn't she?"

"You know it," CK replied. "She'll be down soon. She just has to finish her hair and a cup of coffee."

"Y'all cut her some slack. It's her birthday weekend," Gemma exclaimed while standing by the piano and before popping a praline into her mouth. "I don't diet on weekends. I always start on a Monday. And you know what? Moira can stop drinking on Monday too. You know what Jimmy Buffet says?" She picked up her glass of wine from the piano and finished it off while CK sat on the couch between Nell and Erin.

"Oh, good Lord, please don't let her start with the Jimmy Buffett." CK grabbed Nell's arm in desperation.

"It's always a good time for Jimmy Buffet." Gemma cleared her throat before she started belting out the chorus to "Come Monday."

Erin laughed. "What's with the Jimmy Buffet?"

"I know she's really feeling her oats when she starts the Buffet catalog," Celia Kate answered.

Gemma continued singing off-key.

CK sighed in annoyance at Gemma's usual antics while Nell and Erin laughed.

Moments later Moira glided down the wooden staircase, her beauty as striking as ever from afar, but CK saw the signs of exhaustion etched around her sunken eyes.

"I'm so sorry," she apologized. "Bradford called again. It's been a hard weekend for him. He wants to come home, but I won't let him crash this party." Moira forcefully laughed and did a little dance when she reached the bottom of the stairway.

"Oh, Moira, you should let him come home," Celia Kate urged while standing from the plush couch, knowing Moira was lying. "We would all love to see him."

"Oh no, no, he's perfectly all right." Moira glared at her and forced a smile. "He just needed to hear his mama's voice, that's all."

In reality, Moira had not spoken to either of her sons in nearly two weeks. Brent was seven hours away in Nashville, busy with his first year of college in the premed program. He sent his mom a text every few days, but she missed hearing the sound of his voice. Bradford lived only four hours away, but he likely wouldn't surprise her with a weekend visit like most college kids. In fact, he probably wouldn't come home to see her until Christmas break, if then.

Moira had always been close to her boys, but after Jeffrey died, their relationship changed. During heated arguments, they accused her of neglecting them, claiming she was blinded by her own grief and drinking too much. It was true that she had indulged in a few too many glasses of wine and was late for Brent's high school graduation the previous May, but that day was difficult for her, knowing Jeffrey wasn't there to witness his younger son's accomplishment. Still, she believed they were being dramatic and that they were grappling with their own grief over losing the man they admired most. She held on to the hope that they would come back around when they were older and wiser.

IT WAS FIFTEEN minutes past the scheduled boarding time, but the white catamaran was still waiting at the wooden boat dock that jutted into the calm black waters behind the Allyson house. The captain, a young man named Kevin who was in his early twenties, stood in a starched button-down shirt and khaki shorts, ready to assist the women onto the boat. A table for five was already set on the deck, and delightful aromas wafted up from the galley below, where Antonio was preparing a delicious meal. The lovely dark-haired Renata led the women to their table while Kevin took his place at the helm.

"Let's take a selfie!" Moira insisted as they sat at the rectangular wooden table surrounded by white chairs. They huddled together and smiled brightly. Erin couldn't help but notice Moira's expensive leather phone case pointed at her face, which made her feel self-conscious about her own old device in her hand, marred by water damage and a cracked screen.

Renata offered a cocktail garnished with a wedge of lime, which Moira gladly accepted, and Nell and Celia Kate's disappointment was clearly revealed in their expressions.

Not wanting Moira to drink alone, Gemma also asked Renata for a cocktail, and even though she could feel CK's stare boring into her, she refused to acknowledge it. The others picked up their glasses of water, and together they clinked their drinks in a toast to Moira's fiftieth birthday.

As the Georgia sun lingered on the horizon, it painted a breathtaking display of colors across the evening sky. The air was warm and pleasant, carrying the scent of marsh grass as Kevin stood at the covered helm and sailed them across the tranquil Ogeechee River. The gentle sloshing of the waves provided a soothing soundtrack for their journey toward the open waters of the Atlantic, along with the call of seagulls crying out in the distance.

Southern homes adorned with expansive porches and surrounded by lush, meticulously landscaped gardens lined the coastline. Moira pointed out one particularly large residence featuring an impressive two-story balcony.

"That is where Audria and Raymond McHenry lived before they went bankrupt in the spring," Moira shared, her voice touched with a mix of intrigue and amusement.

"Oh? The ex-senator?" CK asked, taking a sip from her glass of water, her eyes wide with interest. "I read about that."

Moira eagerly launched into a detailed story filled with gossip, painting a vivid picture of the McHenrys' scandalous lives. She shared every juicy detail she could remember, from their extravagant parties where the drugs flowed freely to their public arguments and financial struggles. As she wrapped up her Southern Gothic tale, she concluded, "Long story short, he was cheating on Audria. But I can't say I blamed him. I mean, she really let herself go."

Gemma's anger bubbled to the surface at Moira's callous comment. The surge of frustration and hurt made it impossible for her to contain herself any longer, and she shot back, "Are you suggesting I deserve infidelity just because I have let myself go, Moira?"

The group glanced at one another in shock and then turned back to Gemma, whose face was rigid with hurt and whose eyes were filled with tears that threatened to fall.

Moira stammered, feeling embarrassed, and tried to apologize, but Gemma interrupted her. "Yes, Tyler is cheating on me, and no, I don't want to talk about it—not now or in a week. I didn't mean to mention it because it really isn't any of your business." She gulped down the remainder of her cocktail and then called out, "Renata! Refill, por favore!"

The Italian beauty appeared from the opposite end of the boat holding another cocktail in her hand. The weight of Gemma's words loomed over the group, causing shifting eyes and furrowed brows, while an oblivious Renata checked everyone's glasses before returning to her post below deck.

CK leaned forward in her chair, mouth agape, and whisper-yelled, "Gemma, you cannot possibly expect us not to talk about this."

"Well, we're not. Not right now." Gemma nervously chewed on her lip and avoided eye contact with the women staring at her with bewildered expressions. She held down her olive-green skirt, which threatened to blow upward in the breeze.

The mood shifted dramatically among the friends as they glided from the brackish river into the expansive waters of the Atlantic, where the waves grew slightly larger and caused the boat to rock gently. The vast ocean stretched out before them, an apparently endless expanse of deep blue water. The sun hung lower on the horizon, just one dip away from disappearing altogether. The colors it left behind created a breathtaking display that seemed almost surreal.

Celia Kate, however, paid no attention to the majestic sea and sky. She was too overwhelmed by the shock of what Gemma had revealed. Not only was she sickened by what that jerk Tyler had done to her best friend, but she could not believe her dearest friend on earth had not confided in her about something so monumental.

As Erin watched the sun sink lower over the vast Atlantic, her thoughts veered to her husband and his infidelity. She had discovered Phillip's cheating less than a year after their wedding. He had met the woman in a small dive bar along the coast, a place he often visited after work. He didn't even attempt to hide the affair, and when Erin confronted him, he showed no compassion or remorse.

The tension on the catamaran deck was so thick it felt as though it could be cut with a knife. The silence grew increasingly uncomfortable, oppressive, and suffocating with each passing moment. Erin could hardly stand it any longer, so she decided to speak. All the women, even Gemma, whose cheeks were damp with tears, turned to look at her.

"I was hesitant about coming this weekend. Well, *hesitant* isn't the right word, I guess. I flat out did not want to come."

Erin noticed that Moira looked disappointed at the comment.

"Not because of you, Moira. I was nervous about what to wear," she said, tugging at the cheap navy T-shirt dress she had owned for years. "I worried about being seen as the poor girl, the divorcée from the wrong side of the tracks. I was even scared that I didn't know which fork to use for dinner. But I'm so glad I came. I can relate to Gemma's broken marriage. I understand the constant worry that the other shoe is going to drop, CK. And, Moira"—she smiled at her employer—"I hope you don't take this the wrong way, but I feel that after working for you for a while,

I've come to understand that you're seeking some relief, something to help you cope. That's likely why you pour your first drink before I leave for the evening."

Moira was caught by surprise at Erin's assumption, and her breath hitched in her throat.

Erin nodded at Moira and continued, "I understand that feeling too. I know what it's like to seek relief—perhaps even solace—not in the ways you do, but in the approval of others." She paused. "We have only been together for twenty-four hours, and I have already found friendship among women I normally would have assumed were snobs. I've realized I'm the judgmental one. So I'm thankful for this weekend, and I'm grateful for each one of you."

Her words hung in the air, and before anyone had a chance to respond, Renata returned with an authentic low-country boil, served on large platters for everyone to share.

The spicy aroma of a hearty meal wafted over the boat. They couldn't help but laugh at how the rustic dish of shrimp, crawfish, sausage, potatoes, and corn on the cob contrasted with the elegant atmosphere of the catamaran dinner cruise. It had long been a Southern tradition to drain the seasoned medley and serve it on a table covered in newspaper. Now it made sense why the cloth napkins were patterned with newsprint. Antonio had added a fun surprise with that touch.

Laughter and chatter filled the deck once again, the earlier awkwardness fading as they enjoyed their meal. They took turns serving themselves, steam rising from the platters. The women exchanged stories about low-country boils and other Southern traditions, their voices blending with the sounds of the ocean and the occasional call of a distant seabird.

Moira felt responsible for Gemma's earlier reveal, so she reached under the table and tapped her friend's knee. Their eyes met and Moira mouthed the words, *I'm sorry.* Gemma nodded and quickly looked down at her plate of steaming food. Moira called for Renata and asked for another glass of bourbon and soda.

It came back to Moira in flashes: Moira sitting on their pontoon's deck while the Fourth of July sky began to darken over Tybee Island. The salt air was still warm from the day, sticky and sweet with sunscreen, and the boat rocked gently in place as the sun slid away.

Brent and Bradford were middle schoolers back then—gangly, sunburned, full of energy and loud opinions about everything from fireworks to fried shrimp. They wore matching red, white, and blue swim trunks that Moira had made them put on, but neither would admit they liked them. Brent leaned over the side of the boat, swearing he'd seen a dolphin. Bradford was up near the bow, holding both of the white kittens wrapped in a beach towel like swaddled infants.

Moira had settled against Jeffrey, her back to his chest, his arms wrapped loosely around her stomach. She remembered how safe she felt there.

They had eaten hush puppies and shrimp off paper plates, passing tartar sauce back and forth and watching the shore of the beach become more and more crowded with people. Jeffrey had packed root beers for them all. Brent and Bradford burped competitively all evening.

Then, just after nine, the sky came to life. Fireworks burst over the dunes and reflected in the Atlantic. The boys had gone still for the first time all evening, their faces turned up and eyes wide, the light flickering across their dark hair.

Jeffrey leaned in close to his wife, his voice low against her ear, and said, "Best seat in the world."

Moira remembered that moment clearly—how all four of them stared at the sky while the boat gently rocked, the kittens purring in their towel. Jeffrey might have been gone, and the boys were distant, but they'd had that night—all four of them. And no one could take that away.

Chapter 18

THE SKY ABOVE the Atlantic Ocean was painted in deep indigos and soft purples as the last remainders of sunlight faded into twilight. Stars began to appear, twinkling like tiny diamonds scattered across the sky, while the nearly full moon cast a silvery path across the water.

Antonio emerged from the galley below deck and inquired about the meal. "You've never had fresher crayfish. My friend TJ caught them just this morning. He calls them mudbugs. He catches them by hand! He never uses a trap and never gets pinched."

"Well, tell TJ I've had my fair share of mudbugs, and those were the best," Gemma replied.

Renata cleared away the empty dinner plates and stained newsprint napkins from the table. Antonio disappeared again, but not before promising a dessert he was sure they would love.

A cool breeze settled over the catamaran, prompting CK, Nell, and Erin to pull their jackets around their shoulders. As the silence hung in the air, Gemma's voice broke through, somber and apologetic. "Listen, girls, I'm sorry if I've ruined this beautiful dinner cruise with my marital problems. I had no intention of mentioning Tyler's affair, especially not this weekend. Please don't worry about me. Everything is fine. I'll figure it out."

"It was my fault," Moira added. "I shouldn't have said what I did about Audria McHenry. Infidelity is never justified."

Nell, wrapped in a brown cardigan, responded gently, "From a biblical perspective, you have every reason to leave the marriage, Gemma."

"I stayed with Phillip for so long because I had no income and feared for my safety. But you're a successful woman, Gemma. If you have the chance to leave, then take it. Don't stay and be his doormat," Erin advised.

Gemma shook her head slowly, and her voice was heavy with resignation. "I have thought a lot about this, and I have decided to stay with him until our daughter finishes her senior year of high school. It feels like the right thing to do, at least until she's settled into college. Then I'll consider my options."

"What do you mean you've had a lot of time to think about this? It didn't just happen recently?" Celia Kate cocked her head. The ocean breeze had disheveled her sleek ponytail, and stray hairs danced around her face.

"I found out last October," Gemma answered, embarrassed.

"Nearly a year ago, Gemma?" CK shrieked and leaned into her friend. "You have kept this from me for an entire year?"

"CK," Moira began. "I'm sure she had her reasons. Give her some grace."

"Celia Kate, I didn't—" Gemma began.

CK held up her hand and shook her head in slow disbelief. She was so angry.

"Are you going to let me finish?" Gemma asked while holding down her skirt in the wind.

Celia Kate crossed her arms tightly across her windbreaker and let out a scoff. "I thought we told each other everything, Gemma.

For decades we have shared our lives, our thoughts, our struggles. You call me if you have a stupid ingrown hair, for goodness' sake! How could you not tell me that your husband has been having an affair for nearly a year?"

Gemma looked out at the dark sea, feeling a mix of guilt and sadness. She let out a deep sigh before explaining, "CK, I didn't want to burden you with my problems. You're already a walking bundle of anxiety, and the last thing you needed was to worry about my crumbling marriage. I haven't told anyone except my parents. My dad was so upset that he had to increase his blood pressure medication, and my mom has baked more bundt cakes for me this past year than Nothing Bundt."

CK furiously gnawed on her fingernails while Gemma continued, "After I found out, I begged him to go to marriage counseling, hoping it might help us salvage whatever was left of our relationship, but it was a waste of time. After the third or fourth session, Tyler made it clear that he had no desire to end his affair. He basically told me I could either accept it or leave. I refuse to accept it, but I'm still sticking around, you know, for Carolina." She leaned back in the deck chair as her friends groaned with anger. "I know he's been with her all weekend while I'm away. Carolina has been with friends, so she isn't keeping track of him or what he's up to."

"It's not my business, but is it someone you know, Gemma?" Erin asked as the cool wind whipped through her short dark hair.

Gemma finished off her second cocktail and wryly smiled. "She works in his office. Rebecca. *Becky.*" She scoffed. "Everyone he works with knows about it. I'm a laughingstock. And you know what?" Gemma threw her hands in the air in exasperation.

"I can't for the life of me understand what beautiful Becky sees in him. She's *so* out of his league."

Although she was angry with her, CK said, "So are you, Gemma."

Gemma reached over and grabbed her best friend's hand before she could chew her thumbnail down to the quick. She gave it a reassuring squeeze, silently asking if they could make up now. Celia Kate responded with a clasp of her own, confirming that everything was okay between them.

"You always have been out of Tyler's league," Moira agreed, nodding emphatically. "I'm still mad about that crack he made about the rice at James and Ella's wedding."

Gemma released CK's hand and wiped the tears forming in the corner of her eye. "Seems like we all have our issues. I'm the big one with the cheating, scumbag husband. Erin is the poor one with the cheating, scumbag ex-husband."

Erin laughed.

"CK, you're the paranoid one—just waiting on Armageddon," Gemma finished.

CK shrugged. "It's true that I was the only twenty-five-year-old who had a bathtub stocked with bottled water and army rations for Y2K."

Gemma pressed on, "How many texts have you sent to your kids this weekend? Is the security camera footage of your house streaming on your phone right now? Did you tell Sean to measure out the correct cups of cat food?"

CK grunted when she realized she had forgotten to leave specific feeding instructions for Chipper Jones; he was sure to be a diabetic by the time she returned home. Still, she defended herself. "I see what you're saying, but it's an act of love. It's a responsibility, to see to it that your people are cared for. To see to it that everything is running smoothly."

"But, CK, if you don't see to it that everything is running smoothly, then what?" Gemma asked. "What's the worst that will happen?"

People will die. CK kept the heavy fear to herself.

It was as if Gemma could hear her best friend's thoughts as she continued, "What could you have done to prevent your grandmother from dying? Your mom, CK? What could you have done to stop that ACL from tearing? Nothing."

The words struck a chord with Nell, and she responded, "I'm the exact same way, CK. I understand that some things happen beyond my control. I know I can't live in fear because it's a liar that robs us of our joy. Still, I battle it every single day. I worry about my kids and the choices they make. I spent the first ten minutes of the massage today coming up with worst-case scenarios. I mean, I worried about crepe myrtle disease!" Nell sighed and continued, "I remind myself of God's Word, that he is in control. Even in the hardest times, he weaves everything together for the good of those who love him. And still I find myself overwhelmed with fear rather than embracing my faith. *Fear.* That is the root of all our issues, isn't it?"

Moira, who had been silent throughout this discussion while the sweat from her watered-down cocktail soaked into the napkin in her hand, felt suffocated by her own fears. Instead of sharing them, she resorted to her usual defense mechanism and built a wall around herself. She snapped, "This is supposed to be my birthday party cruise, not an episode of *Dr. Phil.* Can we please talk about happier topics for the rest of the trip?" Her plea hung in the sea air, a mix of frustration and a longing for lighthearted conversation, despite her inner turmoil.

"Of course, Moira," Erin relented just as Antonio and Renata emerged from below deck with dessert: steaming peach cobbler with a spoonful of vanilla bean ice cream melting on top.

"What better to go with a low-country boil than a low-country dessert, yeah?" Antonio declared while he placed the sweets on the table.

"Can't let my blood sugar get too low," Gemma mumbled as she pulled the small plate closer to her.

CK heard Gemma and said, "Moira, I agree that we should steer the conversation toward happier subjects, but I just have to say this once more, even if it won't make a bit of difference." She looked at Gemma. "Listen to what I'm saying and stop putting yourself down. You don't even need Tyler around to make fun of you anymore; you're doing a great job of that yourself."

"CK is right," Nell agreed. "The way you talk about yourself directly influences your mental well-being. Don't be your own worst enemy, Gemma."

"Okay, okay. You ladies know that I cope with humor," Gemma defended herself, poking her spoon at the soupy, melted ice cream. "It's no big deal."

Nell said, "I don't know your husband, but from what I've heard this weekend, it seems like he comments on your weight not out of genuine love or concern for your health, but just to be crass."

"More like just to be a word that rhymes with *crass*," CK grumbled. Erin was the only one who heard her and winked at her.

"It's important to remember, though, that not all advice stems from a negative perspective. Some people truly care, and I think CK is one of those people," Nell continued. She glanced over to Moira, who appeared to be lost in thought, her focus fixed on her dessert and the serene Tybee Island shoreline beyond, seemingly unaware of the deep conversation around her—unaware of a conversation that Nell so desperately wanted to steer toward her specifically.

"I *am* genuinely worried about you, Gemma," CK said, her voice soft. "This isn't about Tyler or what he wants you to look like. This is about your health. And I'm talking about both your physical and mental health."

Gemma sighed, her defenses lowering. "I'm not oblivious to the fact that I need to lose weight. I don't feel good about the way I look, but more importantly, I don't feel good period. I'm not offended by your honesty." She took another bite of her warm cobbler, savoring the sweet flavor as she contemplated her commitment to making her health a priority. "We can talk more about this on Monday." With that, Gemma began to sing off-key, belting out the Jimmy Buffett hit.

Moira had tuned out of the deep conversation, snapping back to reality only when she heard her friends laughing. She noticed that Nell wanted to share a heartfelt moment, evident by the way she kept glancing in Moira's direction. However, Moira wasn't interested in any cliché Hallmark movie scene. Instead, she turned to Renata, her voice steady, and asked for another cocktail, ignoring the awkward glances from those around her.

Before the cruise, while sipping dark coffee in her bathroom, Moira promised herself she would not drink any more alcohol that evening. The setting, however, was too perfect: the warm, gentle breeze; the rhythmic sound of the waves; and the tempting aroma of delicious food. Now she felt the urge for a drink to boost her spirits amid the therapy session taking place around her.

Gemma noticed the downcast look on Moira's tired face and said aloud, "Mo, I'm sorry. You asked us to talk about livelier topics, and we completely ignored you. Let's shift gears, okay? It's your birthday celebration, so let's celebrate, yeah?"

Moira answered with disdain, "Apparently celebrating is frowned upon in this group."

"What's that mean?" asked CK.

"Never mind." Moira pointed to the salon before suggesting, "It's getting quite chilly on the deck. Let's move in there and out of this wind."

They got up from the dining table and settled into the covered lounge area above the bridge deck. Renata returned with Moira's third cocktail of the cruise. As Moira took the drink from Renata's hand, the waves and her unsteadiness caused some of the liquid to spill over the top of the glass, splattering onto her black sandals.

They were now closer to Kevin as he navigated the boat back to Allyson Island. They settled into two semicircular settees and spent a few minutes making small talk with him, inquiring about his background and passion for boats. The moonlight reflected off the polished deck, creating sparkles that resembled stars.

The night's heavy discussions of infidelity, addiction, and anxiety were momentarily forgotten when Moira, Gemma, and CK began reminiscing about a weekend fishing trip they had taken in middle school. They remembered being on that green aluminum boat with Moira's grandfather, Ernest, who had accidentally fallen into Lake Conasauga while trying to reel in a large-mouth bass. Once in the water, he dramatically flailed about and tricked the girls into thinking the fish had latched onto his toe in revenge and was trying to pull him under. Moira recognized his old trick because he had pulled it on her before, but Gemma and CK were completely oblivious.

"Maybe *that's* actually where my anxiety was born. We were having a nice, calm fishing trip and suddenly your old pa was overboard and being attacked by a bass that he convinced us was the size of Jaws."

The five women's laughter blended with the soothing sounds of the sea before drifting into the crisp September air.

Chapter 19

Moira's cozy living room was illuminated by the gentle glow of multiple table lamps and the television, which played quietly in the background. The show—a familiar favorite for each woman—was *The Golden Girls*, its muted sound providing a comforting backdrop to their conversation. The five friends had swapped their cruise dresses for their pajamas and sprawled out on the oversized couch with blankets while passing around a platter of milk chocolate bear claws.

Moira had taken out the white and gold wedding album from a drawer of an antique chest in the living room. For half an hour, they passed the book around, each page serving as a time machine to the past. They laughed and reminisced, pointing out the signature '90s touches: the clothing, the big hair, the heavy makeup. It was hard to ignore how handsome Jeffrey looked as the groom, his smile bright and genuine.

The album also included pictures from the reception, where Moira's hair, decorated with sprigs of baby's breath, had come undone while she danced like a madwoman to Janet Jackson hits. There were several candid photos of Sean and Celia Kate twirling across the parquet floor of the Tunnell Hill Golf and Country Club, and even one of Tyler in the background, next to the punch bowl, looking smug.

"That's him. That's Tyler," Gemma said, tapping on the album page as Nell and Erin leaned in to get a closer look at the evening's villain.

"I do see the resemblance to Jake Ryan," Erin noted while CK suppressed an audible gag.

"He made fun of me that night," Gemma continued, looking away from the album and squinting her dark eyes in an effort to remember. "What was it about? Oh, gosh, I can't recall exactly. But he said something that really hurt my feelings. Maybe it was about the bridesmaid dress?" She frowned, trying to dig deeper into the memory. "Nearly thirty years. Has he really been putting me down for thirty years?"

CK bit the inside of her cheek, feeling angry at the thought of the years of insults Gemma had endured. She wanted to claw Tyler Gardner's eyes out.

"Let's move on," Moira suggested as she turned to the last page of the album.

The final photos were of her and Jeffrey ducking into the back of the limo, caught in the flash as the photographer snapped the shot just before the door closed. In one Moira was halfway in, her veil trailing behind her. Her bouquet of white peonies, eucalyptus, and pale pink roses was clutched in one hand. Her dress was bunched in her lap, messy and beautiful, like she hadn't cared about perfection for hours.

Jeffrey was already inside the car, looking out at her with that smile that crinkled the corners of his eyes. One of his hands reached for her and his other arm was flung casually over the dark leather seat, his bow tie already loosened and his shirt collar opened.

Confetti clung to them both—little specks of gold and ivory

in their hair and on their shoulders. The words "Just Married" were scribbled in white shoe polish on the rear window behind them. There was a blur in the picture, like joy was too excited to hold still. The crowd behind them was out of focus, but Gemma was noticeable, waving with her glass of wine raised.

Moira touched the edge of the photograph and remembered exactly what Jeffrey Allyson had said when the door closed them inside the limo.

"We're going to make a good story, you and me."

And they had.

Soon, the happy feelings turned into sadness for Moira. So she went over to the antique chest and tucked the album away.

"Okay, girls, what do you want to do now?" she said when she returned to the couch. "I thought maybe we could light up the firepit and hang out down by the water?"

"I'm kind of glad to be inside and out of that wind. I don't think my hair can take another tangle," Gemma said.

"Me too. I'd love to just hang out in here," Celia Kate suggested.

"Sure, whatever you all want to do is fine with me." Moira leaned her head back on the tan sofa cushion and sighed. "I can't believe this is the last night of my forties. How did I get here? How did all of us get here?" She looked around the room at her friends. "Those wedding pictures don't seem like they were taken decades ago. In fact, it feels like just yesterday we were carefree high school kids, doesn't it? Back then, we didn't even need to wear bras—just Band-Aids."

Gemma burst into laughter and replied, "Not me. I have been wearing a bra since I was eight! I couldn't get coverage from any kind of bandage unless it was one of those extra-large ones for serious wounds."

"You know what I miss the most about being young?" CK said. "Playing basketball. I have to admit that I'm sad none of my children are interested in sports. I'm proud of my kids and love that they have different interests—fishing, golfing, crafting, drawing—but I was raised in a sports-oriented household. If my parents weren't watching my brother and me play in a game, we would all huddle in the living room and eat pizza and watch basketball or baseball on TV. Tucker and Sean like to watch the Braves, but no part of our life revolves around sports and schedules. Sometimes I wish it did. I mean, I thought it would. I thought I would raise them the way I was raised."

"I played a little," Erin said. "I think I scored a total of twelve points throughout my entire high school career, but I understand where you're coming from, CK. Some of my best memories are from being part of the team and the bond I shared with those girls."

"I still feel like I'm that cheerleader in the Tunnel Hill High School gym," Moira continued, clapping her hands stiffly. "I mean, aside from perimenopause, hot flashes, night sweats, frozen shoulder, and hormone replacement—"

Gemma started clapping and chanted, "We've got razzmatazz! Pep, punch, and pizzazz!"

And then Moira joined her in unison, "Hey, you—you've been had! Tunnel Hill Tornadoes got razzmatazz!"

Erin, her eyes wide with concern, interrupted everyone's laughter. "Wait, go back to what you were saying, Moira. Frozen shoulder? You're traumatizing me," she exclaimed as the others teased her again about being the youngest. "I know you all see me as the baby of the group, but I have to write everything down or set reminders on my phone. My mother went through this too—she struggled to remember things she'd always known, like birthdays and anniversaries. It was so wild to me back then—like, how can you forget your sister's birthday? But now I get it. The other day I couldn't for the life of me remember PJ's phone number. My own son's phone number!"

"I write things down on a calendar *and* put them in my phone and still forget," Gemma confessed. "I'm liable to miss Carolina's graduation."

Gemma's joke made Moira feel a pang of guilt as she recalled dashing up the bleachers at Monterey Prep's football field last May. She could sense the critical, disapproving eyes glaring at her as her heels clicked against the steel seats. The cocktails she'd had while getting ready to watch her youngest receive his diploma that evening made it difficult for her to keep her footing steady. She stumbled as she squeezed down the bleacher row and plopped down next to her son Bradford and her older brothers and their wives. Bradford, MerryLee, and Tabitha immediately scowled at her, both for being late and for the sweet whiskey scent wafting from her breath. She quickly pushed the entire memory back down again.

CK shook her head in bewilderment. "It's strange," she murmured while tracing her fingers across the top of her opposite hand. "I don't feel middle-aged either. But when I look in the mirror, I see my mother. I see her face in mine, in the wrinkles beginning to form. I see her hands when I look at my own. And you know what? I often think I look old and awful, decrepit like the Cryptkeeper. But to me, my mother never looked that way. Mama was beautiful. She was perfect." Feelings of grief and yearning for her mother washed over her. "I miss her so much."

"She was beautiful, CK, both inside and out. And you're just like her," Gemma said. With a wry smile, she added, "I definitely inherited my mother's thighs, all thanks to her biscuits."

"I also see my mother when I look in the mirror," Nell agreed. "I can also hear her, especially when I'm frustrated with the kids. I sound just like her when I say, 'What in Sam Hill were you thinking?'" She imitated her mother's elegant Southern drawl, then ran her hand across the embroidered throw pillow in her lap and said seriously, "We're at the front of the line now, aren't we? Our parents are dying—not our grandparents, but our parents. And we have been pushed right to the front."

Not just our parents, but our husbands too, Moira thought.

"Do men realize how fortunate they are?" CK broke the somber mood. "Sean is more handsome now than when we met two decades ago. I'm slathering fifteen creams on my face every night while he's aging backward like Benjamin Button."

Nell snapped her fingers. "Yes! Besides going a little thin on top, Chip is aging in reverse too. He's two years older than me and still hasn't bought a pair of reading glasses. I need glasses to read the captions on the television because my hearing isn't as good anymore either."

"Most guys age like fine wine, but Tyler Gardner? He's aging more like milk." Gemma immediately clapped a hand over her mouth, surprised that she let that slip, and the other ladies snickered at her. "Oh my goodness! Did I say that out loud?"

"I hope it felt good to say that, because it certainly felt good to hear it," Celia Kate remarked, thinking that Tyler Gardner's athletic physique was long gone and that the thick, dark Jake Ryan hair he once had was now thinning and turning gray.

"It felt good," Gemma confessed, "but I feel guilty. Mama always says to never say something behind someone's back that you wouldn't say to their face."

"Well, I'd like to tell Tyler to his face what I think of him," CK said.

Moira said, "I agree with Mama Linda, but I can't deny that it feels good to hear you take a dig at him."

"Serves him right for being such a jerk all these years. I'm still in shock that he would step out on you, Gemma. He should consider himself lucky that someone like you gave him the time of day!" CK's voice rose and her cheeks flushed hot with anger.

"Okay, okay. Not right now." Gemma shook her head and Celia Kate reluctantly agreed, with a sigh, to save the conversation for later.

Moira glanced across the living room at a shiny silver frame on the round table in the corner. It held one of Moira's favorite photos of her and Jeffrey: a candid shot taken at a charity cocktail event. In the picture, Moira was laughing hysterically, her mouth open and her eyes closed. Her head was leaning on Jeffrey's shoulder as he smiled widely and gazed off-camera.

"Jeffrey aged well too," she said as her lips tightened.

For Jeffrey's fiftieth birthday, he requested no party, no big to-do; he only wanted to be with Moira and his boys. They had dinner at his favorite seafood restaurant, followed by a horse-drawn carriage ride through their beloved Savannah, the city Jeffrey Allyson knew like the back of his hand. They talked more about their boys' future and theirs—that yacht, a trip to Rome. But only two days later, Jeffrey was gone.

Moira's stare wandered from the photo of happier times to the bar that led into the kitchen, where bottles sat neatly lined up like soldiers. A drink would be nice right now—warm and smooth, something that could gently numb the persistent ache of losing her charming husband too soon.

Without consulting her friends or offering to get them anything, she walked to the bar, fully aware that, just like on graduation evening, eyes were focused on her, scrutinizing her every move. She didn't care. This was her home, her party, and she would do whatever she wanted. She pulled down a clean etched glass and poured herself a drink of syrupy brown liquid: Jack Daniel's. It was Jeffrey's libation choice, though he rarely indulged. She couldn't remember ever seeing him heavily intoxicated, even during his fraternity party days. As a college student, he enjoyed having a good time but always kept his wits about him. He looked out for his friends, making sure they stayed safe and didn't get too out of control. That was the kind of guy he'd always been—protective, concerned, generous.

Moira wondered what Jeffrey would say about her drinking habits. She was sure he wouldn't approve. But he wasn't here, was he? If he had been, she wouldn't be drinking so much. This was his fault. His death was nearly killing her.

She reached for a metal stirring stick, and the cubes clinked against the glass while the warm whiskey got to work melting them. She took a sip; it burned her throat. She turned to walk back to the couch. Not wanting to see the disapproval on her friends' faces, she avoided meeting their eyes with her own. She sprawled out on the couch as if she didn't care what they thought—because she truly didn't.

"So what do you ladies want to talk about now?" she asked.

Gemma spotted a couple of decks of cards in a decorative bowl on the coffee table and suggested a game of rummy. The others agreed and tossed throw pillows and their blankets onto the floor around the large coffee table and settled down on them. Dove and Pearl arrived for the card game, kneading their paws into the blankets piled on the rug. Meanwhile, Gemma kept a watchful eye on the "whiskered demons" while shuffling the cards and dealing them out. She also gave Erin a quick refresher on how to play the game.

Chatter and laughter filled the room, accompanied by '80s and '90s hits playing from a speaker in the entertainment center. Several times, before the ice cubes had even melted in her glass, Moira returned to the bar in the butler's pantry for a refill. Each time she made her way to the liquor cabinet, her friends exchanged concerned glances, but they remained silent and continued with their card game, even as Moira's words became slurred and she struggled to remember which card to play.

Without warning, in the middle of the game, Moira turned her head away from the coffee table. The contents of her stomach—a mix of shrimp and sausage and mudbugs and cobbler—splattered all over her expensive silk pajamas and the khaki couch. The cats leapt to their paws and darted out of the room. Nell and Erin, who were sitting closest to her, also jumped up in a panic, while Gemma began to gag at the sight and smell.

Erin and CK rushed to the kitchen to grab towels while Moira moaned and sprawled backward on the floor. She looked up at Nell, her eyes glassy and her nose running, and said, "I bet you're loving this, aren't you?"

Nell replied softly and kindly, "Shh, now. Everything is okay."

Celia Kate and Erin returned, with Erin immediately shifting into work mode. She removed the stained couch cushion, along with a damp blanket and throw pillow, holding them away from her body as she headed to the laundry room at the back of the

house. Meanwhile, Gemma was not helping; she was loudly dry
heaving in the corner while CK shouted at her to stop being so
dramatic. Gemma shouted back at CK, and Moira, lying on the
floor in a drunken stupor, called out, "Not now, you two!"

CK narrowed her eyes at Gemma, who was retching animatedly, and offered to take Moira to her room to get cleaned up.

"I'll do it," Nell eagerly offered.

"No, Nell. CK can help me. I'm not in the mood for an intervention right now." Moira huffed as she sat up from the floor,
wobbling on her elbows, while her messy hair stuck to her forehead.

"I promise, no intervention," Nell said, bending down to gently
grip Moira's arm and help her to her feet. Meanwhile, CK sprayed
carpet cleaner on the rug and groaned at Gemma, who continued
to flail about and make horrible noises.

The French doors in Moira's bedroom were still open to the
balcony, letting the refreshing salty air flow inside. As she and
Nell stepped into the cool room, Moira felt more alert and clearheaded. She gently pulled away from Nell's grasp and shuffled
into the bathroom. There, she removed her filthy pajamas and
tossed them into the hamper before covering herself with a soft
white robe. Still feeling a bit dizzy, she sat down at her bathroom
vanity and asked Nell to bring her another pair of pajamas from
the closet.

Before entering the walk-in closet, Nell paused at Jeffrey's
vanity and noticed that his belongings were still neatly arranged
on the countertop. A wave of sadness washed over her as she
rummaged through Moira's pajama drawer, which was filled
with expensive sets and elegant gowns. She pulled out a pair of
pajamas similar to the pink ones Moira had been wearing, but
in a soft and buttery pastel purple.

"I don't want to talk about it, Nell," Moira insisted, shaking her head and holding up her hand in resistance. Nell recognized that it wasn't the right time for a discussion and placed the clean set of clothes on the counter. As Moira hung her head and massaged her forehead, it became clear to Nell that she was embarrassed by what had happened. Perhaps vomiting shrimp and sausage at her birthday party in front of her friends was precisely what Moira Allyson needed to realize that her drinking had become out of control.

Moira groggily thanked Nell for her help and asked her to give her some privacy while she cleaned up. When Nell left, Moira splashed cold water on her face and brushed her teeth. While looking in the mirror, she suddenly broke down in tears, the heavy reality of her actions hitting her: she had just vomited in front of her friends, and on her couch and living room floor. Feeling completely asinine, she sat down on her vanity stool and buried her face in her hands.

Again she wondered what Jeffrey would think, and guilt swept over her, slow and thick. She pictured him standing in the doorway behind her, watching her like he used to. Only now there would be no soft joke or compliment or smile that wrinkled the corners of his eyes. He would be disappointed.

Moira pressed her fingertips to her cheek and felt the heat there. She felt the shame bubbling within her.

"I'm sorry," she whispered to the mirror, to herself, to him.

The tears came again, and she put her elbows on her knees and cradled her face in her hands once more. She stayed like that while her body shook, not from the alcohol, but from the bondage of it all.

Soon, Dove and Pearl settled onto the top of her bare feet, soft and comforting. She reached down to pet them before she wiped her eyes with tissue and then splashed cold water onto her face again. She looked at her reflection and knew she was still in there somewhere. Beneath the grief and the mess and the blur of everything lost, she was still there.

"I'm going to be better," she whispered to the woman in the mirror, and to Jeffrey. "I have to be."

She didn't know if she believed it. Not yet. But saying it felt like a good start. And saying it brought Jeffrey back into her thoughts. He wasn't angry or even disappointed anymore; he was just waiting for her, for the woman he had loved for so long, to come back.

NELL RETURNED TO the living room, where CK and Erin were still busy cleaning up the area. Gemma had stopped making loud noises and was now quietly standing in the corner, her nose and mouth covered by the collar of her black pajama top.

"I don't know if I'll ever be able to eat a low-country boil again," Gemma griped.

"Should we call it a night?" Erin stood up from the clean, damp rug and pushed the hair that had fallen into her eyes out of the way with her wrist.

"Absolutely not! I was winning that hand," Gemma insisted with a wry smile. "Let's just move to the dining table. I don't know if I'll ever be able to sit on that couch again, either, without picturing corn floating in a pile of whiskey." She shuddered at her own words, and CK told her to be quiet.

The group sat quietly at the mahogany trestle table in the dining room while Erin shuffled the cards before dealing out another hand.

Celia Kate darted her eyes around to ensure they were alone and then asked Nell softly, "Is Moira all right? She must be so embarrassed."

Nell, arranging the cards in her manicured hand, replied, "She's okay. She was washing up when I left her." Nell paused. "Did you happen to notice all of Jeffrey's things still left out when you went up to check on her earlier?"

"Yes," CK said. "It broke my heart. I can't imagine."

Erin added sympathetically, "All of his clothes are still in the closet too. His desk is untouched."

Celia Kate leaned back in her chair to get a better view of the stairway in the foyer, making sure Moira wasn't approaching. "Nell, I completely understand now why you've been worried about her. If you decide to talk to her about her drinking again before the weekend is over, I'll join you."

"I will too," Erin agreed.

CK, Nell, and Erin turned their attention toward Gemma, who still had a sour expression on her face. Sensing their stares, Gemma finally relented, saying, "Okay, I'll talk to her with you. Letting loose on your birthday weekend is one thing, but if she's throwing up on furniture several times a week, then that sounds like a real problem."

"I did the most embarrassing things when I was drinking heavily," Nell said while adjusting the cards in her hands. "I rambled on social media late at night. Once I posted homecoming pictures of Tate and his girlfriend at the time, and I captioned it

'Tate and Jezebel, Homecoming Dance' because the dress she was wearing looked more like a bathing suit from the 1940s."

"Nell! You didn't!" Gemma exclaimed.

"Oh, I did." Nell sighed. "It was up for a couple of hours before my daughter saw it and logged into my account while I was asleep and deleted it. My son was furious, and the poor girl he was dating was so embarrassed. Her mother called me and cussed me up and down. I ruined that relationship for poor Tate. What I did was completely inappropriate."

"It sounds like her dress was inappropriate," Gemma added while focusing on the cards in her hand.

"It wasn't exactly something Emily Post would approve of, but I was still wrong."

"Where I grew up, in the Blue Ridge Mountains, alcohol and drug abuse is everywhere. By some miracle, neither my mama nor daddy were addicts, but I have a lot of cousins who either drink or use drugs," Erin said before taking a sip of water from her glass resting on a coaster. "I'll never forget my birthday. I was turning ten and my cousin Earl showed up drunker than a skunk, and he pulled his gun."

"He what?" Gemma reached for a milk chocolate bear claw on the table.

"Yeah." Erin laughed in amazement. "I still can't believe it. We were at a picnic table in the backyard. Everyone was singing 'Happy Birthday,' and when I was done blowing out the candles, Earl took out his gun, raised it in the air, and fired off a couple of rounds. That was his way of celebrating, I guess. My granddad and some other family sprang into action, not sure what was going on, and wrestled him to the ground and got the gun away from him. My mom always said my tenth birthday came in with a bang."

They all laughed, and Gemma said, "It sure did. That's wild."

"I've got family up in Asheville. Beautiful country up there," Celia Kate added.

"I grew up well north of Asheville, near the Kentucky border, in a very isolated area." Erin scanned her cards, seeing two nearly complete runs and a stubborn queen of spades that refused to fit anywhere. "Moonshine stills were still in operation up there. I don't think we had running water until I was in middle school. My father came from a family of coal miners, and he and my mama were both sick a lot because of the mines and the poor air quality. My mother had a hard time getting pregnant—I was her miracle baby. They were good parents who loved me more than anything, but they couldn't provide much for me. I had to grow up quickly and take care of them.

"This has been my life from the beginning—a never-ending struggle for money and to make ends meet. By the time I met Phillip and he took me out of the mountains, my mother had already passed away and my father was in a care home. He was still young then, but he looked much older, worn down by life in those hills. Even after I moved down here with Phillip, I was still poor. Life was a bit better, but it came at a price. I had running water, but I paid for it in other ways." She drew a card from the stockpile, her skinny fingers slow and deliberate.

"When I look around at this house and ones I cleaned before it, it's mind-blowing. How do people have all this? They must work hard, right? I work too, but I don't have anything left over. People inherit things from their families, passing them down generation to generation, and I guess being poor and having hard luck can be inherited as well. I want to be the one to break that cycle. I don't want my grandchildren to go hungry like I did, or like PJ did some nights. I want this kind of curse to end with me."

"Generational curses," Nell agreed. "My granddaddy was a drinker, so was my daddy, and then me."

"My mama was on anxiety medicine half her life. She did a Prozac trial in the '80s." CK discarded a junk card. "Rummy."

Gemma gathered everyone's cards and shuffled them well. "We're all big. Mama, Daddy, me, my brother."

"I didn't know you had a brother, Gemma," Nell said.

"Oh yes. My big brother, Garrett. He's not only older, but he's actually big—about six three and four hundred pounds. He's divorced and has two kids, and he lives up in Lexington. He works as a football coach there. I haven't told him about Tyler, and I made Mom and Dad promise not to tell him either. He's never been a fan of my husband. He's liable to come down to Atlanta and rip him limb from limb." She dealt the cards across the table, watching them slide gracefully over the smooth mahogany surface.

"I've always thought Garrett was a smart guy," CK added, but Gemma ignored her.

"My father had an affair while I was in high school, which nearly tore our family apart." Nell's green eyes studied the cards in her hand. "Our mother allowed him to stay in the house, but they slept in separate bedrooms for years, living as if they were worlds apart. I can remember them being in the same room together, not speaking a word, as if the other were invisible. My younger brother and sister sensed that something wasn't right, but they didn't know all the details like I did. I tried to protect them from the truth and did my best to keep our home happy for their sake.

"My parents continued living that way for years, even after I moved out to go to college. By then, my brother and sister had figured out that it wasn't normal for a husband and wife to sleep and eat separately and to ignore each other like they did. However, before my younger sister, Candace, graduated high school, God managed to restore our parents' marriage. My dad quit drinking, and peace and love returned to our home. The affair and hitting rock bottom were necessary for him to realize just how serious his problems were. Maybe Moira needed to embarrass herself the way she did tonight to face her issues."

"I don't think it will be like that, like your parents, for me and Tyler. I don't think there's anything left for us," Gemma said matter-of-factly.

Nell nodded. "And that's okay. Some marriages are restored. Some aren't."

"How did you find out, Gemma? I know you said you don't want to talk about it, but I can't get it off my mind," Celia Kate said. "You dropped a pretty big bomb on us."

Gemma tossed a card into the discard pile and said, "He came home late one night last fall, reeking of cheap perfume. You know the kind—like a mix of alcohol and cat urine. Anyway, I asked him about the smell on his clothes, and I swear he didn't even look ashamed. He sat on the bench at the end of our bed, where he always sits to take off his shoes every night. Without a hint of guilt or remorse, he said, 'I have a girlfriend, Gemma.' It was as if he were casually mentioning that he had used the last roll of toilet paper—so nonchalant. I actually laughed, thinking he was joking, but then he looked up at me, dead serious, and repeated it. That's when he told me it was Rebecca from his office and that they had been seeing each other for a couple of months."

"Oh, I could kill him!" CK exclaimed through gritted teeth. "What did you do?"

"Carolina wasn't home that night—she was at Mama and Daddy's house having a sleepover. So Tyler and I had a huge shouting match. He told me that he didn't find me attractive anymore and that he never really did. I told him to get out of the house, and after arguing for a few minutes, he finally grabbed a bag and went to his girlfriend's place. I was so mad. If he hadn't left the house, I probably would have ended up as the subject of an episode of *Dateline*." Gemma ate another bite of bear claw. "I didn't tell anyone, not even my parents, for at least a month, while he kept right on seeing her. I was tempted to tell Carolina what a jerk her dad was, but I didn't, to protect her. Anyway, I don't even remember how I got him to agree to go to marriage counseling with me, but after a few sessions, he told me on the way back home in his truck that he wouldn't be going back. He looked at me and said, 'I just don't love you anymore, Gemma. I don't plan on breaking up with Becky.' I asked him, 'Well, where does that leave me?' And he said to me, 'Stay or go; that's up to you.' And Lord only knows why I've chosen to stay all this time."

CK answered, "Because you're a good mother. You're protective and have considered your daughter's feelings over your own. That's noble, Gemma, but Carolina is a big girl. She can handle this."

"I'm sure, just like my brother and sister, that she can sense that something isn't right in your home," Nell said.

"I'm sure she can," Gemma replied. "We've never discussed it, though."

"So you knew about his affair at the lake this past July? Gemma, I had no idea. You two seemed like your normal selves," CK remarked. "You were kind to him, and yes, he was awful to you."

"And the Oscar goes to . . ." Gemma said sarcastically.

By the time the grandfather clock in the dining room chimed eleven times, the group of friends had played several more rounds of cards and were ready to turn in.

"This sure was a crazy night. It felt like a mash-up of four or five Julia Roberts movies," Gemma said.

"Yeah, and I'm ready for bed." Celia Kate yawned and stretched her arms over her head as the tiredness from their night finally began to set in.

Nell placed the deck of cards back into its box while the others stood and slid the heavy dining chairs under the table.

"Girls?" Moira interrupted them, her voice quiet and hesitant. Her hair had been washed and framed her sleepy face with damp waves.

"Mo? Hey, are you okay?" CK walked toward her and gently touched her elbow.

Moira nodded with a small smile. "Yeah, I'm fine. Completely fine," she reassured them. "Are you all headed to bed, or can we talk for a little while?"

CK was exhausted but wanted to be a good friend and support Moira, so she suppressed a yawn. "Of course."

Erin rubbed her eyes but nodded, and Nell added, "Absolutely."

"Let's go to the hearth room," Moira suggested, much to Gemma's relief, because the faint smell of acidic stomach still lingered in the living room.

With Dove and Pearl following close behind their mother, the group walked through the spacious and beautiful kitchen, where CK offered to make a pot of coffee. The others agreed and moved into the adjoining hearth room, which featured a large bay window that overlooked the backyard. The window had a bench crowded with tall peach cushions.

One wall of the room displayed a brick fireplace with an ornate mantel, and a television was mounted above it. Another wall was decorated with a collection of photographs showcasing the Allyson family. Each image, framed in a variety of wooden styles, captured cherished moments from throughout the years.

In one photo, Bradford and Brent were just little boys. Their hair was fluffy and brown, and they wore bright life jackets, ready for a day of boating on the Ogeechee River. Another picture depicted the middle school boys fishing eagerly at the shoreline of their backyard, their expressions full of excitement as they cast their lines into the water, while another picture of them, older, with height and distinctive jawlines, showed them standing confidently in tall rubber boots, their proud dad beside them, as they explored the salt marsh. One of Moira's favorites, though, was one Brent took only a few years before, of his parents sitting in the chairs at the edge of the yard, beneath the canopy of the centuries-old live oak. Moira remembered how humid it was that late July afternoon because the waves in her hair were more prominent and sweat glistened on Jeffrey's brow.

At the center of the wall hung a large picture of the Allysons, dressed in their Sunday best. The photo was taken by a professional photographer at Chippewa Square on a spring afternoon five years earlier. The boys faked their smiles because Brent still had braces at the time and Bradford hated his short haircut. The smiles on Moira's and Jeffrey's faces, however, were genuine.

Moira pressed a button beside the hearth, and the gas fireplace roared to life. Erin, Nell, and Gemma settled into the white highback chairs arranged around the fireplace. CK soon walked into the room, carrying a wooden tray topped with mismatched cups, along with two small containers of cream and sugar. She set the tray down on an oversized corduroy ottoman at the center of the room, and each woman retrieved a mug and prepared it to her liking. CK then got cozy on the thick peach cushion at the bay window, while Moira carefully took a seat in the last of the white high-back chairs, holding her full cup in hand. One cat bathed herself at Moira's feet while the other perched on the back of Moira's chair.

Gemma, always the one to lighten the mood, said, "Moira, should we get you a bucket? Or get your cats a raincoat? You know, in case there's a round two?"

Nell and Erin lightly giggled as CK growled at Gemma from the bay window. Moira's face flushed red with embarrassment, but she wasn't angry with Gemma. She'd known her friend long enough to know she reverted to humor in somber times. At Jeffrey's funeral, Gemma must have cracked more jokes than Richard Pryor.

Moira felt much more clearheaded with the warmth of the fire blanketing her and the strong coffee in her cup. Although she was still humiliated about what had happened earlier, she was ready to talk about it.

"I want to apologize to you all for, well"—she glanced in the direction of the living room—"*that* debacle. I'm ready to admit that I drank too much tonight. And last night. And the night before you got here. And, well, you get it. There's no excuse for it." She circled her fingertip around the top of the black and white mug as steam rose from it. After a pause, she shook her head, and the waves of her hair spilled over the shoulder of her purple top. She declared, "I'm too young to be a widow. Widows are old, gray-haired grandmothers who drive land yachts and sit in their rocking chairs while knitting and watching *Matlock*. I shouldn't be a widow. Not yet."

"I like *Matlock*." Gemma shrugged.

The other friends remained silent, sipping from their coffee cups and allowing Moira's vulnerability to fill the room. Nell knew this wasn't alcohol talking for her. What they were witnessing, as Moira's eyes glistened with unshed tears, was raw, real, sober emotion that had been pent up for a long time.

"Sometimes," Moira continued, her voice sorrowful as she stared at the steam, "I wake up in the middle of the night, and for a split second, I forget that Jeffrey is dead. I reach across the bed to his side, only to feel the sheets are stark cold. And a dark, foreboding heaviness suffocates me all over again." She caught Gemma's eyes first and noticed they were damp. "I relive it. I relive the phone call telling me he was gone and I relive the blurry, hazy days before we put him in the ground. All of it presses down on me." She quickly wiped the corners of her eyes with her manicured fingers and tried to regain composure. "And I wonder, will I ever stop waking up in the middle of the night and reaching for him? I don't think I will."

Nell wanted to speak to her grieving friend, in hopes of

providing some comfort. But she hesitated, realizing nothing she could say would ease Moira's pain at that moment. In her vulnerable state, Moira reminded Nell of Job, and she understood that they needed to be like Job's friends, who sat quietly with him, simply being present in the face of his immense suffering.

"His brush is still on the vanity, right where he left it the morning he died. There are just a few salt-and-pepper hairs in it, and I don't dare touch that brush because I don't want them to fall to the floor and get sucked up by the vacuum," she said, looking at Erin with sad eyes. "I often stand in the closet and wrap myself in his suit jackets. They still smell like him—like his cologne somewhat, but also just *him*, that distinctive scent of his skin. I'll be in the kitchen cooking or out in the garden, or in our chairs underneath our favorite tree, and I think I catch a whiff of it, Jeffrey's smell. I turn to look, but there's nothing." Moira wiped away the tears that had finally begun to flow freely down her cheeks. "He's not there." She took a sip from her coffee cup while her friends sighed in sadness, all of them with wet eyes of their own. The cat on the back of the chair decided to move and, with one jump, joined the other on the rug in front of the flickering fire.

"And I know. I know, Nell," she continued, looking specifically at her auburn-haired friend. "I know I'll see him again one day. I believe there's more than just this temporary place. I truly do. But still, I want him here. For me . . . and for my boys . . ." Her voice trailed off while Nell nodded sympathetically. Moira rested her coffee cup on her knee that was covered in purple pajama pants. Each word she spoke and each tear that streamed down her cheek felt a little like a release from the feelings she'd kept stuffed down for so long, numbed by alcohol.

"Bradford didn't call me this weekend. I lied," she shamefully admitted. "I asked Erin to cover for me so you, Nell, wouldn't know I was sick from drinking." Her eyes caught Nell's again, and she noticed Nell wore a look of forgiveness instead of anger. "The truth is that my boys rarely call me anymore. They text sometimes because they don't want to hear me slur my words over the phone. They think I've spiraled out of control. I know Bradford and Brent love me, and they worry about me. I mean, they tell me as much when they do speak to me. But that worry makes them resent me. I'm afraid I'm losing them. I'm losing all that I have left of Jeffrey."

Gemma started to crack a joke to ease the tension, but Celia Kate shook her head. This kind of vulnerability felt uncomfortable for Gemma; it was too raw and too serious. Even during the marriage counseling sessions she had attended with Tyler and Dr. Emison, Gemma managed to inject humor into the situation. She joked about the animal-print decor in the office, asking how many cheetahs had lost their lives for the rug. Upon walking into that cheetah-printed office for the first time, she even poked fun at herself for not being able to fit on the couch with Tyler, which made him chuckle in agreement. That was the moment Dr. Emison started writing notes on her notepad.

Her voice still cracking with vulnerability, Moira said, "I am heartbroken, and I'm lonely. I drink because I'm lonely and I'm lonely because I drink. Sounds like a country song, doesn't it?" She shook her head and wiped her damp face with her palm. "I'm sorry," she said before taking a deep drink of her coffee.

"Don't apologize," Nell murmured quietly as she leaned forward in the tall white chair. She reached out and placed a reassuring hand on her friend's arm. "You needed to let all of that out. You have to bring the darkness to light."

"I know . . ." Moira bit her bottom lip and wiped her damp face again. "I just want to be happy again."

Nell placed her half-empty blue cup on the wooden tray on top of the square ottoman. "I know it might seem like I bring my faith into everything we discuss, and maybe I do. I can't apologize for that because it's incredibly important to me, and it applies to every aspect of my life—and all of our lives. The big things, the little things, the serious and the mundane."

"I don't mind it at all," CK said, and the others agreed.

"Hearing you talk, Mo, I just keep thinking how the biblical concept of joy is quite different from what we usually refer to as happiness. Happiness is a fleeting emotion tied to temporary situations, while joy is not just a momentary feeling. Joy remains constant and does not depend on everything being perfect. Instead, joy is a deep sense of peace grounded in who God is and his unchanging promises." Nell scanned the room, noticing everyone was listening intently. "Even after losing everything that he held dear, Job never lost his faith in God. He openly acknowledged that his situation was difficult and didn't shy away from expressing his pain—just like you did tonight, Mo, and like we all have. Job's conversations with God were open and sincere; he even questioned why so much trouble had come on him, and yet he always remembered who God is: the sovereign Creator of the universe, the one in control and the one who holds us close. Despite all the tragedy in his life, Job understood that joy comes from recognizing God's nature. Our God is fair, compassionate, and all-knowing, and his ways, his thoughts and plans, are profoundly different from ours. Job was wise enough to grasp God's character and keep his strong faith, which allowed him to avoid seeing himself as a victim. He didn't wallow in despair; instead, he trusted, and in that trust there was joy."

CK mulled over Nell's words and then added with a nod, "So while this may not be a season of happiness, it can still be a season of joy."

Moira looked around at her friends gathered in her home and smiled. It had been too long since she'd felt this kind of connection. The weight of isolation began to lift, and she longed for the joy Nell was describing.

Moira said, "My mother's favorite scripture was 'Consider it all joy, my brothers and sisters, whenever you face trials of many kinds, because you know that the testing of your faith produces perseverance. Let perseverance finish its work so that you may be mature and complete, not lacking anything.'"

"'Consider it all joy,'" Nell said. "Each one of us should consider it *all* joy."

Chapter 20

"I FEEL LIKE WE'RE having a bonding session, so let's do a trust exercise," CK suggested, rubbing her hands together with a sparkle of mischief in her eyes. "You know, one of those activities where you trust someone to catch you. We used to do this in basketball to help with team bonding."

"Celia Kate, I'm not interested in any hippie trust exercises. Besides, which one of you would dare to volunteer to catch me?" Gemma joked, but CK's expression made her quickly apologize for poking fun at herself again. "Seriously, I'm not into all of this . . . *feeling* things, therapy. Can't we just paint each other's toenails and pig out instead?"

Moira, her face still damp, remembered aloud, "Years ago, Jeffrey and I went to a leadership retreat and did something similar. I couldn't believe they expected me to catch Jeffrey—he was six foot three and weighed two hundred and fifty pounds! Poor thing. He ended up spraining his ankle. It was a running joke that he'd never trust me again."

"Were you drunk when you were supposed to catch him, Mo?" Gemma teased, and Moira playfully stuck out her tongue at her.

"What if," Erin suggested while sitting on her crossed legs, "instead of you old ladies with your bad backs and frozen shoulders trying to catch someone—"

"Watch it, there, Erin, with your high metabolism and normal estrogen levels," Gemma said.

Erin continued, "How about we play 'Fear in a Hat' instead? Everyone writes down their fears, tosses them into a hat, and we can take turns reading them out loud. The idea is that talking about our worries helps us deal with them better."

Gemma raised an eyebrow and argued, "We've been talking about fears all night. I'm over it. We already know Moira's couch is scared it's going to be puked on and CK is scared to cut the cord and—"

"Okay, that cord joke is aging like milk . . . and Tyler," CK said.

"Yeah, we've been talking about the things that worry us, but this is about digging deeper and uncovering things we don't even realize—our subconscious fears, right?" Erin explained. "I read about this online and tried it when I was working up the courage to leave Phillip. It really helped me face why I was scared to leave him. It's like a therapeutic brain dump."

"I'd like to leave my subconscious alone, if you don't mind," Gemma protested.

"A brain dump is like freestyle writing, right?" CK asked, and Erin nodded. "I let my kids do that in our composition class. It's a lot of fun for them. You just let your thoughts flow without worrying about grammar or spelling. As soon as something— anything—pops into your mind, you put it on paper."

"I have carpal tunnel," Gemma said, rubbing her wrists. "Probably from the repetitive movement of digging into potato chip bags and—"

"Moira, Nell, are you in?" CK interrupted, not wanting Gemma's self-criticism to go any further.

"Might as well," Moira said as she stood up and walked over to the large dresser across the hall. She returned with enough pens and sheets of paper for everyone, Dove and Pearl following closely behind her.

Gemma, Nell, and Erin sat on the stools at the kitchen bar while Moira grabbed a magazine from the ottoman in the center of the room and tossed one to CK as well. CK leaned back against the bay window and began to write, while Moira sat back in her chair as one of the fluffy white cats crawled into the crook of Moira's arm and the other resumed her perch on the back of the chair near her head.

After only forty-five seconds or so, Gemma shifted on the hard barstool and complained, "How long are we doing this?"

"There's no time limit. Take as long as you need," Erin answered while continuing to write a streak.

"I may be here all night," Nell mumbled to herself.

Erin continued, "And don't let the fact that someone is going to read them out loud make you hold anything back. Just write whatever pops into your mind."

"What? I thought this was for our eyes only. Someone is going to read it out loud?" Gemma groaned.

"That's the point. If you'd been listening instead of complaining when Erin was explaining, you'd know that," Celia Kate answered.

"I'd rather do that trust exercise where one of you tries to catch me."

The sound of pens scratching on paper filled the kitchen and hearth space. It was a therapeutic noise, with each woman deep in thought.

About ten minutes into the journaling session, Gemma stood up from the uncomfortable stool and stretched her back. She walked back into the warm hearth room, where the fire was still crackling, and settled into a high-back chair with a fresh cup of coffee in hand. She held back from making any jokes while the other women were focused on their writing.

As the minutes passed, one by one, the women began to finish their entries. Moira retrieved a sparkling crystal vase from one of the built-in shelves by the bay window and passed it around. Each woman slid her folded sheet of fears into the vase before returning it to Moira.

A sense of nervousness surrounded them, and Moira said, "Okay, so now we lay it all out there? Do we talk about what we have read when we're done?"

"No, not until we've read what everyone has to say," Erin said. "Who wants to go first?"

CK volunteered, and Moira passed the vase down the line of friends to where she relaxed on the peach cushion in the window seat. Celia Kate shook the vase, took out a sheet of paper from inside, and then set the vase filled with the remaining papers next to her on the cushion. She cleared her throat, sat up straighter, and slowly unfolded the crisp sheet of paper before beginning to read.

> I'm feeling hungry right now, even though I just ate a couple of hours ago. I had two large plates of low-country boil. I haven't had a low-country boil since our Howell family reunion last year, but it wasn't very good. The mudbugs Uncle Gene brought tasted like mud, literally. Anyway, I had some peach cobbler tonight too, but the hunger is still there. Honestly, I don't know if I'll ever eat a low-country boil again after Moira . . . never mind. You'd think that after watching someone barf I wouldn't even be thinking about food, but I am. I'm not sure if it's my

mind messing with me, my blood sugar acting up, or just plain boredom. All I can think about is ice cream, specifically mint chocolate chip ice cream. Tyler can't stand mint chocolate chip—he says it tastes like chocolate toothpaste. He likes butter pecan instead. Mama makes great homemade butter pecan. I like butter pecan too, but not as much as mint chocolate chip. Tyler keeps his butter pecan ice cream in the fridge out in the garage because he thinks it will be safe from me there, but honestly, I wasn't even planning to go for it anyway.

The other night, when Carolina walked in holding a milkshake, Tyler joked, "Oh, Carolina, better hide that from your mom. She's gonna tackle you for it. And you don't want a tackle from her. She could be a defensive lineman for the Falcons!" Carolina laughed, which stung a bit because I thought she would recognize when his jokes turned cruel. Honestly, Carolina has picked up a bully's attitude from her dad. I think back to the email I received a few years ago from Laurie Parton's mom, who said Carolina was giving her daughter a hard time at school. When I brought it up, Carolina admitted it and didn't show any remorse. I wasn't surprised by that email; her mean streak definitely comes from him.

But this is supposed to be about my fears. What am I afraid of? Besides my daughter being known as the mean girl? I'm *not* scared of leaving Tyler or being single. Honestly, I like the idea of living on my own and doing what I want without anyone looking at me with complete disgust. I don't need his money. I don't need him. I have every right and reason to leave. Still, I'm worried about how divorcing him would impact Carolina with so much else happening in her life right now. I worry it will make her more defensive, more of a mean girl. I guess I also worry that our daughter will take his side. I worry she'll agree with him that because I'm big, I don't deserve a faithful husband. If I leave him, I'm scared she'll leave me.

Dr. Dempsey really laid it on the line during my last visit. He talked about how I should fear things like diabetes, high blood pressure, plaque buildup, and dying young. He didn't sugarcoat anything. He called it like it is and sure didn't tell me I'm wearing my weight well, because I'm not. I know I'm not. I don't feel good most of the time and I don't like looking in the mirror either. Seeing myself in that bathing suit today in the bathroom mirror made me want to go to bed and hide under the covers. Even while laughing by the pool and talking about fun stuff, I couldn't help but think every few minutes how much I hate my appearance. I'm tired of that. I'm tired of happy moments being interrupted with depression over how I look in a mirror.

Even though Dr. Dempsey tries to scare me into losing weight, I don't think I will ever lose it. I am well aware that I eat my emotions and my fears. Food has always been my go-to in stressful situations, and what is more stressful than knowing your husband is having an affair and your only child is about to leave home? My word. I'm liable to be six hundred pounds by Christmas. My wrist is starting to hurt. I won't aggravate my carpal tunnel by digging any more into my emotional attachment to food. But one more thing—my biggest fear of all?

Tyler keeps telling me I'll never be thin, or worthy, and I fear that I might prove him right.

Gemma flinched, uneasy, and managed to suppress the overwhelming urge to interrupt Celia Kate's reading with dark humor.

Before she could comment on her brain dump, Nell volunteered to go next and carefully unfolded the sheet of paper she held in her hand, smoothing out the creases as she did so. She leaned closer to decipher the small block letters printed on the page.

I fear death. Not my own. My own death doesn't scare me. I know where I'm going when I die. And I know I'll see my mother and grandmother there. But even though we will be reunited one day, living on this earth without the people I loved so much is a terrible feeling. Like Mo and Jeffrey. Every time she talks about losing him, I panic inside at the thought of losing Sean. I fear the phone call in the middle of the night. I'm afraid if I relax, even for a second, I'll be caught off guard.

I'm worried about Silas leaving me. I have babied him his whole life. He's spoiled more than my other kids. Okay? I admit it. Because of that, I fear I have not equipped him with all he needs to be successful on his own. He can't even boil water. He can't find the cereal in the pantry. The only time he tried to wash clothes, his jeans and T-shirts came out with bleach stains. It's my fault for doing those things for him all the time. It's my fault that he's so dependent. If he goes out into the world and can't take care of himself, Sean will hold that over me forever. He will insist that homeschooling was a bad idea. He will tell me that if Silas had been subjected to public school and spent more time with other kids, then he would be more mature. I know he would because even though he's seen the success of homeschool, Sean is still in the stereo-typical frame of mind that homeschooled kids are oblivious to how the world works and don't get enough social interaction. I know that isn't true, but still, I'm afraid of the "I told you so." I'm afraid of looking like a failure to my husband.

What if Silas is okay, though, living off ramen? What if he manages to not burn down his future apartment? Then that is great, but that will mean he won't ever come home to live with us again. I have full confidence that Sophie and Tucker will do fine on their own one day, but will I ever be able to sleep not knowing where my kids are or what they are doing? How can I protect them when they are out from under my thumb? I can't.

I read a devotional not long ago about Moses's mother putting him in that basket. The story has always made me anxious and put a knot in my throat. A BABY IN A BASKET IN A RIVER. It makes me think of that time when I was little and put our puppy on the pool raft and he toppled right off and disappeared underwater for a minute and it scared me to death. A helpless baby in that same situation? My goodness. That is the point though, isn't it? Moses didn't fall out. He didn't drown. God got him where he wanted him to be, unscathed. He's going to do that for my kids too. And for Nell's kids. All of our kids. Won't he?

But baby Moses drifting safely in deep water isn't the first thing I think of when I read horrible news lines or hear tragic stories. Because sometimes God does allow traumatic things to happen. Like Nell said about Job—God allowed every trial he went through. And I know the story of Job ended with joy. I know the story ends by saying Job lived a long, good life, despite all the bad stuff that happened to him, but knowing that God said to the Enemy, "Have you considered my servant Job?" makes me panic. I don't want to be considered, God. Not me. Not my family. Not my kids.

Being considered. That's my fear.

Celia Kate wiped her eyes at the words she'd written and cleared the lump from her throat while Gemma settled comfortably into the soft pillows on the couch. With a gentle flick of her wrist, Gemma unfolded the sheet of notebook paper from the vase Nell had handed her, bringing it to eye level. After taking a large swig of hazelnut-flavored coffee, she began to read the words written on the page.

I'm scared I'll always be poor. I'll always feel like the help, the maid. I will always be less than. I fear working at the convenience store for the rest of my life. I even fear getting robbed at the convenience store. I fear PJ will always feel responsible for me and that I will be a burden to him. I fear I'll never find a good man to love me. I fear I'll only ever attract abusive men like Phillip. I fear Phillip has changed for the better and is treating his new wife the way I should have been treated. I keep replaying our relationship in my mind, trying to figure out where it went wrong. Did I do something to deserve how he treated me? Was it my fault he became abusive? These thoughts run through my mind all the time and make it hard to move on and find peace.

Is my life ever going to change? When am I going to get over these fears and insecurities? Will I ever move past them? Every time I hop on social media, I see so many people I know making progress, hitting their goals, and living their dreams.

Meanwhile, I feel like I'm treading water, barely keeping my head above the surface. I'm so tired, and honestly, there are times when I just want to throw in the towel.

There's a homeless woman in Forsyth Park who looks about my age. She wears a holey green raincoat and muddy tennis shoes. All she owns is in two big dirty duffel bags. What happened to her to end up there? How many paychecks did she miss to put her in the park? Sometimes she's beaten up. Sometimes it's obvious she has been crying. I want to help her. I wish I could spare a dollar here or there. I wish I could buy her a meal. But I'm barely surviving too. And it scares me. I'm scared I'll become the woman in Forsyth Park.

I want the kind of joy that Nell has talked about. But why would God care about me? I don't have any money to put in the offering plate, and I'm not exactly an expert on religious stuff. I've read the Bible a little bit, but honestly, most of it confuses me. I'm just a poor girl from North Carolina who's been disappointed a lot in the past. I hoped my mom and dad would get better, that Phillip would treat me right, and that my last paycheck would be enough to keep the lights on, but I was let down.

Let down. Down and out. That pretty much sums up my story, and I'm scared I'll look like a fool if I believe things will ever change. Maybe where I belong is with that woman in Forsyth Park.

There were several times over the weekend when Erin had felt vulnerable and scrutinized, but none more so than that moment.

While Erin reeled with humiliation, Moira moved Dove from her lap and sprinted over to the kitchen counter to grab a pair of stylish reading glasses. The frames glimmered in the soft light of the hearth room as she carefully adjusted them on her nose. She sat back in the soft white chair and the cat resumed her spot in Moira's lap, with a look of annoyance at the abrupt move. Moira cleared her throat and read the block print.

I fear the same things that these other women have already talked about this weekend. Everyone fears the same things to some degree, I guess. Rejection, death, tragedy, loss of control, judgment of others, succumbing to temptation, loneliness.

All mothers fear for their children, and I can't stand to think of my son in the military and being deployed to some scary place. I feel nauseated just writing the words. I don't even like the thought of my daughter being on a well-lit college campus with security cameras. Just last month, her sorority sister's drink was spiked. Thankfully she had good friends to see that she got home safely, but I wish Taylor hadn't told me about it because I have been a nervous wreck since. Despite being on my knees, begging for the promises of protection found in the book of Psalms over both my children, I usually have a sense of dread hovering over me and it just won't release me from its grip.

Worry is a sin, isn't it? God's Word clearly tells us not to do it, that worry is a lack of faith, but I disobey and do it anyway. It's our fleshly nature to worry, and our flesh is constantly at war with our spirit, with the part of us that knows the doubts and fears that consume us are nothing but lies—strongholds designed by the Enemy to keep us shackled in a state of bondage and insecurity, to rob us of joy and peace.

I know I talk about God a lot, and that portrays me as a woman of great faith. I say the expected things that good Christians should say, but I have to admit that I sometimes feel a deep disconnect from my faith, from my God who loves me so. I'm a hypocrite to preach to CK about trust when my own mind is a constant battleground of anxiety and mistrust.

I used to drink to ease my anxieties, so I understand why Moira does the same. I'm thankful God has been so good and so kind to give me the strength to stay on the wagon, because some days I just want to jump off, numb my thoughts, and quiet my mind. I know alcohol does that well. Even if it's only temporary.

God, forgive me of my unbelief, my doubt, my skepticism. I have seen firsthand how good you are, but sometimes I have bouts of amnesia. I forget that you always show up right on time. I forget that you are who you say you are. I forget that you are always working, even when I don't feel it. I forget there really is truth in what I preach to others.

Father, forgive me where I have failed you, Nell continued to pray silently while Erin unfolded the crisp letter she had removed from the vase, its paper slightly crinkled from being held tightly. She began to read the elegant penmanship in thick black ink.

I'm afraid of growing old and looking old, and I'm also afraid of doing it alone.

I'm afraid my boys hate me.

I'm afraid to stop drinking.

I'm afraid the grief will never go away.

What Nell said about happiness and joy being two different things is true for me. I'm certainly not happy most of the time, but I know I'm not joyful either. I'm just numb and empty and everything feels dark and heavy.

I have lost not only Jeffrey, but also Brent and Bradford. I ache for them and for the way things used to be. I was truly blessed to have such a caring husband and kind boys. Forgive me, God, for the times I took that for granted. Forgive me, God, for the moments I ranted and raved, complaining about towels on the floor and lights left on upstairs.

I'm afraid that Bradford won't come back to Savannah after he graduates from college because he won't want to be anywhere near me. And if that happens, what will that mean for the business? Thankfully, there are capable people—Jeffrey's most trusted employees—at the helm right now, but Jeffrey and his dad and granddad dedicated so many years to building that company, and all their hard work could be lost, taken from our family, if Bradford doesn't step up. If that happens, I would have no one to blame but myself.

I know my friends meant well with their constant calls and texts after Jeffrey died. But their concern for me, the grieving widow, just kept reminding me that Jeffrey was gone and eventually, I started to resent it. That's why I stopped responding to their messages. That's why my sisters-in-law and other friends didn't show up this weekend. It's not about drapes and detailing cars and mums and other ridiculous excuses. They simply don't want to be around me anymore. When I wasn't ignoring them, I was calling them in the middle of the night with drunk, bold criticisms and opinions, expressing things I probably shouldn't have. I've lost the respect of so many because of my actions.

It started out so harmless—a glass of wine in my and Jeffrey's favorite spot under the oak tree, watching the sunset. Then he was gone, and I found myself alone under that oak. Soon that one glass turned into two, then three, and eventually a whole bottle. More than once I've woken up in the middle of the night in that hard Adirondack chair, surrounded only by cicadas and bullfrogs. Jeffrey would be so disappointed to see what I have become.

I'm so embarrassed about this weekend. I was hungover and ended up ruining the evening, which has made it clear that I need to quit. I know that. Still, I have to be honest: I do not want to stop. I enjoy the forgetfulness and the deep sleep that drinking brings. It feels like medication to me. I don't know how to go on without it.

I'm not happy, but I fear that I may never be joyful again either.

And without joy, and without Jeffrey and my boys, I don't know if life is worth living.

Moira's sorrowful words lingered as her friends quietly wiped away the tears pooling in their eyes, the soft sounds of sniffles filling the warm room. One of the cats in Moira's lap stirred awake, meowing in frustration.

"Mo?" Nell's voice broke the silence.

Moira raised her finger and shook her head slightly to show she wasn't ready to talk yet. "I'm not sure what the rules are here,

Erin, but I think I have said enough tonight. We all have. Let's go to bed, okay? It's really late and we're all old . . . except for Erin," she said with a firm but gentle tone.

Moira wearily rose from her chair, and as she did, Dove and Pearl jumped to the floor. Nell, CK, Gemma, and Erin also stood up, and together they made their way up the staircase. When they reached the top of the landing, they exchanged hugs and said their good nights.

Moira walked slowly down the hallway to her room, the soft glow of the bedside lamp casting shadows on the eggshell-colored walls. Once her pets were inside the room with her, she gently closed the door and leaned against it for a moment as she took a deep breath. Her mind wandered back to earlier that evening when she tossed her cobbler, and the familiar dark, heavy shame pressed down on her again. The same shame she'd felt each time she'd woken up in the movie theater, her head spinning while she watched the VHS of her dancing with Jeffrey to Etta James on the parquet dance floor at their wedding reception. The same shame she felt when she hovered over a trash can in the middle of the night or felt aching in her back from passing out in the hard Adirondack chair. She shook her head, as if to physically shake the memories away, and walked into her bathroom, where she caught a glimpse of herself in the mirror. Her eyes were red from crying all night, and her face looked tired and worn. For once, she didn't look so beautiful.

In the other bedrooms on Allyson Island, all was quiet except for the noise in the women's minds. Nell lay in bed, staring at the ceiling and replaying the events of the long day. She silently spoke to the Lord, laying every burdensome thought at his feet.

In the shared room of Gemma and CK, CK sat on the edge of the bunk bed, checking the alarm app to make sure her home was armed while also trying to recall the details of each letter. She had so many questions about Tyler's affair, but she knew it wasn't the right time to ask Gemma to confide in her.

Gemma, usually full of humor, lay in the bunk opposite CK, gazing at Tyler's whereabouts on the location app. He was at Rebecca's apartment and had been for hours. Despite her typical joking demeanor, she felt a deep sadness and couldn't find it in her broken heart to crack any jokes.

Meanwhile, in the other room, Erin felt safe, unlike at her apartment, but still, she couldn't rest. She tried to escape the emotional weight of the night by playing solitaire on her cracked phone. It was past 1:00 a.m. when she received a text from Savannah Power, warning her that she would lose service if her bill wasn't paid by Monday.

"'Come Monday,'" she said, quietly echoing the lyrics Gemma had sung several times that evening.

Chapter 21

ON SUNDAY MORNING, the golden sunlight shone through the sheer curtains hanging over the tall windows and woke Nell. After going to the palm-leafed bathroom, she reached for her well-worn Bible in her bag next to the bed and slipped back under the warm covers. As she read from the book of Job, she thought about her church family, the families in her Sunday school class, who were so special to her, and sweet old Mrs. Conway, with her numerous costume bracelets that jingled like wind chimes in Nell's ear when she reached down to hug the petite lady. The bonds Nell had formed within Oglethorpe's walls were treasures she held close to her heart.

She missed being with her church family that morning, but that hadn't always been the case. As a child, she was forced to attend Sacred Heart Catholic Church every time the doors were open, so when she became an adult, she expressed her independence by sleeping in on Sunday mornings. When she married Chip and was expected to attend church with him, she rebelled against it because it felt like an obligation once again. Gradually, though, her mindset began to change. Church soon became a place that held her accountable and nurtured her faith. Nell started to realize that while one doesn't need to be inside a building to be a Christian, attending church with others—imperfect people in need of guidance—certainly helps. She wished Moira would come to this realization and return to Oglethorpe.

When she was done reading her Bible, Nell dressed in an over-size T-shirt and comfortable, stretchy leggings before grabbing a small pink and white gift bag and heading downstairs. There she found Erin sitting alone in her Pearl Jam T-shirt and pajama shorts at the breakfast table. Erin looked up from her cup of coffee and offered a faint smile.

"Good morning, friend," Nell said while she poured her own mug from the pot that Erin had made. She sat with her at the round wooden table and looked out the nook's windows to the fog settling over the confluence of the Ogeechee and the stream. "How'd you sleep?"

"Not very good, actually," Erin said. "I don't know how long I stayed awake. I just kept thinking. I couldn't turn off my mind. I felt like I do at night back at home. Restless."

Nell carefully sipped the scalding liquid and replied, "I didn't sleep well either."

"Hearing everyone's fears last night, I don't know." Erin drooped her shoulders beneath the faded T-shirt. "It all left me unsettled. I wish we'd talked about what we'd written down. Cleared the air, you know?"

"I have been thinking a lot about you, Erin," Nell said. "What you talked about reminded me of something Jesus mentioned in the Sermon on the Mount. He said, 'Blessed are the poor in spirit, for theirs is the kingdom of heaven,' and 'Blessed are the meek, for they will inherit the earth.' Basically, it's about how those who realize they need help and stay humble, even when things get tough, are blessed by God and will eventually receive his kingdom. Even though the poor and meek may not have had much to give Jesus when he walked the earth, that didn't matter. He just wanted their hearts, and that is still true today."

Erin blew the steam rising from her coffee mug. "I want to believe in the stuff you talk about, Nell—all the stuff you told me by the pool yesterday and how God has done all these great things in your life—but like I said last night, I don't want to get my hopes up and then find out this religion stuff doesn't work."

Nell answered, "I don't like the term *religion* because it can be associated with negativity and many attitudes that aren't Christlike. Instead of using the word *religion*, I like to say *relationship*. That's what I've told you about this weekend—my relationship with Jesus. Unlike human relationships, Jesus is incapable of letting us down. He is the one you can truly place your hope in because he embodies hope itself. I forget that sometimes, but it's the truth. He is our only source of hope."

Erin was still a bit unsure, but she promised herself she would dig into this more and see whether what Nell was saying actually held any truth.

"Let me tell you a little bit of the story about doubting Thomas," Nell began.

⌒

WHILE NELL AND Erin refilled their coffee cups and continued talking at the kitchen table, CK and Gemma entered Moira's room to find her standing at the balcony door and looking out over the morning fog. She was dressed in black leggings and a white jacket and neon running shoes, and her hair was in a messy ponytail.

"Happy birthday!" Gemma called out as they walked to Moira.

CK chimed in with her birthday greeting. They hugged one another, and Moira apologized for being sweaty.

"I haven't gone for a run all weekend. Figured I might as well start my fiftieth off right. It was good to get out there this morning."

"It's easy to get up early when you haven't been puking up pinot all night," Gemma teased.

"Enough with the vomit jokes," CK said as she took on her role as Gemma's adviser. "Either get some new material or be a little more sensitive."

"She'll never let me live this down, CK," Moira replied, gesturing for her friends to sit in the plaid chairs of the bedroom's sitting nook, which overlooked the beautiful backyard and the river in the distance. "So how did you all sleep?"

Gemma shrugged and CK responded, "We both tossed and turned all night."

"Those letters had us all tossing and turning, yeah?" Moira took a swig from her glass water bottle. Then she sat at the foot of her bed across from them. Both cats quietly and stealthily appeared, seemingly out of nowhere, and nuzzled against her legs.

Gemma scooted back in her chair and said, "Keep those furry assassins over there."

"Your letter." CK looked at Moira. "You're okay, aren't you?"

Mo let out a deep sigh. "Yeah, my letter did end on a dramatic note, didn't it? Very Meg Ryan–esque." She thought of the last line she had written, expressing her uncertainty about whether life was worth living. "I can't deny that some days I wonder if I'll ever feel whole again, but I'm going to be okay. I'm not okay yet, but I will be. I promise."

"You will be okay, Mo," Gemma assured her. "But you've got

to reach out to us when you're not." She pointed to herself and CK. "Please let us know if you're having a hard time. I know we're both hours away, but we're also just a call or text away. We have leaned on each other for years, and we can't stop now. I'm sure I can come up with some dark humor for whatever you're facing."

"I know," Moira replied with a smile. "I just don't want to burden you two."

CK interjected, "There are no burdens between friends."

"I'm glad to hear that, because I'll probably be going through a nasty divorce soon, and I'm sure there will be times when I call you screaming or crying or threatening to eat an entire lasagna on my own," Gemma said.

"Why didn't you call us screaming and crying and making dumb jokes sooner, Gemma?" Moira asked. "What you just told me about reaching out to you applies to you reaching out to us too, doesn't it?"

Gemma looked at her hands in her lap and said, "Just like you said, Mo. I didn't want to bother anyone with it."

"No more of that from any of us, okay? Iron sharpens iron, right? We have to tell each other what's going on. We need each other," CK said. "And you have us, Mo, but you also need to connect with people here too. That's why you should think about going back to church. Let those people love and support you in ways that Gemma and I can't. And what about Nell? I don't know the extent of what is going on between you two, but she's a gem. You need each other."

"I know." Moira nodded in agreement, and then she let out a deep, buried sigh. "It's been a good weekend."

"Not for your couch," Gemma said.

Moira and Celia Kate rolled their eyes and Moira said, "Thank you for coming. I've always been able to count on you two. I won't take that for granted again."

"You're just lucky I didn't have to hang drapes this weekend." Gemma smirked.

"Oh my goodness." Moira gasped and covered her face in embarrassment. "Last night while lying in bed I remembered what happened between me and Tabitha. I guess writing all that other stuff down unlocked my subconscious or something."

"Oh, what?" Gemma leaned in. "Did you throw up on her old curtains and she had to replace them?"

"In a way, I did," Moira admitted, removing her hands from her flushed face. "A few months back, she sent me pictures of her newly redecorated living room, and I had been drinking a bit too much when I saw them. You know what they say: a drunk man's words are a sober man's thoughts."

"Oh no, Mo. What did you say?" Celia Kate asked, biting her lip.

"I told her the new drapes looked like cigarettes. I mean, they were white on top and had a wide yellow trim at the bottom. That's why—that's why she said she had to hang new ones this weekend."

Gemma let out a loud, boisterous laugh and said, "I always liked that Tabitha. That's good."

"I don't know. It's kind of tacky," CK said while holding out her hand for the cats to come to her, but they refused to leave Moira's ankles.

"Celia Kate, does your nose ever bleed from taking the high road all the time?" Gemma rolled her dark eyes.

The trio rose from their seats to go downstairs for breakfast, and Gemma paused mid-step and said, "Oh yeah. One more thing. That birthday gift we gave you when we arrived on Friday?" She flinched. "It's a bottle of wine."

"We didn't realize . . . well . . ." Celia Kate shrugged awkwardly.

"Just take it back home with y'all. One of Erin's jobs tomorrow will be to clean out the bar." The very thought of that made Moira anxious, but she pushed the uneasy feeling aside and decided to deal with it later.

They left Moira's room and walked down the staircase together, closely followed by the long-haired cats that playfully pranced behind them. The house, although large and grand, felt cozy and welcoming, with the promise of a new day ahead.

When they entered the kitchen, they found Nell and Erin sitting at the table in a stream of sunlight, and the rich aroma of freshly brewed coffee filled the air.

Nell and Erin greeted Moira by singing "Happy Birthday" and stood up from their chairs to give her hugs. Moira then went into the pantry and grabbed a large white box of Antonio's homemade breakfast pastries, with "Sunday Morning" scrawled in marker across the top. She placed the box on the table, along with a jug of orange juice next to the coffee that Erin had already prepared. They all commented on how Antonio's chocolate-drizzled biscotti and sugar-dusted bomboloni were too beautiful to eat.

"Mimosas were on the menu for breakfast this morning. Who am I kidding? Mimosas have been a part of my breakfast every day for months." She pinched off a piece of the fluffy Italian donut and placed it in her mouth. As she glanced around, she realized that her house was stocked with the finest wines and liquors, items she had always considered to be signs of sophistication, not dependency.

Moira looked at Nell and said, "I want to apologize to you. I have pushed you away and treated you unfairly because I felt like you were judging me. My anger came from my pride and my refusal to accept that I could be wrong. I have been playing the victim—the widow who deserves a drink now and then. That's how it all started, and it snowballed from there. You loved me enough to call me out multiple times, Nell. You didn't give up on me; you didn't raise your voice when I raised mine at you, and you even showed up this weekend when you certainly didn't have to. You are a precious person, and I'm truly thankful for you."

Nell nodded in appreciation at the apology and said, "I got this for you." She picked up the small pink and white bag that was sitting near her tennis shoes on the hand-scraped hardwood floor.

"It's a devotional specifically for widows. The title, *Cry Out for the Widow*, comes from Isaiah 1:17, where the people are instructed to plead with God on behalf of the widow. I haven't pleaded with God on your behalf the way I should have, and I owe you an apology for that."

"That is a beautiful gift," Celia Kate remarked. "I know I haven't pleaded for you the way I should have either, Mo."

Moira sniffed back tears. "Thank you, ladies, for your prayers. And thank you for this devotional, Nell. It's exactly what I need." She examined the book with a floral cover in her hands.

"So Nell gave you a devotional and we gave you a twenty-five-ounce bottle of temptation. Yikes!" Gemma growled and popped a bite of the sugary dough into her mouth while the group chuckled.

"At least they got you *something*, Moira. I want to apologize for coming empty-handed," Erin said, her cheeks flushed with embarrassment as she fidgeted with the hem of her T-shirt. She looked down, unable to meet Moira's eyes, her voice quiet. "I just didn't have the extra cash this month to—"

"Stop that," Moira said, cutting her off. She reached out and placed her hand on top of Erin's, which rested on the table. "There's no need for that apology. Being here this weekend was the gift I needed."

"We've talked, we've written letters, we've been open books, and now we all know each other's problems, so what do we do about it? I'm scared of this, and you're scared of that, but what's the solution?" Celia Kate asked, her tone vulnerable as she wrapped her fingers around her warm ceramic mug.

"Pray," Nell said firmly and with conviction. "Plead. For each other. For ourselves. There's power when we share our burdens with each other, but even more so when we share them with our God."

"Nell, would you mind doing that over us now? Just . . . pray for us?" CK asked while the others silently nodded in agreement.

Without hesitation, they joined hands on top of the round table, fingers interlaced among the clutter of coffee cups, juice glasses, and sweet Italian pastries. Nell began the prayer with heartfelt thanks for the precious time they were able to spend together, for the bonds of their friendship, and even for their struggles. "Thank you for our trials, Lord," she said, her voice steady and soothing. "For it is through these challenges that we draw closer to each other and to you."

As Nell continued to call on the God of the universe, she couldn't stop the tears that fell from her green eyes, a release of pent-up worries and anxieties. A warmth seemed to wrap around each woman like a comforting blanket. It was supernatural how the room, which had been filled the night before with shared fears and sadness, was now bursting with a sense of hope, joy, and peace.

Chapter 22

Artist Rober Becker's weathered white van pulled into Moira's driveway right on time at 10:30 a.m. He stepped out wearing splattered striped overalls and stretched his long arms overhead. In his late sixties, Rober possessed a unique charm that set him apart. He wore flip-flops year-round, and his shaggy white hair cascaded over his forehead, matching the wildness of his equally unruly beard.

Rober's business, Monet on the Move, was quite popular in the area, and he was well-known in Savannah not only for his artistic talents but also for his warm and inviting spirit. Through his work, he found a renewed sense of purpose after the loss of his beloved wife and fellow artist, Gertie. He carried her memory with him to every gig in town and infused it into every brushstroke. Before Gertie passed away, the eccentric duo had spent their lives in the workshop behind their home in the swamp, creating beautiful abstract art that adorned residences along the Georgia coast.

One notable piece, a large blue and white seascape painting, hung on Jeffrey's office wall in the Allyson home—the same office that had remained untouched and sealed off since his death, with his pens and papers still scattered on the mahogany desk, just as they were the last time he sat there. Rober was also responsible for the oversized watercolor of Moira's feathered friend, the great heron, which decorated the wall of the pool house.

"Moira, my love!" Rober called as he entered the courtyard garden on Allyson Island. The space was filled with lush greenery, vines, and ivy, complemented by the sultry and sweet smell of creamy-colored gardenias. A fountain stood at the center of the garden, surrounded by brick pavers and a bed of thriving hosta plants. "Are those gardenias I see blooming in late September? This truly is paradise!"

"Let me help you," Moira said, reaching out to take a stack of twelve-by-sixteen blank canvases from Rober's tanned, wrinkled hands.

"Happy birthday, dear woman!" He placed a satchel of paints down on a wrought iron bench and greeted Moira with a kiss on the cheek. "I assume these are your lovely friends?" He looked at each woman standing nearby and offered them warm smiles. "I hope you all are wearing your subpar clothing, yes?" He eyed their casual outfits. "Still, I have smocks. Moira, be a dear." He pointed to a frayed army duffel bag that he had dropped onto the soft green grass.

The women fastened the clean but paint-stained smocks over their clothes while Rober set up easels in a semicircle around the picturesque garden and explained that they would all be painting the same subject in their own unique interpretation: the grand old three-tiered fountain.

Moira had almost stayed home that humid Saturday morning they found the fountain, probably fifteen years before, but Jeffrey lured her out with the promise of antiques and a café au lait from the little shop downtown that she loved. They found the fountain at the back of the estate sale, half swallowed by unruly wisteria.

It was three levels of weathered limestone, streaked with rust and green moss clinging to the nicks and grooves. It stood nearly six feet tall, topped with a cupid that looked more sorrowful than sweet, with its eyes downcast and one hand resting on an urn from which water poured. Moira thought it looked like it had come straight from Bonaventure Cemetery, and she froze the moment she saw it. Jeffrey grinned at her, knowing how much she loved it. They had walked slowly around the fountain while Moira ran her fingers over the chipped edge of the bottom bowl.

It took two men, a dolly, and a borrowed trailer to get it home. They placed it right in the center of the courtyard, beneath the crepe myrtle that turned the air pink in the summertime. Jeffrey even ran the plumbing himself, and after buying a book on plumbing at the hardware store, breaking two pipes, and swearing a blue streak, he finally brought the fountain bubbling to life.

The first night it ran, they dragged their kids and their lawn chairs out and sat under the stars to listen to the water spill from tier to tier in a steady rhythm. Brent and Bradford pressed their ears to the stone base like they were listening to the ocean in a conch shell.

"It sounds like old Savannah," Moira murmured.

Jeffrey agreed and placed his warm hand on hers. "It is old Savannah, Mo. It just happens to be in our backyard."

⸻

GEMMA WAS AT her easel, fiddling with the smock tightly knotted at her waist, as she frowned at the blank canvas. "I can't even draw a straight line," she muttered quietly, her gaze wandering to the intricate designs of the water feature.

On the other end of the semicircle, Erin was transforming her canvas with bold, confident strokes of her brush. Each movement was skilled, capturing the way the Sunday-morning light danced on the water flowing from one limestone tier to another.

Nell noticed Erin's talent, leaned in, and said, "Hey, that is really good."

"Yes, very good," Rober said, joining the conversation. "I see what you're trying to capture here. You have a nice eye." He pinched his chin between his first finger and thumb as he analyzed her easel.

"CK's son could help you set up an online shop like he did for his sister. Extra cash would be good, wouldn't it?" Nell continued after Rober shuffled across the garden to look at Celia Kate's work.

Erin shrugged and said, "Extra cash is always good. I'll think about it."

Moira, who was at the easel next to Erin, overheard their conversation. The pool house caught her eye and an idea began to form in her mind. Without taking the time to consider the pros and cons, she turned to Erin and asked, "What would you think about moving into the pool house? There would be no rent and no electricity bills, free room and board."

Everyone in the garden ceased their conversations and paused their paint strokes. The only sound that filled the air was the gentle trickling of water. Even Rober, who was beginning his own painting of the fountain, turned his head to Moira to listen in.

Erin stared at Moira, shocked and confused. "Moira, that is— that is too much. I mean, why would you do that?"

"Why not?" Moira asked. "I have an extra bedroom, an extra house, just sitting there not being used. That's a shame."

"I couldn't," Erin replied, shaking her head firmly before she turned her gaze back to the canvas of color.

"Why not, Erin? It would be—" Moira began, but Rober interrupted.

"Ladies? I would hate for our time together to end and you still weren't done with your art. Focus on the task at hand, *s'il vous plait!*"

Moira, in a hushed tone, like a child who'd just been scolded by an elementary school teacher, said to Erin, "We'll talk more on this later." And she shifted her eyes back to the grand fountain.

For the next half hour, the women worked in silence, broken only by the calming sound of water trickling from tier to tier. Rober moved slowly among them, offering whispered directions and encouragement. When he gave Gemma a vague compliment, saying, "Nice technique," she replied, "Rober, you are a lovely man, but you're also a liar. We both know this looks more like a first grader's version of a crashed spaceship than an elegant water feature."

Rober's hearty laugh filled the garden and spilled over the box hedge border as he shouted, "I like you!" He patted her on the back and added, "However, I would say this is more akin to the work of a kindergartner."

When the time was up, the women gathered together, holding their unique canvases, while Rober snapped multiple pictures with his antique camera, framing them against the backdrop of the impressive fountain. After capturing the final shot, the hippie artist shook each woman's hand firmly and leaned in to kiss Moira lightly on the cheek. He then busied himself loading his van with supplies, wearing a contented smile and humming to himself.

He waved out the window as his van disappeared down the shaded cobblestone driveway, and the sound of another vehicle approaching could be heard. Antonio's catering van soon appeared and parked in the spot Rober had just vacated. He excitedly hopped out of the vehicle and greeted Moira with a warm embrace, his bright white teeth gleaming against his tanned face as he wished her a happy birthday.

"What's for lunch, Antonio?" Gemma asked, her "*Elementary Spaceship*, on canvas" tucked under her arm.

"It's a surprise, Mrs. Gemma, but I promise it's *molto bene!*" he exclaimed, waving his hands around wildly with excitement as he and Renata entered the kitchen.

"Why don't we get our things together while they prepare lunch?" CK suggested, looking at Gemma.

"That's a good idea," she replied. "That way we can hit the road as soon as we're done eating. Mo, where's your burn pile?" Gemma asked, holding up her painting.

The group laughed.

"You can just leave it in your room. I'll find a place to hang it around here," Mo promised.

"It would look good hanging in a garbage can," Gemma joked as she entered the French doors at the back of the house, followed by CK and Nell.

"Erin, wait." Moira gently tugged at her arm. "Let's go look at the pool house."

"I just don't know if that's a good idea, Moira," Erin replied. "PJ and I wouldn't want to impose—"

"Would I have offered it if I thought it would be an imposition? Now, come on," she said, pulling on Erin's soft gray Coastal Cleaning Co. T-shirt.

They walked along the soft green grass, passing the pool and the courtyard where they had just painted, and approached the quaint building that resembled a beachside cottage. As they stepped onto the smooth slate floors, they were greeted by the smell of essential oils that Kaylee had diffused during the spa treatments the day before.

"Now, you know there's only one bedroom." Moira pointed to the double doors on the far wall. "But this couch"—she tapped on one of the velvety tan cushions in the main living area—"folds out into a bed. And it's not one of those uncomfortable sofa beds with the rod in your back all night. MerryLee slept on it and couldn't even gripe about it the next day. My crabby sister-in-law not complaining about something . . . well, that is a miracle in itself! Would it be okay for PJ?"

Erin looked around at the luxury surrounding her: the beautifully decorated space, the view of the calm water, and the enormous oak tree hanging over a row of wooden Adirondack chairs visible through the floor-to-ceiling windows. Suddenly, she turned to Moira, and tears started streaming down her cheeks without warning. She leaned in and wrapped her arms around her boss, who quickly pulled her into a comforting embrace. In that moment, Erin was overwhelmed by gratitude and found herself speechless.

As Moira held her vulnerable friend, she was reminded of cradling her own boys during thunderstorms and comforting them when nightmares woke them from deep sleep. She realized she should have held them like this when their father passed away. No one is ever too old or too strong to be held.

"Is this a yes?" Mo laughed and pulled away before she wiped the tears from Erin's face in a motherly way. "You're free to come and go as you please. You won't be any bother to me. You make this place your home, a space for you and your boy."

Erin cleared the knot from her throat and struggled to form words. "Moira, I just can't thank you enough. I won't have to sleep with one eye open like I do at the apartment. There were three break-ins last week."

"Unless you're scared of herons, I think you'll sleep just fine out here. And you can thank me by quitting your job at Family Pantry." Mo squeezed Erin's thin shoulders.

"Oh, I don't know if I can do that," Erin replied and shook her head. Then she wiped her damp cheeks again.

"Why would you stay there? What's your take-home pay? Enough for the rent? Well, you don't have rent anymore. You can't continue to work there. It's too dangerous."

Erin gasped. "Moira, I know you offered to let PJ and me stay here for free, but I won't let you do that. We don't take handouts. We never have. We will pay our way."

Moira paused for a moment before suggesting, "Okay, then. PJ can help me out around here. My boys aren't here to do it, and the boat dock has some boards that need to be replaced. Now that I'm an old widow, I could really use some help keeping the ivy vine and wisteria under control—pulling weeds and working the gardens and that kind of thing. I was going to hire someone to pressure wash the house and drive next spring. He could do that too." She smiled.

"Whatever you need around here, Moira. He'd earn his keep. He's always been a hard worker." Erin sniffled and then glanced out the window. While staring at the oak leaves swaying in the marsh breeze, she thought out loud, "This would help me save enough to catch up on PJ's payments for school. I could get the car fixed. Pay what I owe the dentist and—" She stopped when the tears began to fall again.

"I know you're appreciative, Erin, but it's my honor to do this for you," Moira replied as they hugged once more.

Erin was truly grateful for Moira's kindness. However, she realized that by accepting the offer, she would also be doing Moira a favor. Her and PJ's full-time presence on Allyson Island would help ease the loneliness that had been weighing on Moira since Jeffrey passed away.

Chapter 23

THE TRANQUILITY OF the late morning was suddenly disrupted when CK's phone rang on top of the chest of drawers. She stepped out of the bathroom, where she had been packing her toiletry bag, and answered the call. Sophie's anxious voice came across the line. "Mom, my stomach is hurting so bad! I looked on the internet and think I have appendicitis!"

CK's heart pounded as she began to pace the bedroom. "Sophie, baby, where does it hurt, honey?"

"What's going on?" Gemma asked while attempting to zip her overflowing suitcase.

"Lower right quadrant, Mom! Lower right quadrant!" the little girl groaned.

"Put your dad on the phone!" CK frantically searched the room for her wristlet with her keys attached to the strap. She said to Gemma, "We have to go now. Sophie's appendix is—"

Suddenly, Celia Kate could not speak. Her mind was clouded with images of her beautiful, dark-haired little Sophie in a hospital bed, a faceless doctor in a white coat speaking in hushed, concerned tones about sepsis and emergency surgery. Her heart was about to pound out of her chest, and her vision went blurry. The pink and green bedroom spun around her. Celia Kate gasped for air while Gemma rushed to her side.

"Hey, sis. Breathe with me. In and out. Slow and steady."
Gemma gently took her by the arm and stood close to her. "Let's
sit down."

"No!" CK shouted and wrestled against Gemma. "We have
to go. We have to get home. Sophie is sick. If her appendix rup-
tures . . . sepsis. She could—"

Gemma interrupted by gently saying, "Give me the phone.
Let me find out what's going on." She pulled the small rectangle
from CK's white-knuckle grip and pressed the speakerphone button while CK rapidly took in air.

Sean's voice interrupted the panicked scene with a casual,
"Hello?"

"Sean! Why haven't you taken her to the emergency room
yet?" CK shouted into the phone that Gemma was holding while
CK continued to frantically search through the blankets on the
bed for her keys. "What are you thinking? Get her there now! Or
call an ambulance!"

"Call an ambulance for gas?" he asked. "That is dramatic, even
for you, Celia Kate."

"Gas? Her appendix is about to rupture!" Spit flew from her
lips when she shouted.

"Okay, okay, calm down." Gemma lightly touched CK's arm
and then asked calmly, "Sean, what's happening there?"

"Sophie has gas. The kid put down two beef burritos and half
a container of chunky guac after church."

"From Tortilla Town or El Patio?" Gemma asked while she
picked at her nails.

Sean grunted. "Do you even have to ask?"

"El Poot-o?" Gemma laughed. "You know, that's why the seats
outside in the courtyard are always taken. Inside it smells like—"

"Sean!" CK angrily interrupted their banter. "She said her appendix was hurting! The lower right side of her stomach? Is that where the pain is? Is it worse when she coughs? When it's pressed?"

Gemma handed the phone back to CK and continued working on the stuck suitcase zipper.

"Honey, do you know why Sophie thinks she needs an appendectomy? Because our kids can't fart without thinking they have a debilitating disease. You have talked about rupturing appendixes since Silas had colic. You've rushed our kids to the emergency room for mosquito bites, heat rashes, skinned knees—"

"Tucker's kneecap was hanging off, Sean! What was I supposed to do? Tape it back on?" Celia Kate defended herself and then sat down on the bed.

"Sophie is fine. The pain isn't even in her lower right quadrant, I promise. There's nothing to worry about. She has gas, CK. She's okay."

CK remained quiet for several moments, steadying her breath while her mind raced.

"Babe? Are you there? Did you hear me? Sophie is fine."

"I have done this to them, haven't I?" she asked her husband.

Gemma glanced at her quickly before returning her attention to the bags on the made bed.

"Done what?" he asked.

"I have made them terrified." She stared past Gemma and out the window, focusing on the top of a palm tree. "I have unleashed all my anxieties and worries onto them. I have made them a mess."

Sean sighed. "No, CK, you— Our kids are fine," he said. "I shouldn't have said all of that. She started searching for stuff on the internet and that's when she got worried. This isn't your fault."

"Isn't it?" she asked in a low voice laced with guilt.

"No, it really isn't. Listen to me. Sophie is fine. Don't worry about a thing here at home. Enjoy the rest of the afternoon with Mo and your friends, and we'll see you tonight, okay?"

"Yeah."

"Silas is going to make supper for us, and Tucker is helping me clean the house before you get home. Chipper Jones is purring on the couch, and Sophie will be fine as soon as she lets a big one rip."

"Wait a minute. Silas is doing what?" She looked at Gemma in shock.

"He's going to make supper for us tonight. I taught him how to work the grill, and he's ready to man it on his own. We've already got chicken marinating, and he said he's making scalloped potatoes. Oh, some of your ranch and bacon pasta too. We love you and we'll see you soon. And don't let Gemma Earnhardt take the wheel!"

"That's Mrs. Gemma Earnhardt to you!" she called before Sean hung up the phone.

"Silas is making supper. Humph." CK tossed the phone onto the bed.

"The kid can't even boil water, huh? Can't take care of himself? He may starve?" Gemma teased as she sat next to her friend on the bed and took her hand. "What's going on in your mind right now?"

CK shook her head. "I've made my kids neurotic, haven't I? My daughter just needs to fart, but she thinks she's dying. That's my fault. They've picked up on my fears and adopted them as their own. I'm the reason they'll all need therapy."

"Celia Kate, stop talking like that. I have eaten enough El Patio to know that, while it's delicious, it can make you feel like you're about to give birth to an alien baby. I'm not at all surprised that she freaked out," Gemma said with a smile.

"Sheer panic. That is what I felt. You, on the other hand, love my kids like they're your own, but you stayed rational. Why didn't I? Why didn't I calmly ask more questions before picturing my child being rushed down a hallway on a gurney with a ruptured appendix and sepsis, with me pacing in an ICU? I felt faint. I thought I was going to pass out. I was that scared," CK said, beginning to cry.

Gemma wrapped her arm around CK and pulled her close. CK rested her head on Gemma's soft shoulder, and they sat in comfortable silence. After a few minutes, Gemma began to whisper a prayer, echoing Nell's earlier words about trust, faith, and being anxious for nothing. CK slowed her breathing and focused on the comforting words Gemma spoke. By the time Gemma concluded with "Amen," CK's heart rate had returned to normal.

Chapter 24

EVERYONE'S BAGS HAD been packed and placed by the front door in preparation for heading back to their homes. But first, they gathered in the kitchen for one last lunch together. Antonio had arranged a spread of chicken salad on buttery croissants alongside an elaborate charcuterie board topped with homemade potato chips, dips, and pickles. The centerpiece on the marble countertop was a two-tiered chocolate birthday cake, crowned with fresh strawberries, elegantly displayed on a gleaming crystal cake stand.

Moira and her friends moved down the buffet line at the kitchen island, filling their pink and blue floral ceramic plates before sitting together at the table. A sweet silence settled over them as they enjoyed their meal. Through the row of tall kitchen windows, the September sun shone brightly on the Ogeechee River.

As Erin ate her lunch, she gazed at the charming white brick pool house in the corner of the yard, feeling a rush of excitement knowing it would soon be her new home.

"Well, Mo," Gemma said, breaking the quiet before popping a plump grape into her mouth with a satisfied crunch, "fifty looks fantastic on you, but of course, we knew it would."

A chorus of agreement filled the kitchen.

"This weekend has been nothing short of amazing, Mo. The delicious food, the friendship, the laughter, and even the tears—it has all been just wonderful," CK added with a warm smile.

"Hear, hear!" Nell exclaimed as she lifted her glass of sweet tea, a wedge of lemon sinking to the bottom. The ladies clinked their glasses together in a celebratory toast. While they continued to enjoy their lunch and reflect on the weekend, Antonio and Renata were busy loading their catering van in the driveway. When they returned inside, Moira and her friends praised them for the delicious recipes from the weekend. Renata offered to take photos of the ladies posing with the beautiful birthday cake before it was sliced.

After Antonio and Renata left and the last piece of cake had been enjoyed and plates cleared, Celia Kate noticed the time on the clock on the stove and sighed. "Gemma, I think it's time for us to head out. Weekend traffic is going to be a nightmare, I'm sure."

"Yeah, you're right," Gemma said as they both stood from the table. The two women headed to the foyer, where their suitcases were waiting, and sounds of cheerful camaraderie followed them.

Moira turned to Gemma, concern clear in her eyes. "What do you think you'll do about Tyler? We never discussed it."

Gemma grabbed one of her bags and bobbed her shoulders. "I thought about it all night, and I'm still not sure yet. It's going to take time and prayer. I'm most concerned about Carolina and how her parents splitting up her senior year will affect her, but I also know Tyler doesn't love me, and he sure doesn't respect me, and he isn't interested in working on our marriage. It's not good for her to continue living in a household with a man who treats his wife like garbage. Right now I can't answer your question, but I'm committed to praying about it. I need wisdom and clarity."

"Then that's what we'll all pray for you," Nell said.

"You've been a good wife. And you're a good mother," Moira added.

"You are too, Moira," Gemma said. "Don't tell yourself otherwise, okay?"

Moira shrugged her shoulders, not fully believing the words.

"It's going to work out, right?" Gemma said as she pulled another heavy bag onto her shoulder. A drip of paint had missed her smock and left a small green dot on her beige top, just beside the bag's strap. "And I'm going to lose weight, to prove Tyler wrong, and to prove Dr. Dempsey wrong too."

"You have always found great satisfaction in proving people wrong." Moira looked to CK and said with a smile, "Remember when Jake Martin and Buddy Dalton said Gemma would never make the cheerleading squad? They were sure mistaken."

CK nodded with remembrance, and Gemma added, "Well, it wasn't a mistake when I let my baton slip and hit Jake Martin right between the eyes."

"I see ol' Baton Brow at church every week. He's still got the scar," CK said as they all laughed. "So who do we want to be when we come back to Allyson Island next year for Moira's fifty-first birthday? I thought about this while I was tossing and turning and listening to Gemma toss and turn all night. I want to be a woman of more faith and less fear, without her phone glued to her hand and her nerves on edge."

Gemma shifted the large carry-on that was boring into her

shoulder and said, "I want to lose 350 pounds—250 of that being Tyler Gardner."

"I'm with you, CK," Nell agreed. "More faith, less fear. Less doubting and worrying, and more fully trusting in God's plan and will, even if it doesn't line up with my own."

"Amen," CK replied. "Erin, what about you? What do you want when you come back next year?"

"Financial stability," she said confidently. "No debt. It's possible now, with Moira's help." She smiled at her boss, her friend. "What about you, Mo?"

"I want to be sober." Moira's words hung in the air.

"Then that is what's going to happen for all of us. With the Lord's help and with each other's. We're going to stay in touch, hold each other accountable, pray for each other, plead"—CK looked to Moira—"for the widow. That is the kind of friend I want to be. That is the kind of friend I need."

After one last hug, CK and Gemma walked out the wooden front door and into the warm sun that was beaming onto the front porch. As they descended the tall stairs, Gemma complained about the weight of her luggage, prompting CK to fuss at her for bringing so much. When they reached the bottom of the steps, Gemma looked back at Moira, Erin, and Nell, who were standing on the porch, and rolled her eyes while CK continued to tease her. The rolling suitcases bumped noisily behind them on the brick driveway. Soon they disappeared around the side of the house where CK's SUV was parked.

"They're fun, aren't they?" Moira giggled.

Erin turned to Moira with a grateful smile. "I guess I should get going too. I can't thank you enough, Moira, for this weekend and for your offer to let me stay here. PJ will be so excited, and thankful as well. I can't believe how perfect the timing is. Our lease at the apartment is up next month, and I'm so glad I don't have to renew it. I just can't thank you enough—"

"Erin, you really don't have to keep thanking me," Moira interrupted, smiling. "I'll see you bright and early in the morning. We've got a lot of bottles to pour out."

"That sounds like a plan. I'll take care of all the linens and dishes tomorrow too. You enjoy the day. Don't lift a finger," she said before hugging Moira tightly. She grabbed her duffel bag from the porch floor and soon disappeared around the side of the house, where her beat-up hatchback was parked.

This left Moira and Nell alone on the wide porch that housed multiple rocking chairs and terra-cotta pots of trailing sweet potato vine and impatiens. Moira looked at her friend and asked, "Nell, do you think you could stay for a while? Do you have anywhere you need to be?"

Nell shook her head. "No, I'll be glad to stay for a bit."

Moira quickly brewed a fresh pot of coffee, and she and Nell walked out the back door, crossing the soft grass to reach the Adirondack chairs in the shade of the live oak tree. Moira ran her hand across a chair, disturbing the dust and pollen that had settled on it.

"What a beautiful spot," Nell said while gripping her mug and gazing out over the water. The wind rustled the moss that clung to the twisted branches of the tree and the leathery, yellow-green fern leaves that crawled along the trunk. "I believe Chip and I sat out here with you and Jeffrey one evening after dinner?"

"Yes," Moira remembered with a smile. "The night I overcooked the leg of lamb. It was like chewing on a tire."

A blue heron landed in the far corner of the yard, near the

spot where the stream joined the Ogeechee River. Moira quietly pointed it out to Nell. They admired the majestic bird, perched gracefully on the grass, with the marsh providing a picturesque backdrop.

"I remember being out on the marsh with my daddy when I was a little girl, and he told me that the blue coloring on the bird represents calmness, peace, and harmony. The white stripe down its back symbolizes purity, while the bird's black beak represents strength and determination." Nell chuckled. "Of course, my dad was probably drunk when he told me that, but it sounds good, doesn't it?" They both laughed, the tension between them easing.

"Yeah, it does. I'll have to tell Erin that. Rober did that water-color painting of the heron hanging in the pool house. Maybe when she looks at it, she'll think about those things."

"It was so good-hearted of you to offer her the place, Mo." Nell took a sip of coffee.

"Oh, it's nothing," Moira said. "I'm just glad someone will be out there. It was Jeffrey's idea to turn it into both a pool house and a guesthouse. He intended it to be a suite for Mama to live in one day." She paused for a moment. "You know, I'm thankful my mother hasn't been here to see how I've reacted to his death. When Daddy died, she mourned with quiet dignity, like a lady—wearing dark clothes and bowing her head in prayer at her bedside night after night. She didn't dance on a coffee table at a Sunday school party or hug a trash can or pass out on the couch. I've certainly been an embarrassment to her and to our family name."

"I think if your mama had been here, she would have loved you just the same. Mine too," Nell said. "Unconditionally."

"I hope so," Moira said on an exhale. "Anyway, I also asked

Erin to stay there for the same reason I asked you to stay with me for a little while today," Mo admitted.

"Why is that?"

"I wanted you to stay because I didn't want to be in this house alone. I'm afraid if I'm alone, I will drink. Honestly, I could use one right now."

Nell said with empathy, "I get that."

Moira thought of the outdoor bar on the covered porch only a hundred or so yards behind her, a whitewashed brick structure with a black hanging sconce that made the bottles of liquor on the marble top sparkle enticingly.

"Oglethorpe hosts Celebrate Recovery meetings every Sunday night. I've shared my testimony with the group several times, and there is such a sweet and encouraging spirit in those meetings. If you'd like to join me, I would be happy to go with you," Nell offered.

Moira sipped from the hot ceramic mug and said, "I'll think about it."

"What better time to start than on your birthday?" Nell smiled.

Moira hesitated. "Maybe next Sunday. Tonight I just want to eat cake and watch home movies with the cats. Bradford and Brent might call."

"You just told me that you don't want to be alone. You won't be if—" Nell stopped when she realized Moira's excuses were driven by her fear of taking the first real step toward change. Refraining from pushing further, Nell said, "Okay, just let me know when you're ready."

"I want to apologize to you again, Nell, for being so angry and prideful," Moira began, but Nell interrupted her by holding up her hand.

"Forgiven and forgotten. Quit picking up what you've already laid down. Amen?"

Moira bobbed her head in agreement, thankful for Nell's grace. They sat quietly while the leaves rustled and egrets squawked in the distance.

"Jeffrey and I spent a lot of time here." Moira leaned her blonde head against the tall wooden slats of the chair. "I hauled these other chairs down here from the patio for us all to sit in after our walk on Saturday morning," She referred to the matching Adirondacks on either side of her and Nell. "But I was upstairs drinking headache powder and using eye drops instead."

Nell remained quiet and watched a swarm of flies hovering over the cordgrass.

"That was my plan, anyway. Jeffrey and I made a lot of plans right here in these chairs. I remember my mother saying, whenever her intentions fell through, that we may make our plans but God has the last word. I guess I didn't realize the truth in that until Jeffrey died."

"His will is best," Nell added. "Even when it's hard, when we don't understand it. His plan is good, simply because he is good. I know it. I believe it. And still, I sometimes forget it."

"I'm still trying to find the good in my husband's death," Moira confessed before looking to her friend in desperation. "I don't know if I can."

Nell sat in silence with her grieving friend before Moira muttered, "I miss my boys, Nell."

Nell turned slightly in her chair and looked at Moira.

"You mentioned a moment ago our mothers' unconditional love. I worry that I have embarrassed my sons, and I don't know if they love me unconditionally anymore. I haven't spoken to either of them in weeks. They don't come home for long weekends, and they rarely reply to my texts in a timely manner. Sometimes they don't respond at all. We used to be so close, but over the past year and a half, I feel like I've lost them. The thought of it makes me sick."

"Because of the drinking?" Nell asked gently.

Moira nodded. "They have seen me at my worst. In the first few months after Jeffrey died, they showed me grace and understood how deeply I was grieving. But my grace period with them ended a while ago."

"You will get them back, Mo. When they see the effort you're putting in and your commitment to stay sober for them, you will get them back. My daddy got me back, and even when I didn't like him very much because of his actions and his addiction, I still loved him. It's the same with Tate, Taylor, and me. I embarrassed them so much with my drunken ramblings on social media and my silly behavior when they had friends over, but they never gave up on me. We're as close as ever," Nell assured her. "Your boys may seem distant right now, but they still love you, Mo. You are their mother—the same mother in all those beautiful memories framed all over your house. You have not lost them, not for good. I promise you that."

Moira stopped the tears before they streamed down her cheeks and said, "I hope so."

"I was telling Erin this morning the story of Thomas in the Bible. You remember it?" Nell asked.

"Doubting Thomas?"

"Yeah." Nell nodded. "He heard that Jesus had risen from the dead, but he still doubted it had happened. And he spent over a week doubting. But finally, Jesus appeared to him and told him to touch the wounds on his hands. You see that? Thomas had to reach out. He had to take action, effort. He reached out, placed his finger where the nails had been, and immediately, Thomas knew. His doubt was gone, and he worshiped the Lord. But he had to reach out. You've got to do your part, Mo. We all do."

"I will," Moira said. "I will."

They looked at the marsh stretched out in front of them. The air seemed even thicker now with the smell of salt and earth, and a few egrets silently stalked the shallow water. A breeze stirred the moss hanging in long veils from the branches above them, swaying like it was alive and breathing.

Moira looked at Nell, whose red hair was pulled into a messy ponytail that bobbed slightly as she leaned back and took a sip from her chipped mug, and said, "I know it sounds ridiculous, but I saw a light in my room one night last summer. It was just . . . there. Like a flash, but soft and quiet. And I felt . . . I don't know quite how to explain it. Contentment, I guess. The kind I didn't have to earn or chase after. It just settled on me, and then it was gone."

Nell smiled. "You already know what I think it probably was. What do you think?"

Moira scoffed lightly, but not with conviction. "You think God's in the business of indoor light shows?"

"I think he's in the business of meeting people right where they are," Nell said, soft but certain.

Moira closed her eyes for a second. "I wasn't drinking, surprisingly. That's what has stuck with me. I didn't have a drop that night. I was just lying there, completely sober and thinking about how I used to be someone's wife. How I used to matter to someone."

Nell reached for her mug resting on the Adirondack arm as she said, "You still matter. And maybe that light was the Lord telling you just that. That he sees you and that you're not forgotten. Maybe he knew, in that moment, you would believe a flash of light more than a whisper in your heart."

Moira didn't respond right away. She looked out at the marsh instead, blinking faster now to keep back tears. She finished her last swallow of coffee and asked, "You think it'll come back?"

"Maybe," Nell said, "but even if it doesn't, you saw it once. Maybe that's all it took."

The wind moved through the moss again, quiet and soft. The sun was setting a little lower now, warming their shoulders. For the next hour, the two women rekindled their friendship on the edge of the marsh, both trying, in their own way, to believe in light.

They finally moved inside to Moira's kitchen, where they finished off the leftover pastries dusted with sugar. When their stomachs were full and the coffeepot was empty, Moira noticed Nell check the gold and silver watch on her wrist.

"It's getting late, Nell. You can go. I'm sorry for keeping you this long," Moira said as she pushed the cats off her lap and stood up, her bare feet touching the floor.

"I really don't want to leave you," Nell began.

"Honestly, I'm okay," Moira replied. She gathered the empty coffeepot and plates from the table and walked to the sink. "I'm going to keep myself busy for the rest of the afternoon. I might go for another run to work off that birthday cake and the leftover bomboloni."

"You won't hesitate to call me if you need anything, will you? Why don't we go ahead and pour out those bottles now, while I'm still here?" Nell suggested.

"No, I'm fine, really," Moira replied as she walked her friend to the front door, where Nell's luggage was still sitting.

"I'm committed to praying for you. Maybe I'll see you next Sunday?" Nell asked hopefully as she grabbed her bags and Moira opened the front door for her.

"Maybe so." Moira dipped her head. "I'm glad you came, Nell. You had no reason to show up, but you did. That means a lot to me. And I'm glad we are, well, okay again."

"Answered prayer, yeah?" Nell asked.

After Moira shut the heavy door behind Nell, Dove and Pearl rubbed their thick, furry bodies against Moira's ankles, and she let out a sigh.

"It's just us again, girls," she said to her feline friends, who looked up at her with wide, trusting eyes.

Moira walked farther into the house and sat down on the large, cozy sectional in the living room. She raked her hand across the cushion that Erin had cleaned the night before and felt a twinge of shame. As she reflected on some of the conversations from the weekend, she couldn't help thinking that her best friends had carried the same emotional baggage for decades—could they finally be set free from it? Would Gemma actually leave her emotionally abusive husband and commit to her weight-loss goals? Would Celia Kate ever stop stressing out and waiting for the other shoe to drop? Could she be freed from her grief? And could Erin find her confidence? Moira felt, for the first time, that it was possible if they listened to Nell's advice and looked to the Lord to fill their voids.

Her eyes scanned the room before landing on a five-by-seven photo in a silver frame on the antique table at the end of the couch. The picture was taken at her fortieth birthday party—her and the love of her life along with their two young boys, all standing on the dock behind their home. Jeffrey had planned a special surprise evening, inviting family and a small group of friends. It was typical of him; he always pampered her on her birthdays. The surprise trip to St. Croix, the new sedan, the starlit symphony in the park.

As she continued to stroke Dove's and Pearl's soft white fur, her teary eyes shifted to the butler's pantry, which was stocked with bottles of alcohol. The temptation was strong, so she decided to go for a second brisk run of the day to clear her mind.

MOIRA JOGGED DOWN the path along the river, her footsteps muffled by the soft silt beneath her neon sneakers. She had always loved the way the mossy oaks formed a cool, lush canopy overhead, their ancient branches intertwined. She slowly breathed in the air that was thick with the earthy scent of the river and sea salt. A pontoon boat drifted lazily on the water, and the distant strains of classic rock floated to her from the boat, mingling with the rustle of marsh weeds swaying in the wind.

She reflected on how everything—the music and the fresh air—seemed perfect for enjoying a drink. Whether it was wine or whiskey didn't matter; either would satisfy her longing at that moment. Her thoughts raced faster than her feet until she suddenly stopped, her sneakers sinking into the silt. She had arrived at the shady bend between her home and the senator's estate, and just five feet away stood the familiar, magnificent blue heron.

Moira must have seen this same bird a hundred times in the far corner of her yard, but she had never been this close to such a spectacular creature before. The heron did not startle or fly away in panic. Instead, its sharp, inquisitive eyes were fixed on her with a calm, steady gaze. Its tall, slender frame was graceful, and up close, the delicate blend of blue and white feathers looked even more striking, almost magical, than they had from a distance.

She remembered Nell's words—specifically, her father's drunken words—about the symbolism of the heron: purity, strength, and determination. These were the very qualities she had needed this weekend, what she needed to successfully stay sober. God's purity and strength, her own determination. It was as if this bird stood there as a reminder.

They continued to study each other for what felt like an eternity, an unspoken understanding passing between them. Then, with sudden grace, the heron spread its large wings. Moira heard the rustling of feathers and even the whooshing of wind catching beneath them and watched as the bird took flight. Its long, slender legs trailed behind as it soared over the Savannah marsh, disappearing into the golden hue of the afternoon sun. A sense of peace washed over Moira as she stood silently by the water. She reached into the pocket of her pink windbreaker, pulled out her cell phone, and dialed Nell's number.

"Hey, I've changed my mind," she said, her voice resolute. "Will you meet me at the church tonight?"

Moira could tell Nell was smiling on the other end of the line as she said, "Six o'clock sharp at the south entrance."

After ending the call, Moira slipped her phone into her pocket and resumed her pace, starting with a slow jog that quickly turned into a sprint.

She crossed the small bridge. It wasn't much—just a simple wooden arc that spanned the narrow tributary, hardly wide enough to justify its existence. However, Jeffrey had insisted it was necessary.

He said it gave the place a sense of ceremony and reminded him of something from a Faulkner novel. Moira laughed at that because Jeffrey had never actually finished a Faulkner novel in his life.

He drew plans for the bridge on a napkin one night while they sat on the cobblestone porch and cicadas sounded like static in the trees. The next weekend he was at the lumberyard bright and early, talking angles and slats with a man named Roy who called everyone "chief."

For days, their side yard looked like a construction site: sawdust in the air, wood stacked in crooked piles, and Jeffrey out there in an old Braves hat and jeans, hammering away.

Moira had brought him lemonade and Tylenol, and stood at the kitchen window watching him mutter to himself, argue with the level, and finally step back to admire the little bridge with a look of such ridiculous pride that it made her laugh out loud.

"Come stand on it!" he called to her. "Behold what I've done here!"

The boards smelled like pine, and the railings were slightly uneven. The whole thing was charmingly crooked, but she crossed it, barefoot, praying it would hold her since it had been constructed by a man who wore a suit and tie and sat behind a cherry desk five days out of the week.

"This will still be here long after I'm dead and gone." He leaned on the railing, beaming ear to ear.

And it was.

Just then, as she crossed the weathered wood, gray and splintered, her phone chimed. She pulled it out of her windbreaker and felt her heart flutter when she saw Bradford's name and number lighting up the screen.

"Hello, son," she greeted him, her voice cracking with emotion.

His deep voice, which she had longed to hear for weeks, bathed her in contentment when he said, "Happy birthday, Mama."

She quickly wiped her eyes and walked to one of the wooden chairs where she and Nell had sat earlier. There she talked with Bradford for nearly an hour—about the weekend, about her plans to attend the church that evening. She offered apologies, she accepted his, and for the first time in a long time, all felt right on Allyson Island.

Chapter 25

On a late September afternoon, laughter echoed from the edge of the water and hovered over the marsh. Moira and her friends relaxed in wooden chairs beneath the large tree. Their hearts were full, and so were their stomachs, satisfied with the lunch of homemade pimento cheese, crackers, and vegetable sticks, along with a coconut cream birthday cake Antonio had baked. Like all his other dishes, the dessert was almost too beautiful to eat. They drank from Mason jars filled with pink, fruity punch made with strawberries, ginger ale, and lemonade.

With a sip, Moira closed her eyes for just a second, and the taste carried her somewhere she hadn't been in such a long time— the row house on Chatham Square. It was narrow, creaky, and perfect, with ivy climbing the iron railings and light that poured through the tall transom windows.

Jeffrey made a similar punch there one sweltering Saturday afternoon, shirtless in the tiny kitchen, humming off-key with the Red Hot Chili Peppers on the radio and determined to beat the heat without turning on the ancient AC that rattled and gurgled and put out only semi-cool air. He tossed in cut-up strawberries, lemon slices, and a splash of whatever white wine had survived the night before, and he stirred it all in a big glass mixing bowl.

"Trust the process," he'd said, grinning. "I'm an innovator."

Moira raised her eyebrows. "You're winging it."

"Same thing." He shrugged his broad, tanned shoulders.

He proudly handed her a glass. It was so cold and so sweet that it hurt her teeth, but they drank it anyway, barefoot on the front steps, while watching the world pass by under the Spanish moss. Tourists walked the square with cameras, and a street musician played jazz from a bench across the way.

Jeffrey leaned in and rested his forehead against hers. "If we can make it through a Savannah summer in this house without central air, we can make it through anything, Mo."

She had laughed, and he had kissed her like they had forever.

Moira returned to reality and looked to Celia Kate. "Tell us about your trip. Did you get your hair braided? Did you try the conch salad like I suggested? Did you swim with the pigs?"

"I did get my hair braided, and the Bahamian woman who did it was sweet as pie, but she pulled it so tight my eyebrows lifted three inches and I looked surprised the rest of the trip."

Celia Kate's skin had developed a radiant tan from her recent trip to Nassau. She and Sean's second honeymoon was a much-needed relaxing getaway, especially since Silas had buckled down and doubled his studies so he would graduate from high school a year early. With his extra credits, he began classes at Cumberland State just four weeks ago. While CK and Sean enjoyed hang gliding over the Caribbean and napping on the white sand beaches, and even swimming with spotted pigs in the turquoise water off Rose Island, Silas had responsibly and successfully taken care of his younger siblings, and Chipper Jones, without any incidents. During her trip, CK checked the security cameras only a handful of times instead of keeping the footage playing on her phone like a television show.

She felt a profound sense of relief knowing her oldest child was thriving. He was getting to classes on time, completing his assignments, not going hungry, and even dating a sweet girl whom CK and Sean approved of. On top of all that, Silas was doing some freelance graphic design work, which meant his bank account was growing. He was even discussing the possibility of getting his own apartment closer to campus instead of commuting back and forth.

Whenever anxiety crept in about this stage of her son's life, Celia Kate would make it a priority to talk to God about it, and then she would send a group text to the women who were now lounging under the magnificent live oak with her. The immediate replies and prayers she received always helped CK feel less overwhelmed. Her faith had finally become stronger than her fears.

"I would love to do that. Swim with pigs, I mean," Gemma said, and CK waited for the joke—the obvious one—but she was relieved Gemma didn't take the chance to make a single self-critical remark. It was truly an answered prayer that she rarely talked down on herself anymore.

The group text had become a lifeline for Gemma too, being a safe place for her to talk about her feelings and vent her hurt and frustration over her husband's disrespect. Over the past year, whenever she checked his location and found him at his mistress's apartment, she would fire off messages to her friends, often filled with pain and at times strong language. They allowed her to blow off steam, and then they helped her work through her emotions. Ultimately, they greatly boosted her courage to walk away from her crumbling marriage.

Gemma and Tyler had been separated for just over six months, and for the first time in as long as she could remember, she felt truly free. She continued to live in their suburban farmhouse, while he had moved into the apartment that Gemma had been eyeing on her location app for over a year. She wasn't bothered at all that he was with another woman. Becky could have him, along with his offensive attitude and comments.

Carolina was both infuriated and heartbroken by her father's affair and the way he mistreated her mother. Although he may have been a bad husband, Tyler had always been a loving father, so Gemma encouraged Carolina to reconcile with her dad and to forgive him. He continually asked for forgiveness, but she wasn't ready.

Carolina decided to postpone her college plans, work at a local boutique, and live at home for another year. While Gemma urged her to attend school in Chattanooga to pursue her own dreams, Carolina felt that she and her mother needed each other during this tough time. This decision turned out to be a beautiful blessing for them both, as they were growing closer than they had been in years.

With the help of her Christian counselor and the support of the Allyson Island group, Gemma discovered healthier ways to handle her frustrations. Instead of turning to food, she began using prayer and engaging in physical activities. When the emotions from her divorce felt too heavy to bear, she would take a walk around her neighborhood, jog on the local track, or enjoy a stroll along the downtown sidewalks of Atlanta, where her office was located. This change in focus helped her drop sixty pounds since last September, making her feel significantly better both physically and emotionally.

"Speaking of pigs, Tate told me the last time we spoke that Camp Arifjan rejected a proposal by a lawmaker to ban the serving of pork in the dining hall. He was so glad because he said he didn't know how he'd get through without his bacon every morning," Nell said.

Nell frequently reached out to the group about Tate's recent deployment to Kuwait. Being out of contact with him, except for infrequent letters and poorly connected, glitchy phone calls every few days, caused her a lot of anxiety. In addition to worrying about her son, Nell was really worried about Taylor, who had started dating a college guy who was pretty wild and not a great influence on her. Nell often opened up about her concerns in the group chat, and her friends responded with encouraging reminders and Bible verses that reassured her that God was in control of everything, even their kids' futures.

Erin said, "I'm really glad that Tate and PJ got to know each other while we were all hunkered down at Oglethorpe during the hurricane last year. Those following few months they spent hanging out at church over the winter were awesome for PJ. It helped him take his mind off his worries about work and money and even me."

Erin was happy to still be living in the pool house on Moira's property. Because Moira refused to accept rent payments from Erin, she was able to pay off all her debt and begin saving money with the goal of buying her very first home. She also had some income from painting small seascape canvases and selling them on the website that Silas Stokes had created for her, free of charge. With her current savings and earnings, she was on track to afford a down payment in about six months.

PJ had begun a new chapter in his life and had a new job earning good money working at an auto shop. Since she no longer relied on PJ's income to make ends meet, he was able to get a car and rent an apartment across the river in Charleston.

He visited his mother every few days and helped around Moira's estate on weekends or as needed. Tate Rehman had encouraged him to find a church after he moved to Charleston, and he did. He really enjoyed the young adult ministry and had met some great people his age.

Over the last year Erin and Moira developed a close friendship, a sisterhood. Not only did Erin help keep Moira's house tidy, but she also regularly attended church and Bible study at Oglethorpe with Moira. When Phillip's new wife contacted Erin, worried about her safety because of Phillip's violent behavior, Moira offered Erin advice on how to help without getting too involved. There were also vulnerable moments when Erin's presence and support helped Moira stay on track and avoid slipping back into old habits.

"Hunkered down in that hurricane. Mercy, that sure tested my sobriety! I think I blew up our group chat three million times in the twelve hours I was with MerryLee." Moira's brother insisted on being with her when the storm barreled through, and he brought MerryLee along with him. "I should have listened to you, Erin, and gone with you and PJ to Oglethorpe and left my brother and MerryLee here alone to batten down the hatches." Moira groaned as she watched Dove and Pearl sit at the Ogeechee shore, observing a swarm of gnats hovering over the black water.

Moira Allyson had managed to stay sober for a whole year—precisely 365 days—not taking a single sip of alcohol since last year's birthday weekend. Whenever she felt the overwhelming urge to drink, she would lean on God and her friends and even her boys for support.

Moira praised the Lord that she and her boys had mended their fractured relationship. Brent, still deep into his premed program at Vanderbilt, made it a point to call her often, their conversations longer with each passing week. Bradford came home from the University of Georgia for several weeks during the summer, eager to spend quality time with his mom. They cooked together, took walks, and talked about their life with Jeffrey. They also talked about the hopeful future. Bradford was sure that after he graduated from UGA next year, he wanted to return home and take over Allyson Supply. Moira didn't just have her sobriety—she had her family back.

Through the Celebrate Recovery program at Oglethorpe Church, she started up relationships with people she could reach out to during vulnerable moments. One of those friends was Dr. David Marlow, who had been sober for seven years and shared her faith in the Lord. He also thought Moira was beautiful.

Dr. Marlow was a widower whose wife had died of cancer ten years earlier. Like Moira, he drank heavily to numb his sadness and didn't believe he would ever find love again. What began as a friendship—going to the movies, enjoying steaks at local restaurants, drinking sweet tea with lemon under her favorite live oak—soon developed into something unexpected. In Moira's presence, Dr. Marlow felt his heart, once hardened by grief, gradually begin to soften. Similarly, Moira started to believe she could love again too—not in the same way she had loved her dear Jeffrey, but in a new way, a different way.

A few months into her relationship with the handsome salt-and-pepper-haired David, Moira stood under the bright lights of her bathroom vanity, her heart anxious and her mind racing with sad but determined thoughts. It was finally time for her to confront the reminders of her late husband. Taking a deep breath, she reached for his toothbrush, which was still sitting by the sink, along with his watch and shaving kit. As she carefully placed everything into a rubber tote, she felt a bittersweet sense of relief. It was a small but significant step forward. It wasn't about erasing memories but rather about moving on. She didn't love Jeffrey any less, even though he was gone. Love didn't vanish with people. It just changed shape.

She turned her attention to the closet, where Jeffrey's clothes were still hanging. Slowly she began to pull out his fancy suits, favorite shirts, comfortable jeans, and the casual jacket he always wore on chilly nights by the firepit in the backyard. She neatly folded each item and placed it into a cardboard box to take to the local donation center. As she checked the pockets, she found hard candies, peppermints, scraps of paper, and crumpled tissues. It was emotionally exhausting as she remembered times and places associated with each piece of clothing. Even after all his clothes were boxed up, the closet still held his scent, causing tears to well up in her blue eyes. It felt as if she was packing away parts of her heart, but she knew this was a necessary step toward healing.

Later that same day, as she cleared off the desk piled high with Jeffrey's papers and keepsakes, Erin came in, took her hands, and led her in a beautiful prayer. Together, they thanked God for the love Moira and Jeffrey had shared and asked that Moira continue to be surrounded by joy, and even excitement, for the new beginnings, the new plans, that the Lord was preparing for her.

That same night Moira had the most vivid, lifelike dream. In it, she was in the courtyard, standing barefoot on the damp grass, with the scent of jasmine heavy in the air. The fountain bubbled behind her, and the moonlight made everything glow in silver. The crepe myrtle rustled in the wind, and then Jeffrey appeared.

Moira couldn't bring herself to say anything. Her throat felt tight, and her body froze at the sight of him. He flashed that same smile that had undone her a thousand times before—the same one that had swept her off her feet back at the fraternity house in '92.

"You always get that look when you're overthinking," he said softly while stepping closer to her. "It's the same look you had when you bought that awful red couch."

She laughed lightly and finally said, "I miss you."

He reached out, and his hand took hers.

"It feels like I'm leaving you behind," she admitted.

"No," he responded tenderly. "You're not."

He stepped around to face her completely, the moonlight illuminating him, making him look almost angelic.

"I was yours, Moira, and you were mine. That will never change. But if he's good to you, if he makes you laugh . . . if he sees you the way I did, then it's okay to be his now."

She blinked back tears. "But what if it changes how I remember you?"

"It won't," he replied. "Don't waste your future on our past. It gave you all it could."

And just like that, the silvery light shifted and Jeffrey was gone.

Moira woke up with the smell of jasmine still in her hair and the feeling of his hand still in hers. For the first time in a long while, she didn't cry. She simply breathed and allowed herself to wonder what might come next.

***

"HAPPY BIRTHDAY, MOIRA Allyson," Celia Kate said while she held up the Mason jar of pink punch. "You're even more beautiful than you were last year!"

"Hear, hear," Nell answered, also lifting her drink.

"Hear, hear!" Erin repeated.

"I'm just thankful you survived another year with those homicidal fleabags." Gemma nodded to the white cats at the shore.

The five of them sat under the broad, reaching arms of the live oak, its limbs swaying just enough to catch the afternoon light. The sun was low, spilling gold across the Ogeechee River as it wound through the marshes. In the stillness, only the sound of cicadas and the occasional splash of a mullet jumping broke the quiet.

Nell had kicked off her shoes, her legs tucked under her, a jar of tangy punch cradled in both hands. Celia Kate was leaning back, legs stretched out and ankles crossed, closing her eyes behind her tortoiseshell sunglasses as she slowly sipped her drink. Moira's laugh came soft, directed at something Gemma had just said. Gemma, ever the storyteller, twirled the straw in her jar, the ice clinking gently. Erin, quiet for now, gazed out over the marsh, her expression a peaceful look of rest.

Each woman sitting there was an improved version of the person she had been a year earlier, no longer grappling with fear and longing for faith. Because of the gracious Author of joy, the sweet support they provided each other, and a soul-nurturing weekend on Allyson Island, everything had changed.

Their jars of sweet-and-tart pink liquid caught the light and glowed like the stained glass windows at Oglethorpe Church. No one was in a rush to speak. No one was in a rush to leave. The river, the oak, the marsh, and the friends—they'd all stay a while longer.

Author's Note

SAVANNAH, WITH ITS moss-draped oaks and salty breeze, claimed a piece of my heart on my first visit. It felt only natural to set *A Weekend on Allyson Island* in a place where the beauty of the South meets the peace of the sea.

This story is fictional, but the struggles are deeply personal.

I see myself in each of these characters. I've battled insecurity and doubt, the need for control, anxiety, overeating and the regret that comes after succumbing to temptations. I've wrestled with shame—and by God's grace—I've also encountered the quiet, steady presence of Jesus in the middle of every single one of those battles.

This book is for anyone who sees a little of themselves in these flawed, searching women. My prayer is that as you turn the final page, you are reminded of this truth:

"Where the Spirit of the Lord is, there is freedom" (2 Corinthians 3:17).

Not perfection. But freedom.

Thank you for spending the weekend with us on Allyson Island. I hope you leave with a lighter heart and renewed hope.

With love and gratitude,
Susannah B. Lewis

Acknowledgments

THIS BOOK WOULD not exist without the help, grace, and encouragement of many.

To Jenaye Meridia, my literary agent—thank you for rooting for me.

To my editors, Kimberly and Julie, at Thomas Nelson—your thoughtful insight, patience through multiple POV shifts and re-writes, and your attention to detail have helped shape this book into something that I am proud of.

To my family—thank you for your patience and support through late nights and moments of doubt.

To beautiful Savannah, Georgia—you gave this story its heartbeat.

And to Jesus—thank you for never leaving me in the dark. Thank you for redemption, for grace, and for turning every broken piece into something beautiful.

Discussion Questions

1. Moira's drinking problem is evident from the beginning. How did each character approach that issue throughout the course of the weekend? Which approach would you have taken?

2. Gemma struggled with her self-esteem and with her husband's treatment of her. Was that a situation you could relate to? Or did you find yourself relating more to CK and her desire to encourage her friend (and her frustration with Gemma's husband)? Explain how that storyline impacted you.

3. Marriage plays an integral part in each of the women's stories. Which of their marriages resonated the most with you? Which one frustrated you the most?

4. Erin was reluctant to partake in the weekend with Moira and her friends. If you had been in a similar position, would you have accepted such an invitation? Why or why not?

5. Losing her husband devastated Moira. Did you find her response to that loss understandable? Why or why not?

6. How did Nell's faith impact her relationships and how she dealt with Moira's drinking during that weekend?

7. CK had a very difficult time letting go of control, particularly regarding her children. Is that something you have had to wrestle with? What has helped you surrender that control?

8. Which character do you think made the most significant transformation over the course of the year following the weekend? Explain what stood out to you the most.

9. Toward the end of the novel, each character writes a letter about their most significant fears. Is that something you would do with a group of your closest friends? Why or why not?

10. Did you find the conclusion of the novel satisfying? Why or why not? Were there other endings you had imagined for any of the characters?

About the Author

SUSANNAH B. LEWIS is a humorist, blogger for *Whoa! Susannah*, and freelance writer whose work has appeared in numerous publications. The author of *Can't Make This Stuff Up!*, *Bless Your Heart, Rae Sutton*; and *Della and Darby*, Lewis studied creative writing at Jackson State Community College and earned her bachelor's degree in business management from Bethel College. She lives in Tennessee with her husband, Jason, their three children, and three dogs.

~

Visit her online at whoasusannah.com
Facebook: @whoasusannah
Instagram: @whoasusannahblog
TikTok: @susannahblewis